# THE
# TEAHOUSE
# DETECTIVE

## THE CASE OF MISS ELLIOTT

BARONESS ORCZY (1865–1947) was a Hungarian-born British author, best known for the Scarlet Pimpernel novels. Her Teahouse Detective, who features in *The Case of Miss Elliott*, was one of the first fictional sleuths created in response to the Sherlock Holmes stories' huge success. Initially serialized in magazines, the stories were later published in book form and have since been adapted for radio, television and film. Two more collections of Teahouse Detective mysteries are available or forthcoming from Pushkin Vertigo.

# THE TEAHOUSE DETECTIVE

## THE CASE OF MISS ELLIOTT

## BARONESS ORCZY

PUSHKIN VERTIGO

Pushkin Press
71–75 Shelton Street
London WC2H 9JQ

These stories were first published as
*The Case of Miss Elliott* by T. Fisher Unwin in 1905

First published by Pushkin Press in 2019

1 3 5 7 9 8 6 4 2

ISBN 13: 978-1-78227-533-6

Text designed and typeset by Tetragon, London
Printed in Great Britain by the CPI Group, UK

www.pushkinpress.com

# CONTENTS

# *The Case of Miss Elliott*

**1**

The man in the corner was watching me over the top of his great bone-rimmed spectacles.

"Well?" he asked, after a little while.

"Well?" I repeated with some acerbity. I had been wondering for the last ten minutes how many more knots he would manage to make in that same bit of string, before he actually started undoing them again.

"Do I fidget you?" he asked apologetically, whilst his long bony fingers buried themselves, string, knots, and all, into the capacious pockets of his magnificent tweed ulster.

"Yes, that is another awful tragedy," he said quietly, after a while. "Lady doctors are having a pretty bad time of it just now."

This was only his usual habit of speaking in response to my thoughts. There was no doubt that at the present moment my mind was filled with that extraordinary mystery which was setting all Scotland Yard by the ears, and had completely thrown into the shade the sad story of Miss Hickman's tragic fate.

*The Daily Telegraph* had printed two columns headed "Murder or Suicide?" on the subject of the mysterious death of Miss Elliott, matron of the Convalescent Home, in Suffolk

Avenue – and I must confess that a more profound and bewildering mystery had never been set before our able detective department.

"It has puzzled them this time, and no mistake," said the man in the corner, with one of his most gruesome chuckles, "but I dare say the public is quite satisfied that there is no solution to be found, since the police have found none."

"Can you find one?" I retorted with withering sarcasm.

"Oh, my solution would only be sneered at," he replied. "It is far too simple – and yet how logical! There was Miss Elliott, a good-looking, youngish, ladylike woman, fully qualified in the medical profession and in charge of the Convalescent Home in Suffolk Avenue, which is a private institution largely patronized by the benevolent.

"For some time, already, there had appeared vague comments and rumours in various papers, that the extensive charitable contributions did not all go towards the upkeep of the Home. But, as is usual in institutions of that sort, the public was not allowed to know anything very definite, and contributions continued to flow in, whilst the Honorary Treasurer of the great Convalescent Home kept up his beautiful house in Hamilton Terrace, in a style which would not have shamed a peer of the realm.

"That is how matters stood, when on 2nd November last the morning papers contained the brief announcement that at a quarter past midnight two workmen walking along Blomfield Road, Maida Vale, suddenly came across the body of a young lady, lying on her face, close to the wooden steps of the narrow footbridge which at this point crosses the canal.

"This part of Maida Vale is, as you know, very lonely at all times, but at night it is usually quite deserted. Blomfield Road, with its row of small houses and bits of front gardens, faces the canal, and beyond the footbridge is continued in a series of small riverside wharves, which is practically unknown ground to the average Londoner. The footbridge itself, with steps at right angles and high wooden parapet, would offer excellent shelter at all hours of the night for any nefarious deed.

"It was within its shadows that the men had found the body, and to their credit, be it said, they behaved like good and dutiful citizens – one of them went off in search of the police, whilst the other remained beside the corpse.

"From papers and books found upon her person, it was soon ascertained that the deceased was Miss Elliott, the young matron of the Suffolk Avenue Convalescent Home; and as she was very popular in her profession and had a great many friends, the terrible tragedy caused a sensation, all the more acute as very quickly the rumour gained ground that the unfortunate young woman had taken her own life in a most gruesome and mysterious manner.

"Preliminary medical and police investigation had revealed the fact that Miss Elliott had died through a deep and scientifically administered gash in the throat, whilst the surgical knife with which the deadly wound was inflicted still lay tightly grasped in her clenched hand."

## 2

The man in the corner, ever conscious of any effect he produced upon my excited imagination, had paused for a while, giving me time, as it were, to co-ordinate in my mind the few simple facts he had put before me. I had no wish to make a remark, knowing of old that my one chance of getting the whole of his interesting argument was to offer neither comment nor contradiction.

"When a young, good-looking woman in the heyday of her success in an interesting profession," he began at last, "is alleged to have committed suicide, the outside public immediately want to know the reason why she did such a thing, and a kind of freemasonic, amateur detective work goes on, which generally brings a few important truths to light. Thus, in the case of Miss Elliott, certain facts had begun to leak out, even before the inquest, with its many sensational developments. Rumours concerning the internal administration, or rather maladministration of the Home began to take more definite form.

"That its finances had been in a very shaky condition for some time was known to all those who were interested in its welfare. What was not so universally known was that few hospitals had had more munificent donations and subscriptions showered upon them in recent years, and yet it was openly spoken of by all the nurses that Miss Elliott had on more than one occasion petitioned for actual necessities for the patients – necessities which were denied to her on the plea of necessary economy.

"The Convalescent Home was, as sometimes happens in institutions of this sort, under the control of a committee of benevolent and fashionable people who understood nothing about business, and less still about the management of a hospital. Dr Kinnaird, president of the institution, was a young, eminently successful consultant; he had recently married the daughter of a peer, who had boundless ambitions for herself and her husband.

"Dr Kinnaird, by adding the prestige of his name to the Home, no doubt felt that he had done enough for its welfare. Against that, Dr Stapylton, honorary secretary and treasurer of the Home, threw himself heart and soul into the work connected with it, and gave a great deal of his time to it. All subscriptions and donations went, of course, through his hands, the benevolent and fashionable committee being only too willing to shift all their financial responsibilities on to his willing shoulders. He was a very popular man in society – a bachelor with a magnificent house in Hamilton Terrace, where he entertained the more eminent and fashionable clique in his own profession.

"It was the evening papers, however, which contained the most sensational development of this tragic case. It appears that on the Saturday afternoon Mary Dawson, one of the nurses in the Home, was going to the house surgeon's office with a message from the head nurse, when her attention was suddenly arrested in one of the passages by the sound of loud voices proceeding from one of the rooms. She paused to listen for a moment, and at once recognized the voices of Miss Elliott and of Dr Stapylton, the honorary treasurer and chairman of committee.

"The subject of conversation was evidently that of the eternal question of finance. Miss Elliott spoke very indignantly, and Nurse Dawson caught the words:

"'Surely you must agree with me that Dr Kinnaird ought to be informed at once.'

"Dr Stapylton's voice in reply seems to have been at first bitingly sarcastic, then threatening. Dawson heard nothing more after that, and went on to deliver her message. On her way back she stopped in the passage again, and tried to listen. This time it seemed to her as if she could hear the sound of someone crying bitterly, and Dr Stapylton's voice speaking very gently.

"'You may be right, Nellie,' he was saying. 'At any rate, wait a few days before telling Kinnaird. You know what he is – he'll make a frightful fuss and –'

"Whereupon Miss Elliott interrupted him.

"'It isn't fair to Dr Kinnaird to keep him in ignorance any longer. Whoever the thief may be it is your duty or mine to expose him, and if necessary bring him to justice.'

"There was a good deal of discussion at the time, if you remember, as to whether Nurse Dawson had overheard and repeated this speech accurately: whether, in point of fact, Miss Elliott had used the words '*or* mine' or '*and* mine'. You see the neat little point, don't you?" continued the man in the corner. "The little word 'and' would imply that she considered herself at one with Dr Stapylton in the matter, but 'or' would mean that she was resolved to act alone if he refused to join her in unmasking the thief.

"All these facts, as I remarked before, had leaked out, as such facts have a way of doing. No wonder, therefore, that on the day fixed for the inquest the coroner's court was filled to overflowing, both with the public – ever eager for new sensations – and with the many friends of the deceased lady, among whom young medical students of both sexes and nurses in uniform were most conspicuous.

"I was there early, and therefore had a good seat, from which I could comfortably watch the various actors in the drama about to be performed. People who seemed to be in the know pointed out various personages to one another, and it was a matter of note that, in spite of professional engagements, the members of the staff of the Convalescent Home were present in full force and stayed on almost the whole time. The personages who chiefly arrested my attention were, firstly, Dr Kinnaird, a good-looking Irishman of about forty, and president of the institution; also Dr Earnshaw, a rising young consultant, with boundless belief in himself written all over his pleasant rubicund countenance.

"The expert medical evidence was once again thoroughly gone into. There was absolutely no doubt that Miss Elliott had died from having her throat cut with the surgical knife which was found grasped in her right hand. There were absolutely no signs of a personal struggle in the immediate vicinity of the body, and rigid examination proved that there was no other mark of violence upon the body; there was nothing, therefore, to prove that the poor girl had not committed suicide in a moment of mental aberration or of great personal grief.

"Of course, it was strange that she should have chosen this curious mode of taking her own life. She had access to all kinds of poisons, amongst which her medical knowledge could prompt her to choose the least painful and most efficacious ones. Therefore, to have walked out on a Sunday night to a wretched and unfrequented spot, and there committed suicide in that grim fashion seemed almost the work of a mad woman. And yet the evidence of her family and friends all tended to prove that Miss Elliott was a peculiarly sane, large-minded, and happy individual.

"However, the suicide theory was at this stage of the proceedings taken as being absolutely established, and when Police Constable Fiske came forward to give his evidence no one in the court was prepared for a statement which suddenly revealed this case to be as mysterious as it was tragic.

"Fiske's story was this: close upon midnight on that memorable Sunday night he was walking down Blomfield Road along the side of the canal and towards the footbridge, when he overtook a lady and gentleman who were walking in the same direction as himself. He turned to look at them, and noticed that the gentleman was in evening dress and wore a high hat, and that the lady was crying.

"Blomfield Road is at best very badly lighted, especially on the side next to the canal, where there are no lamps at all. Fiske, however, was prepared to swear positively that the lady was the deceased. As for the gentleman, he might know him again or he might not.

"Fiske then crossed the footbridge, and walked on towards the Harrow Road. As he did so, he heard St Mary Magdalen's church clock chime the hour of midnight. It was a quarter of an hour after that that the body of the unfortunate girl was found, and clasping in her hand the knife with which that awful deed had been done. By whom? Was it really by her own self? But if so, why did not that man in evening dress who had last seen her alive come forward and throw some light upon this fast thickening veil of mystery?

"It was Mr James Elliott, brother of the deceased, however, who first mentioned a name then in open court, which has ever since in the minds of everyone been associated with Miss Elliott's tragic fate.

"He was speaking in answer to a question of the coroner's anent his sister's disposition and recent frame of mind.

"'She was always extremely cheerful,' he said, 'but recently had been peculiarly bright and happy. I understood from her that this was because she believed that a man for whom she had a great regard was also very much attached to her, and meant to ask her to be his wife.'

"'And do you know who this man was?' asked the coroner.

"'Oh yes,' replied Mr Elliott, 'it was Dr Stapylton.'

"Everyone had expected that name, of course, for everyone remembered Nurse Dawson's story, yet when it came, there crept over all those present an indescribable feeling that something terrible was impending.

"'Is Dr Stapylton here?'

"But Dr Stapylton had sent an excuse. A professional case of the utmost urgency had kept him at a patient's bedside. But Dr Kinnaird, the president of the institution, came forward.

"Questioned by the coroner, Dr Kinnaird, however, who evidently had a great regard for his colleague, repudiated any idea that the funds of the institution had ever been tampered with by the Treasurer.

"'The very suggestion of such a thing,' he said, 'was an outrage upon one of the most brilliant men in the profession.'

"He further added that, although he knew that Dr Stapylton thought very highly of Miss Elliott, he did not think that there was any actual engagement, and most decidedly he (Dr Kinnaird) had heard nothing of any disagreement between them.

"'Then did Dr Stapylton never tell you that Miss Elliott had often chafed under the extraordinary economy practised in the richly endowed Home?' asked the coroner again.

"'No,' replied Dr Kinnaird.

"'Was not that rather strange reticence?'

"'Certainly not. I am only the Honorary President of the institution – Stapylton has chief control of its finances.'

"'Ah!' remarked the coroner blandly.

"However, it was clearly no business of his at this moment to enter into the financial affairs of the Home. His duty at this point was to try and find out if Dr Stapylton and the man in evening dress were one and the same person.

"The men who found the body testified to the hour: a quarter past midnight. As Fiske had seen the unfortunate girl alive a little before twelve, she must have been murdered or had committed suicide between midnight and a quarter past. But there was something more to come.

"How strange and dramatic it all was!" continued the man in the corner, with a bland smile, altogether out of keeping with the poignancy of his narrative; "all these people in that crowded court trying to reconstruct the last chapter of that bright young matron's life and then – but I must not anticipate.

"One more witness was to be heard – one whom the police, with a totally unconscious sense of what is dramatic, had reserved for the last. This was Dr Earnshaw, one of the staff of the Convalescent Home. His evidence was very short, but of deeply momentous import. He explained that

16

he had consulting rooms in Weymouth Street, but resided in Westbourne Square. On Sunday, 1st November, he had been dining out in Maida Vale, and returning home a little before midnight saw a woman standing close by the steps of the footbridge in the Blomfield Road.

"'I had been coming down Formosa Street and had not specially taken notice of her, when just as I reached the corner of Blomfield Road, she was joined by a man in evening dress and high hat. Then I crossed the road, and recognized both Miss Elliott and –'

"The young doctor paused, almost as if hesitating before the enormity of what he was about to say, whilst the excitement in court became almost painful.

"'And –?' urged the coroner.

"'And Dr Stapylton,' said Dr Earnshaw at last, almost under his breath.

"'You are quite sure?' asked the coroner.

"'Absolutely positive. I spoke to them both, and they spoke to me.'

"'What did you say?'

"'Oh, the usual, "Hello, Staplyton!" to which he replied, "Hello!" I then said "Good night" to them both, and Miss Elliott also said "Good night." I saw her face more clearly then, and thought that she looked very tearful and unhappy, and Stapylton looked ill-tempered. I wondered why they had chosen that unhallowed spot for a midnight walk.'

"'And you say the hour was –?' asked the coroner.

"'Ten minutes to twelve. I looked at my watch as I crossed the footbridge, and had heard a quarter to twelve strike five minutes before.'

"Then it was that the coroner adjourned the inquest. Dr Stapylton's attendance had become absolutely imperative. According to Dr Earnshaw's testimony, he had been with deceased certainly a quarter of an hour before she met her terrible death. Fiske had seen them together ten minutes later; she was then crying bitterly. There was as yet no actual charge against the fashionable and rich doctor, but already the ghostly bird of suspicion had touched him with its ugly wing."

### 3

"As for the next day," continued the man in the corner after a slight pause, "I can assure you that there was not a square foot of standing room in the coroner's court for the adjourned inquest. It was timed for eleven a.m., and at six o'clock on that cold winter's morning the pavement outside the court was already crowded. As for me, I always manage to get a front seat, and I did on that occasion, too. I fancy that I was the first among the general public to note Dr Stapylton as he entered the room accompanied by his solicitor, and by Dr Kinnaird, with whom he was chatting very cheerfully and pleasantly.

"Mind you, I am a great admirer of the medical profession, and I think a clever and successful doctor usually has a most delightful air about him – the consciousness of great and good work done with profit to himself – which is quite unique and quite admirable.

"Dr Stapylton had that air even to a greater extent than his colleague, and from the affectionate way in which Dr Kinnaird finally shook him by the hand, it was quite clear that the respected chief of the Convalescent Home, at any rate, refused to harbour any suspicion of the integrity of its Treasurer.

"Well, I must not weary you by dwelling on the unimportant details of this momentous inquest. Constable Fiske, who was asked to identify the gentleman in evening dress whom he had seen with the deceased at a few minutes before twelve, failed to recognize Dr Stapylton very positively: pressed very closely, he finally refused to swear either way. Against that, Dr Earnshaw repeated, clearly and categorically, looking his colleague straight in the face the while, the damnatory evidence he had given the day before.

"'I saw Dr Stapylton, I spoke to him, and he spoke to me,' he repeated most emphatically.

"Everyone in that court was watching Dr Stapylton's face, which wore an air of supreme nonchalance, even of contempt, but certainly neither of guilt nor of fear.

"Of course, by that time *I* had fully made up my mind as to where the hitch lay in this extraordinary mystery; but no one else had, and everyone held their breath as Dr Stapylton quietly stepped into the box, and after a few preliminary questions the coroner asked him very abruptly:

"'You were in the company of the deceased a few minutes before she died, Dr Stapylton?'

"'Pardon me,' replied the latter quietly, 'I last saw Miss Elliott alive on Saturday afternoon, just before I went home from my work.'

"This calm reply, delivered without a tremor, positively made everyone gasp. For the moment coroner and jury were alike staggered.

"'But we have two witnesses here who saw you in the company of the deceased within a few minutes of twelve o'clock on the Sunday night!' the coroner managed to gasp out at last.

"'Pardon me,' again interposed the doctor, 'these witnesses were mistaken.'

"'Mistaken!'

"I think everyone would have shouted out the word in boundless astonishment had they dared to do so.

"'Dr Earnshaw was mistaken,' reiterated Dr Stapylton quietly. 'He neither saw me nor did he speak to me.'

"'You can substantiate that, of course?' queried the coroner.

"'Pardon me,' once more said the doctor, with utmost calm, 'it is surely Dr Earnshaw who should substantiate *his* statement.'

"'There is Constable Fiske's corroborative evidence for that,' retorted the coroner, somewhat nettled.

"'Hardly, I think. You see, the constable states that he saw a gentleman in evening dress, etc., talking to the deceased at a minute or two before twelve o'clock, and that when he heard the clock of St Mary Magdalen chime the hour of midnight he was just walking away from the footbridge. Now, just as that very church clock was chiming that hour, I was stepping into a cab at the corner of Harrow Road, not a hundred yards *in front* of Constable Fiske.'

"'You swear to that?' queried the coroner in amazement.

"'I can easily prove it,' said Dr Stapylton. 'The cabman who drove me from there to my club is here and can corroborate my statement.'

"And amidst boundless excitement, John Smith, a hansom-cab driver, stated that he was hailed in the Harrow Road by the last witness, who told him to drive to the Royal Clinical Club, in Mardon Street. Just as he started off, St Mary Magdalen's Church, close by, struck the hour of midnight.

"At that very moment, if you remember, Constable Fiske had just crossed the footbridge, and was walking towards the Harrow Road, and he was quite sure (for he was closely questioned afterwards) that no one overtook him from behind. Now there would be no way of getting from one side of the canal to the other at this point except over that footbridge; the nearest bridge is fully two hundred yards further down the Blomfield Road. The girl was alive a minute *before* the constable crossed the footbridge, and it would have been absolutely impossible for anyone to have murdered a girl, placed the knife in her hand, run a couple of hundred yards to the next bridge and another three hundred to the corner of Harrow Road, all in the space of three minutes.

"This alibi, therefore, absolutely cleared Dr Stapylton from any suspicion of having murdered Miss Elliott. And yet, looking on that man as he sat there, calm, cool and contemptuous, no one could have had the slightest doubt but that he was lying – lying when he said he had not seen Miss Elliott that evening; lying when he denied Dr Earnshaw's statement; lying when he professed himself ignorant of the poor girl's fate.

"Dr Earnshaw repeated his statement with the same emphasis, but it was one man's word against another's, and as Dr Stapylton was so glaringly innocent of the actual murder, there seemed no valid reason at all why he should have denied having seen her that night, and the point was allowed to drop. As for Nurse Dawson's story of his alleged quarrel with Miss Elliott on the Saturday night, Dr Stapylton again had a simple and logical explanation.

"'People who listen at keyholes,' he said quietly, 'are apt to hear only fragments of conversation, and often mistake ordinary loud voices for quarrels. As a matter of fact, Miss Elliott and I were discussing the dismissal of certain nurses from the Home, whom she deemed incompetent. Nurse Dawson was among that number. She desired their immediate dismissal, and I tried to pacify her. That was the subject of my conversation with the deceased lady. I can swear to every word of it.'"

### 4

The man in the corner had long ceased speaking and was placing quietly before me a number of photographs. One by one I saw the series of faces which had been watched so eagerly in the coroner's court that memorable afternoon by an excited crowd.

"So the fate of poor Miss Elliott has remained wrapt in mystery?" I said thoughtfully at last.

"To everyone," rejoined the funny creature, "except to me."

"Ah! What is your theory, then?"

"A simple one, dear lady; so simple that it really amazes me that no one, not even you, my faithful pupil, ever thought of it."

"It may be so simple that it becomes idiotic," I retorted with lofty disdain.

"Well, that may be. Shall I at any rate try to make it clear?"

"If you like."

"For this I think the best way would be, if you were to follow me through what transpired before the inquest. But first tell me, what do you think of Dr Earnshaw's statement?"

"Well," I replied, "a good many people thought that it was he who murdered Miss Elliott, and that his story of meeting Dr Stapylton with her was a lie from beginning to end."

"Impossible!" he retorted, making an elaborate knot in his bit of string. "Dr Earnshaw's friends, with whom he had been dining that night, swore that he was *not* in evening dress, nor wore a high hat. And on that point – the evening dress, and the hat – Constable Fiske was most positive."

"Then Dr Earnshaw was mistaken, and it was not Dr Stapylton he met."

"Impossible!" he shrieked, whilst another knot went to join its fellows. "He spoke to Dr Stapylton, and Dr Stapylton spoke to him."

"Very well, then," I argued; "why should Dr Stapylton tell a lie about it? He had such a conclusive alibi that there could be no object in his making a false statement about that."

"No object!" shrieked the excited creature. "Why, don't you *see* that he had to tell the lie in order to set police, coroner, and jury by the ears, because he did not wish it to be even remotely hinted at, that the man whom Dr Earnshaw saw with Miss Elliott, and the man whom Constable Fiske saw with her ten minutes later, were *two different persons?*"

"Two different persons!" I ejaculated.

"Ay! two confederates in this villainy. No one has ever attempted to deny the truth of the shaky finances of the Home; no one has really denied that Miss Elliott suspected certain defalcations and was trying to force the hands of the Honorary Treasurer towards a full enquiry. That the Honorary Treasurer knew where all the money went to was pretty clear all along – his magnificent house in Hamilton Terrace fully testifies to that. That the President of the institution was a party to these defalcations and largely profited by them I for one am equally convinced."

"Dr Kinnaird?" I ejaculated in amazement.

"Ay, Dr Kinnaird. Do you mean to tell me that he alone among the entire staff of that Home was ignorant of those defalcations? Impossible! And if he knew of them, and did neither enquire into them nor attempt to stop them, then he must have been a party to them. Do you admit that?"

"Yes, I admit that," I replied.

"Very well, then. The rest is quite simple; those two men, unworthy to bear the noble appellation of doctor, must for years have quietly stolen the money subscribed by the benevolent for the Home, and converted it to their own use: then, they suddenly find themselves face to face with immediate discovery in the shape of a young girl determined to unmask the systematic frauds of the past few years. That meant exposure, disgrace, ruin for them both, and they determine to be rid of her.

"Under the pretence of an evening walk, her so-called lover entices her to a lonely and suitable spot; his confederate is close by, hidden in the shadows, ready to give his assistance if the girl struggles and screams. But suddenly Dr Earnshaw appears. He recognizes Stapylton and challenges him. For a moment the villains are nonplussed, then Kinnaird – the cleverer of the two – steps forward, greets the two lovers unconcernedly, and after two minutes' conversation casually reminds Stapylton of an appointment the latter is presumed to have at a club in St James's Street.

"The latter understands and takes the hint, takes a quick farewell of the girl, leaving her in his friend's charge, then, as fast as he can, goes off, presently takes a cab, leaving his friend to do the deed, whilst the alibi he can prove, coupled with Dr Earnshaw's statement, was sure to bewilder and mislead the police and the public.

"Thus it was that though Dr Earnshaw saw and recognized Dr Stapylton, Constable Fiske saw Dr Kinnaird, whom he did *not* recognize, on whom no suspicion had fallen, and whose name had never been coupled with that of Miss Elliott. When Constable Fiske had turned his back, Kinnaird murdered the girl and went off quietly, whilst Dr Stapylton, on whom all suspicions were bound to fasten sooner or later, was able to prove the most perfect alibi ever concocted.

"One day I feel certain that the frauds at the Home will be discovered, and then who knows what else may see the light?

"Think of it all quietly when I am gone, and tomorrow when we meet tell me whether if *I* am wrong what is *your* explanation of this extraordinary mystery."

Before I could reply he had gone, and I was left wondering, gazing at the photographs of two good-looking, highly respectable and respected men, whom an animated scarecrow had just boldly accused of committing one of the most dastardly crimes ever recorded in our annals.

# *The Hocussing of Cigarette*

**1**

Quite by chance I found myself one morning sitting before a marble-topped table in the ABC shop. I really wondered for the moment what had brought me there, and felt cross with myself for being there at all. Having sampled my tea and roll, I soon buried myself in the capacious folds of my *Daily Telegraph*.

"A glass of milk and a cheesecake, please," said a well-known voice.

The next moment I was staring into the corner, straight at a pair of mild, watery blue eyes, hidden behind great bone-rimmed spectacles, and at ten long bony fingers, round which a piece of string was provokingly intertwined.

There he was as usual, wearing – for it was chilly – a huge tweed ulster, of a pattern too lofty to be described. Smiling, bland, apologetic, and fidgety, he sat before me as the living embodiment of the reason why I had come to the ABC shop that morning.

"How do you do?" I said, with as much dignity as I could command.

"I see that you are interested in Cigarette," he remarked, pointing to a special column in *The Daily Telegraph*.

"She is quite herself again," I said.

"Yes, but you don't know who tried to poison her and succeeded in making her very ill. You don't know whether the man Palk had anything to do with it, whether he was bribed, or whether it was Mrs Keeson or the groom Cockram who told a lie, or why –?"

"No," I admitted reluctantly; "I don't know any of these things."

He was fidgeting nervously in the corner, wriggling about like an animated scarecrow. Then suddenly a bland smile illuminated his entire face. His long bony fingers had caught the end of the bit of string, and there he was at it again, just as I had seen him a year ago, worrying and fidgeting, making knot upon knot, and untying them again, whilst his blue eyes peered at me over the top of his gigantic spectacles.

"I would like to know what your theory is about the whole thing," I was compelled to say at last; for the case had interested me deeply, and, after all, I had come to the ABC shop for the sole purpose of discussing the adventures of Cigarette with him.

"Oh, my theories are not worth considering," he said meekly. "The police would not give me five shillings for any one of them. They always prefer a mystery to any logical conclusion, if it is arrived at by an outsider. But you may be more lucky. The owner of Cigarette did offer £100 reward for the elucidation of the mystery. The noble Earl must have backed Cigarette for all he was worth. Malicious tongues go even so far as to say that he is practically a ruined man now, and that the beautiful Lady Agnes is only too glad to find herself the wife of Harold Keeson, the son of the well-known trainer.

"If you ever go to Newmarket," continued the man in the corner after a slight pause, during which he had been absorbed in unravelling one of his most complicated knots, "anyone will point out the Keesons' house to you. It is called Manor House, and stands in the midst of beautiful gardens. Mr Keeson himself is a man of about fifty, and, as a matter of fact, is of very good family, the Keesons having owned property in the Midlands for the past eight hundred years. Of this fact he is, it appears, extremely proud. His father, however, was a notorious spendthrift, who squandered his property, and died in the nick of time, leaving his son absolutely penniless and proud as Lucifer.

"Fate, however, has been kind to George Keeson. His knowledge of horses and of all matters connected with the turf stood him in good stead: hard work and perseverance did the rest. Now, at fifty years of age, he is a very rich man, and practically at the head of a profession, which, if not exactly that of a gentleman, is, at any rate, highly remunerative.

"He owns Manor House, and lived there with his young wife and his only son and heir, Harold.

"It was Mr Keeson who had trained Cigarette for the Earl of Okehampton, and who, of course, had charge of her during her apprenticeship, before she was destined to win a fortune for her owner, her trainer, and those favoured few who had got wind of her capabilities. For Cigarette was to be kept a dark horse – not an easy matter in these days, when the neighbourhood of every racecourse abounds with rascals who eke out a precarious livelihood by various methods, more or less shady, of which the gleaning of early information is perhaps the least disreputable.

"Fortunately for Mr Keeson, however, he had in the groom, Cockram, a trusted and valued servant, who had been in his employ for over ten years. To say that Cockram took a special pride in Cigarette would be but to put it mildly. He positively loved the mare, and I don't think that anyone ever doubted that his interest in her welfare was every bit as keen as that of the Earl of Okehampton or of Mr Keeson.

"It was to Cockram, therefore, that Mr Kesson entrusted the care of Cigarette. She was lodged in the private stables adjoining the Manor House, and during the few days immediately preceding the Coronation Stakes the groom practically never left her side, either night or day. He slept in the loose box with her, and ate all his meals in her company; nor was anyone allowed to come within measurable distance of the living treasure, save Mr Keeson or the Earl of Okehampton himself.

"And yet, in spite of all these precautions, in spite of every care that human ingenuity could devise, on the very morning of the race Cigarette was seized with every symptom of poisoning, and although, as you say, she is quite herself again now, she was far too ill to fulfil her engagement, and, if rumour speaks correctly, completed thereby the ruin of the Earl of Okehampton."

## 2

The man in the corner looked at me through his bone-rimmed spectacles, and his mild blue eyes gazed pleasantly into mine.

"You may well imagine," he continued, after a while, "what a thunderbolt such a catastrophe means to those whose hopes of a fortune rested upon the fitness of the bay mare. Mr Keeson lost his temper for an instant, they say – but for one instant only. When he was hastily summoned at six o'clock in the morning to Cigarette's stables, and saw her lying on the straw, rigid and with glassy eyes, he raised his heavy riding-whip over the head of Cockram. Some assert that he actually struck him, and that the groom was too wretched and too dazed to resent either words or blows. After a good deal of hesitation he reluctantly admitted that for the first time since Cigarette had been in his charge he had slept long and heavily.

"'I am such a light sleeper, you know, sir,' he said in a tear-choked voice. 'Usually I could hear every noise the mare made if she stirred at all. But, there – last night I cannot say *what* happened. I remember that I felt rather drowsy after my supper, and must have dropped off to sleep very quickly. Once during the night I woke up; the mare was all right then.'

"The man paused, and seemed to be searching for something in his mind – the recollection of a dream, perhaps. But the veterinary surgeon, who was present at the time, having also been hastily summoned to the stables, took up the glass which had contained the beer for Cockram's supper. He sniffed it, and then tasted it, and said quietly:

"'No wonder you slept heavily, my man. This beer was drugged: it contained opium.'

"'Drugged!' ejaculated Cockram, who, on hearing this fact, which in every way exonerated him from blame, seemed more hopelessly wretched than he had been before.

"It appears that every night Cockram's supper was brought out to him in the stables by one of the servants from the Manor House. On this particular night Mrs Keeson's maid, a young girl named Alice Image, had brought him a glass of beer and some bread and cheese on a tray at about eleven o'clock.

"Closely questioned by Mr Keeson, the girl emphatically denied all knowledge of any drug in the beer. She had often taken the supper tray across to Cockram, who was her sweetheart, she said. It was usually placed ready for her in the hall, and when she had finished attending upon her mistress' night toilet she went over to the stables with it. She had certainly never touched the beer, and the tray had stood in its accustomed place on the hall table looking just the same as usual. 'As if I'd go and poison my Cockram!' she said in the midst of a deluge of tears.

"All these somewhat scanty facts crept into the evening papers that same day. That an outrage of a peculiarly daring and cunning character had been perpetrated was not for a moment in doubt. So much money had been at stake, so many people would be half-ruined by it, that even the non-racing public at once took the keenest interest in the case. All the papers admitted, of course, that for the moment the affair seemed peculiarly mysterious, yet all commented upon one fact, which they suggested should prove an important clue: this fact was Cockram's strange attitude.

"At first he had been dazed – probably owing to the after-effects of the drug; he had also seemed too wretched even to resent Mr Keeson's very natural outburst of wrath. But then, when the presence of the drug in his beer was detected, which proved *him*, at any rate, to have been guiltless in the matter, his answers, according to all accounts, became somewhat confused; and all Mr Keeson and the 'vet', who were present, got out of him after that, was a perpetual ejaculation: 'What's to be done? What's to be done?'

"Two days later the sporting papers were the first to announce, with much glee, that thanks to the untiring energy of the Scotland Yard authorities, daylight seemed at last to have been brought to bear upon the mystery which surrounded the dastardly outrage on the Earl of Okehampton's mare Cigarette, and that an important arrest in connection with it had already been effected.

"It appears that a man named Charles Palk, seemingly of no address, had all along been suspected of having at least a hand in the outrage. He was believed to be a bookmaker's tout, and was a man upon whom the police had long since kept a watchful eye. Palk had been seen loafing around the Manor House for the past week, and had been warned off the grounds once or twice by the grooms.

"It now transpired that on the day preceding the outrage he had hung about the neighbourhood of the Manor House the whole afternoon, trying to get into conversation with the stable-boys, or even with Mr Keeson's indoor servants. No one, however, would have anything to do with him, as Mr Keeson's orders in those respects were very strict: he had often threatened any one of his *employés* with instant dismissal if he found him in company with one of these touts.

"Detective Twiss, however, who was in charge of the case, obtained the information that Alice Image, the maid, had been seen on more than one occasion talking to Palk, and that on the very day before the Coronation Stakes she had been seen in his company. Closely questioned by the detective, Alice Image at first denied her intercourse with the tout, but finally was forced to admit that she had held conversation with him once or twice.

"She was fond of putting a bit now and again upon a horse, but Cockram, she added, was such a muff that he never would give her a tip, for he did not approve of betting for young women. Palk had always been very civil and nice-spoken, she further explained. Moreover, he came from Buckinghamshire, her own part of the country, where she was born; anyway, she had never had cause to regret having entrusted a half-sovereign or so of her wages to him.

"All these explanations delivered by Alice Image, with the flow of tears peculiar to her kind, were not considered satisfactory, and the next day she and Charles Palk were both arrested on the charge of being concerned in the poisoning of the Earl of Okehampton's mare Cigarette, with intent to do her grievous bodily harm."

### 3

"These sort of cases," continued the man in the corner after a slight pause, during which his nervous fingers toyed incessantly with that eternal bit of string – "these sort of cases always create a great deal of attention amongst the public, the majority of whom in this country have very strong sporting proclivities. It was small wonder, therefore, when Alice Image and Charles Palk were brought before the local magistrates, that the court was crowded to overflowing, both with pressmen and with the general public.

"I had all along been very much interested in the case, so I went down to Newmarket, and, in spite of the huge crowd, managed to get a good seat, whence I could command a full view of the chief personages concerned in this thrilling sporting drama.

"Firstly, there was the Earl of Okehampton – good-looking, but for an unmistakable air of the broken-down sporting man about his whole person; the trainer, Mr Keeson – a lean, clean-shaven man, with a fine, proud carriage, and a general air of ancient lineage and the Domesday Booke about him; Mrs Keeson – a pale, nervous-looking creature, who seemed very much out of place in this sporting set; and, finally, the accused – Alice Image, dissolved in tears, and Charles Palk, overdressed, defiant, horsey, and unsympathetic.

"There was also Cockram, the groom. My short-sighted eyes had fastened on him the moment I entered the court. A more wretched, miserable, bewildered expression I have never seen on any man's face.

"Both Alice Image and Charles Palk flatly denied the charge. Alice declared, amid a renewed deluge of tears, that she was engaged to be married to Cockram, that she 'no more would have hurt him or the pretty creature he was in charge of, for anything'. How could she? As for Palk – conscious, no doubt, of his own evil reputation – he merely contented himself with shrugging his shoulders and various denials, usually accompanied with emphatic language.

"As neither of the accused attempted to deny that they had been together the day before the outrage, there was no occasion to call witnesses to further prove that fact. Both, however, asserted emphatically that their conversation was entirely confined to the subject of Alice's proposed flutters on the favourite for the next day's race.

"Thus the only really important witness was the groom, Cockram. Once again his attitude as a witness caused a great deal of surprise, and gradually, as he gave his evidence in a peculiarly halting and nervous manner, that surprise was changed into suspicion.

"Questioned by the magistrate, he tried his hardest to exonerate Alice from all blame; and yet when asked whether he had cause to suspect anyone else he became more confused than ever, said, 'No,' emphatically first, then, 'Yes,' and finally looked round the court appealingly, like some poor animal at bay. That the man was hiding something, that he was, in point of fact, lying, was apparent to everyone. He had drunk the beer, he said, unsuspectingly on that fatal night; he had then dropped off to sleep almost immediately, and never woke until about six a.m., when a glance at the mare at once told him that there was something very wrong.

"However, whether Cockram was lying or not – whether he suspected anyone else or was merely trying to shield his sweetheart, there was, in the opinion of the magistrate, quite sufficient evidence to prove that Alice Image, at any rate, had a hand in the hocussing of Cigarette, since it was she who had brought the drugged beer to Cockram. Beyond that there was not sufficient evidence to show either that she was a tool in the hands of Palk, or that they both were merely instruments in the hands of some third person.

"Anyway, the magistrate – it was Major Laverton, JP, a great personal friend of the Earl of Okehampton, and a remarkably clever and acute man – tried his hardest to induce Alice to confess. He questioned the poor girl so closely and so rigorously that gradually she lost what little self-control she had, and everyone in the court blamed Major Laverton not a little, for he was gradually getting the poor girl into a state of hysterics.

"As for me, I inwardly commended the learned JP, for already I had guessed what he was driving at, and was not the least astonished when the dramatic incident occurred which rendered this case so memorable.

"Alice Image, namely, now thoroughly unnerved, harassed with the Major's questions, suddenly turned to where Cockram was sitting, and, with hysterical cry, she stretched out both her arms towards him.

"'Joe! my Joe!' she cried; 'you know I didn't do it! Can't you do anything to help me?'

"It was pathetic in the extreme: everyone in the court felt deeply moved. As for Cockram, a sudden change came over him. I am accustomed to read the faces of my fellow men, and in that rough countenance I saw then emerging, in response to the girl's appeal, a quick and firm resolution.

"'Ay, and I will, Alice!' he said, jumping to his feet. 'I have tried to do my duty. If the gentlemen will hear me I will say all I know.'

"Needless to say, 'the gentlemen' were only too ready to hear him. Like a man who, having made up his mind, is now resolved to act upon it, the groom Cockram began his story.

"'I told your worship that, having drunk the beer that night, I dropped off to sleep very fast and very heavy-like. How long I'd been asleep I couldn't say, when suddenly something seemed not exactly to wake me but to dispel my dreams, so to speak. I opened my eyes. and at first I couldn't see anything, as the gas in the stable was turned on very low; but I put out my hand to feel the mare's fetlocks, just by way of telling her that I was there all right enough, and looking after her – bless her! At that moment, your worship, I noticed that the stable door was open, and that someone – I couldn't see who it was – was goin' out of it. "Who goes there?" says I, for I still felt very sleepy and dull, when, to my astonishment, who should reply to me but –'

"The man paused, and once more over his rough, honest face came the old look of perplexity and misery.

"'But –?' queried the magistrate, whose nerves were obviously as much on tension as those of everyone else in that court.

"'Speak, Joe – won't you?' appealed Alice Image pathetically.

"'But the mistress – Mrs Keeson, sir,' came from the groom in an almost inaudible whisper. 'You know, ma'am,' he added, while the gathering tears choked his voice, 'I wouldn't 'ave spoke. But she's my sweetheart, ma'am; and I couldn't bear that the shame should rest on her.'

"There was a moment's deadly silence in that crowded court. Everyone's eyes wandered towards the pale face of

Mrs Keeson, which, however, though almost livid in colour, expressed nothing but the most boundless astonishment. As for Mr Keeson, surprise, incredulity, then furious wrath at the slander, could be seen chasing one another upon his handsome face.

"'What lie is this?' burst involuntarily from his lips, as his fingers closed more tightly upon the heavy riding whip which he was holding.

"'Silence, please!' said the Major with authority. 'Now, Cockram, go on. You say Mrs Keeson spoke to you. What did she say?'

"'She seemed rather upset, sir,' continued Cockram, still looking with humble apology across at his mistress, 'for she only stammered something about: "Oh, it's nothing, Cockram. I only wanted to speak to my son – er – to Mr Harold – I –"'

"'Harold?' thundered Mr Keeson, who was fast losing his temper.

"'I must ask you, Mr Keeson, to be silent,' said the Major. 'Go on, Cockram.'

"And Cockram continued his narrative:

"'"Mr Harold, ma'am?" I said. "What should 'e be doing 'ere in the stables at this time of night?" "Oh, nothing," says she to me, "I thought I saw him come in here. I must have been mistaken. Never mind, Cockram; it's all right. Good night."

"'I said good night, too, and then fell to wondering what Mr 'Arold could have wanted prowling round the stables at this hour of the night. Just then the clock of St Saviour's struck four o'clock, and while I was still wondering I fell asleep again, and never awoke until six, when the mare was as sick as she could be. And that's the whole truth, gentlemen; and I would never have spoke – for Mr and Mrs Keeson have always been good to me, and I'd have done anything to save them the disgrace – but Alice is goin' to be my wife, and I couldn't bear any shame to rest upon 'er.'

"When Cockram had finished speaking you might have heard a pin drop as Major Laverton asked Mrs Keeson to step into the witness-box. She looked fragile and pale, but otherwise quite self-possessed as she quietly kissed the book and said in a very firm tone of voice:

"'I can only say in reply to the extraordinary story which this man has just told that the drug in the beer must have given him peculiarly vivid dreams. At the hour he names I was in bed fast asleep, as my husband can testify; and the whole of Cockram's narrative is a fabrication from beginning to end. I may add that I am more than willing to forgive him. No doubt his brain was clouded by the opiate; and now he is beside himself owing to Alice Image's predicament. As for my son Harold, he was absent from home that night; he was spending it with some bachelor friends at the Stag and Mantle hotel in Newmarket.'

"'Yes! By the way,' said the magistrate, 'where is Mr Harold Keeson? I have no doubt that he will be able to give a very good account of himself on that memorable night.'

"'My son is abroad, your worship,' said Mrs Keeson, while a shade of a still more livid hue passed over her face.

"'Abroad, is he?' said the magistrate cheerfully. 'Well, that settles the point satisfactorily for him, doesn't it? When did he go?'

"'Last Thursday, your worship,' replied Mrs Keeson.

"Then there was silence again in the court, for that last Thursday was the day of the Coronation Stakes – the day immediately following the memorable night on which the mare Cigarette had been poisoned by an unknown hand."

### 4

"I doubt whether in all the annals of criminal procedure there ever occurred a more dramatic moment than that when so strange a ray of daylight was shed on the mysterious outrage on Cigarette. The magistrate, having dismissed Mrs Keeson, hardly dared to look across at the trainer, who was a personal friend of his, and who had just received such a cruel blow through this terrible charge against his only son – for at that moment I doubt if there were two people in that court who did not think that Mrs Keeson had just sworn a false oath, and that both she and her son had been in the stables that night – for what purpose only they and their own conscience could tell.

"Alice Image and Charles Palk were both discharged; and it is greatly to the credit of Cockram that in the midst of his joy in seeing his sweetheart safe he still remained very gloomy and upset. As for Mr Keeson, he must have suffered terribly at all this mud cast at his only son. He had been wounded in what he worshipped more than anything else in the world – his family honour. What was the use of money and the old estates if such a stain rested upon his name?

"As for Mrs Keeson, public sympathy was very much overshadowed with contempt for her stupidity. Had she only held her tongue when Cockram challenged her, suspicion would never have fastened upon Harold. The fact that she had lied in the witness-box in order to try and remedy her blunder was also very severely commented upon. The young man had gone abroad on that memorable Thursday accompanied by two of his bachelor friends. They had gone on a fishing expedition to Norway, and were not expected home for three weeks. As they meant to move from place to place they had left no address: letters and telegrams were therefore useless.

"During those three weeks pending Harold Keeson's return certain facts leaked out which did not tend to improve his case. It appears that he had long been in love with Lady Agnes Stourcliffe, the daughter of the Earl of Okehampton. Some people asserted that the young people were actually – though secretly – engaged. The Earl, however, seems all along to have objected to the marriage of his daughter with the son of a trainer, and on more than one occasion had remarked that he had not sunk quite so low yet as to allow so preposterous a *mésalliance*. Mr Keeson, whose family pride was at least equal to that of the Earl, had naturally very much resented this attitude, and had often begged his son to give up his pretensions, since they were manifestly so unwelcome.

"Harold Keeson, however, was deeply in love; and Lady Agnes stuck to him with womanly constancy and devotion. Unfortunately a climax was reached some days before the disastrous events at Newmarket. The Earl of Okehampton suddenly took up a very firm stand on the subject of Harold Keeson's courtship of his daughter. Some hot words were exchanged between the two men, ending in an open breach, the Earl positively forbidding the young man ever to enter his house again.

"Harold was terribly unhappy at this turn of events. Pride forbade him to take an unfair advantage of a young girl's devotion, and, acting on the advice of his parents, he started for his tour in Norway, ostensibly in order to try and forget the fair Lady Agnes. This unhappy love affair, ending in an open and bitter quarrel between himself and the owner of Cigarette, did – as I said before – the young man's case no good. At the instance of the Earl of Okehampton, who determined to prosecute him, he was arrested on landing at Harwich.

"Well," continued the man in the corner, "the next events must be still fresh in your mind. When Harold Keeson appeared in the dock, charged with such meanness as to wreak his private grievance upon a dumb animal, public sympathy at once veered round in his favour. He looked so handsome, so frank and honest, that at once one felt convinced that *his* hand, at any rate, could never have done such a dastardy thing.

"Mr Keeson, who was a rich man, moreover had enlisted the services of Sir Arthur Inglewood, who had, in the short time at his disposal, collected all the most important evidence on behalf of his client.

"The two young men who had been travelling in Norway with Harold Keeson had been present with him on the memorable night at a bachelor party given by a mutual friend at the Stag and Mantle. Both testified that the party had played Bridge until the small hours of the morning, that between two rubbers – the rooms being very hot – they had all strolled out to smoke a cigar in the streets. Just as they were about to re-enter the hotel two church clocks – one of which was St Saviour's – chimed out the hour – four o'clock.

"Four o'clock was the hour when Cockram said that he had spoken to Mrs Keeson. Harold had not left the party at the Stag and Mantle since ten o'clock, which was an hour before Alice Image took the drugged beer to the groom. The whole edifice of the prosecution thus crumbled together like a house of cards and Harold Keeson was discharged, without the slightest suspicion clinging to him.

"Six months later he married Lady Agnes Stourcliffe. The Earl, now a completely ruined man, offered no further opposition to the union of his daughter with a man who, at any rate, could keep her in comfort and luxury; for though both Mr Keeson and his son lost heavily through Cigarette's illness, yet the trainer was sufficiently rich to offer his son and his bride a very beautiful home."

The man in the corner called to the waitress, and paid for his glass of milk and cheesecake, whilst I remained absorbed in thought, gazing at *The Daily Telegraph*, which, in its 'London Day by Day', had this very morning announced that Mr and Lady Agnes Keeson had returned to town from 'The Rookery', Newmarket.

5

"But who poisoned Cigarette?" I asked after a while; "and why?"

"Ah, who did, I wonder?" he replied with exasperating mildness.

44

"Surely you have a theory," I suggested.

"Ah, but my theories are not worth considering. The police would take no notice of them."

"Why did Mrs Keeson go to the stables that night? Did she go?" I asked.

"Cockram swears she did."

"She swears she didn't. If she did why should she have asked for her son? Surely she did not wish to incriminate her son in order to save herself?"

"No," he replied; "women don't save themselves usually at the expense of their children, and women don't usually 'hocus' a horse. It is not a female crime at all – is it?"

The aggravating creature was getting terribly sarcastic; and I began to fear that he was not going to speak, after all. He was looking dejectedly all around him. I had one or two parcels by me. I undid a piece of string from one of them, and handed it to him with the most perfectly indifferent air I could command.

"I wonder if it was Cockram who told a lie?" I then said unconcernedly.

But already he had seized on that bit of string, and nervously now, his long fingers began fashioning a series of complicated knots.

"Let us take things from the beginning," he said at last. "The beginning of the mystery was the contradictory statements made by the groom Cockram and Mrs Keeson respectively. Let us take, first of all, the question of the groom. The matter is simple enough: either he saw Mrs Keeson or he did not. If he did not see her then he must have told a lie, either unintentionally or by design – unintentionally if he was mistaken; but this could not very well be since he asserted that Mrs Keeson spoke to him, and even mentioned her son, Mr Harold Keeson. Therefore, if Cockram did not see Mrs Keeson he told a lie by design for some purpose of his own. You follow me?"

"Yes," I replied, "I have thought all that out for myself already."

"Very well. Now, could there be some even remotely plausible motive why Cockram should have told that deliberate lie?"

"To save his sweetheart, Alice Image," I said.

"But you forget that his sweetheart was not accused at first, and that, from the very beginning, Cockram's manner, when questioned on the subject of the events of that night, was strange and contradictory in the extreme."

"He may have known from the first that Alice Image was guilty," I argued.

"In that case he would have merely asserted that he had seen and heard nothing during the night, or, if he wished to lie about it, he would have said that it was Palk, the tout, who sneaked into the stables, rather than incriminate his mistress, who had been good and kind to him for years."

"He may have wished to be revenged on Mrs Keeson for some reason which has not yet transpired."

"How? By making a statement which, if untrue, could be so easily disproved by Mr Keeson himself, who, as a matter of fact, could easily assert that his wife did not leave her bedroom that night, or by incriminating Mr Harold Keeson, who could prove an alibi? Not much of a revenge there, you must admit. No, no; the more you reflect seriously upon these possibilities the deeper will become your conviction that Cockram did not lie either accidentally or on purpose; that he did see Mrs Keeson at that hour at the stable door; that she did speak to him; and that it was she who told the lie in open court."

"But," I asked, feeling more bewildered than before, "why should Mrs Keeson have gone to the stables and asked for her son when she must have known that he was not there, but that her enquiry would make it, to say the least, extremely unpleasant for him?"

"Why?" he shrieked excitedly, jumping up like a veritable jack-in-the-box. "Ah, if you would only learn to reflect you might in time become a fairly able journalist. Why did Mrs Keeson momentarily incriminate her son? – for it was only a momentary incrimination. Think, think! A woman does not incriminate her child to save herself; but she might do it to save someone else – someone who was dearer to her than that child."

"Nonsense!" I protested.

"Nonsense, is it?" he replied. "You have only to think of the characters of the chief personages who figured in the drama – of the trainer Keeson, with his hasty temper and his inordinate family pride. Was it likely when the half-ruined Earl of Okehampton talked of *mésalliance*, and forbade the marriage of his daughter with his trainer's son, that the latter would not resent that insult with terrible bitterness? and, resenting it, not think of some means of being even with the noble Earl? Can you not imagine the proud man boiling with indignation on hearing his son's tale of how

47

Lord Okehampton had forbidden him the house? Can you not hear him saying to himself:

"'Well, by —— the trainer's son *shall* marry the Earl's daughter!'

"And the scheme – simple and effectual – whereby the ruin of the arrogant nobleman would be made so complete that he would be only too willing to allow his daughter to marry anyone who would give her a good home and him a helping hand?"

"But," I objected, "why should Mr Keeson take the trouble to drug the groom and sneak out to the stables at dead of night when he had access to the mare at all hours of the day?"

"Why?" shrieked the animated scarecrow. "Why? Because Keeson was just one of those clever criminals, with a sufficiency of brains to throw police and public alike off the scent. Cockram, remember, spent every moment of the day and night with the mare. Therefore, if he had been in full possession of his senses and could positively swear that no one had had access to Cigarette but his master and himself, suspicion was bound to fasten, sooner or later, on Keeson. But Keeson was a bit of a genius in the criminal line. Seemingly he could have had no motive for drugging the groom, yet he added that last artistic touch to his clever crime, and thus threw a final bucketful of sand in the eyes of the police."

"Even then," I argued, "Cockram might just have woke up – might just have caught Keeson in the act."

"Exactly. And that is, no doubt, what Mrs Keeson feared.

"She was a brave woman, if ever there was one. Can you not picture her knowing her husband's violent temper, his indomitable pride? and guessing that he would find some means of being revenged on the Earl of Okehampton? Can you not imagine her watching her husband and gradually guessing, realizing what he had in his mind when, in the middle of the night, she saw him steal out of bed and out of the house? Can you not see her following him stealthily – afraid of him, perhaps – not daring to interfere – terrified above all things of the consequences of his crime, of the risks of Cockram waking up, of the exposure, the disgrace?

"Then the final tableau – Keeson having accomplished his purpose, goes back towards the house, and she – perhaps with a vague hope that she might yet save the mare by taking away the poison which Keeson had prepared – in her turn goes to the stables. But this time the groom is half awake, and challenges her. Then her instinct – that unerring instinct which always prompts a really good woman when the loved one is in danger – suggests to Mrs Keeson the clever subterfuge of pretending that she had seen her son entering the stables.

"She asks for him, *knowing well that she could do him no harm*, since he could so easily prove an alibi, but thereby throwing a veritable cloud of dust in the eyes of the keenest enquirer, and casting over the hocussing of Cigarette so thick a mantle of mystery that suspicion, groping blindly round, could never fasten tightly on anyone.

"Think of it all," he added as, gathering up his hat and umbrella, he prepared to go, "and remember at the same time that it was Mr Keeson alone who could disprove that his wife never left her room that night, that he did not do this, that he guessed what she had done and why she had

49

done it, and I think that you will admit that not one link is missing in the chain of evidence which I have had the privilege of laying before you."

Before I could reply he had gone, and I saw his strange scarecrow-like figure disappearing through the glass door. Then I had a good think on the subject of the hocussing of Cigarette, and I was reluctantly bound to admit that once again the man in the corner had found the only possible solution to the mystery.

# III

# *The Tragedy in Dartmoor Terrace*

## 1

"It is not by any means the Law and Police Courts that form the only interesting reading in the daily papers," said the man in the corner airily, as he munched his eternal bit of cheesecake and sipped his glass of milk, like a frowsy old tom-cat.

"You don't agree with me," he added, for I had offered no comment to his obvious remark.

"No?" I answered. "I suppose you were thinking –"

"Of the tragic death of Mrs Yule, for instance," he replied eagerly. "Beyond the inquest, and its very unsatisfactory verdict, very few circumstances connected with that interesting case ever got into the papers at all."

"I forget what the verdict actually was," I said, eager, too, on my side to hear him talk about that mysterious tragedy, which, as a matter of fact, had puzzled a good many people.

"Oh, it was as vague and as wordy as the English language would allow. The jury found that 'Mrs Yule had died through falling downstairs, in consequence of a fainting attack, but *how* she came to fall is not clearly shown'.

"What had happened was this: Mrs Yule was a rich and eccentric old lady, who lived very quietly in a small house in Kensington; No. 9 Dartmoor Terrace is, I believe, the correct address.

"She had no expensive tastes, for she lived, as I said before, very simply and quietly in a small Kensington house, with two female servants – a cook and a housemaid – and a young fellow whom she had adopted as her son.

"The story of this adoption is, of course, the pivot round which all the circumstances of the mysterious tragedy revolved. Mrs Yule, namely, had an only son, William, to whom she was passionately attached; but, like many a fond mother, she had the desire of mapping out that son's future entirely according to her own ideas. William Yule, on the other hand, had his own views with regard to his own happiness, and one fine day went so far as to marry the girl of his choice, and that in direct opposition to his mother's wishes.

"Mrs Yule's chagrin and horror at what she called her son's base ingratitude knew no bounds; at first it was even thought that she would never get over it.

"'He has gone in direct opposition to my fondest wishes, and chosen a wife whom I could never accept as a daughter; he shall have none of the property which has enriched me, and which I know he covets.'

"At first her friends imagined that she meant to leave all her money to charitable institutions; but oh! dear me, no! Mrs Yule was one of those women who never did anything that other people expected her to. Within three years of her son's marriage she had filled up the place which he had vacated, both in her house and in her heart. She had adopted a son, preferring, as she said, that her money should benefit an individual rather than an institution.

"Her choice had fallen upon the only son of a poor man – an ex-soldier – who used to come twice a week to Dartmoor Terrace to tidy up the small garden at the back: he was very respectable and very honest – was born in the same part of England as Mrs Yule, and had an only son whose name happened to be William; he rejoiced in the surname of Bloggs.

"'It suits me in every way,' explained Mrs Yule to old Mr Statham, her friend and solicitor. 'You see, I am used to the name of William, and the boy is nice-looking and has done very well at the Board School. Moreover, old Bloggs will die within a year or two, and William will be left without any encumbrances.'

"Herein Mrs Yule's prophecy proved to be correct. Old Bloggs did die very soon, and his son was duly adopted by the rich and eccentric old lady, sent to a good school, and finally given a berth in the Union Bank.

"I saw young Bloggs – it is not a euphonious name, is it? – at that memorable inquest later on. He was very young and unassuming, and used to keep very much out of the way of Mrs Yule's friends, who, mind you, strongly disapproved of his presence in the rich old widow's house, to the detriment of the only legitimate son and heir.

"What happened within the intimate and close circle of 9 Dartmoor Terrace during the next three years of course nobody can tell. Certain it is that by the time young Bloggs was nearing his twenty-first birthday, he had become the very apple of his adopted mother's eye.

"During those three years Mr Statham and other old friends had worked hard in the interests of William Yule.

Everyone felt that the latter was being very badly treated indeed. He had studied painting in his younger days, and now had set up a small studio in Hampstead, and was making perhaps a couple of hundred or so a year, and that with much difficulty, whilst the gardener's son had supplanted him in his mother's affections, and, worse still, in his mother's purse.

"The old lady was more obdurate than ever. In deference to the strong feelings of her friends she had agreed to see her son occasionally, and William Yule would call upon his mother from time to time – in the middle of the day when Bloggs was out of the way at the Bank – stay to tea, and part from her in frigid, though otherwise amicable, terms.

"'I have no ill-feeling against my son,' the old lady would say, 'but when he married against my wishes, he became a stranger to me – that is all – a stranger, however, whose pleasant acquaintanceship I am pleased to keep up.'

"That the old lady meant to carry her eccentricities in this respect to the bitter end, became all the more evident when she sent for her old friend and lawyer, Mr Statham, and explained to him that she wished to make over to young Bloggs the whole of her property by deed of gift, during her lifetime – on condition that on his twenty-first birthday he legally took up the name of Yule.

"Mr Statham subsequently made public, as you know, the whole of this interview which he had with Mrs Yule.

"'I tried to dissuade her, of course,' he said, 'for I thought it so terribly unfair on William Yule and his children. Moreover, I had always hoped that when Mrs Yule grew older and more feeble she would surely relent towards her only son. But she was terribly obstinate.'

"'It is because I may become weak in my dotage,' she said, 'that I want to make the whole thing absolutely final – I don't want to relent. I wish that William should suffer, where I think he will suffer most, for he was always over-fond of money. If I make a will in favour of Bloggs, who knows I might repent it, and alter it at the eleventh hour? One is apt to become maudlin when one is dying, and has people weeping all round one. No! – I want the whole thing to be absolutely irrevocable; and I shall present the deed of gift to young Bloggs on his twenty-first birthday. I can always make it a condition that he keeps me in moderate comfort to the end of my days. He is too big a fool to be really ungrateful, and after all I don't think I should very much mind ending my life in the workhouse.'

"'What could I do?' added Mr Statham. 'If I had refused to draw up that iniquitous deed of gift, she only would have employed some other lawyer to do it for her. As it is, I secured an annuity of £500 a year for the old lady, in consideration of a gift worth some £30,000 made over absolutely to Mr William Bloggs.'

"The deed was drawn up," continued the man in the corner, "there is no doubt of that. Mr Statham saw to it. The old lady even insisted on having two more legal opinions upon it, lest there should be the slightest flaw that might render the deed invalid. Moreover, she caused herself to be examined by two specialists in order that they might testify that she was absolutely sound in mind, and in full possession of all her faculties.

"When the deed was all that the law could wish, Mr Statham handed it over to Mrs Yule, who wished to keep it by her until 3rd April – young Bloggs' twenty-first birthday – on which day she meant to surprise him with it.

"Mr Statham handed over the deed to Mrs Yule on 14th February, and on 28th March – that is to say, six days before Bloggs' majority – the old lady was found dead at the foot of the stairs in Dartmoor Terrace, whilst her desk was found to have been broken open, and the deed of gift had disappeared."

## 2

"From the very first the public took a great interest in the sad death of Mrs Yule. The old lady's eccentricities were pretty well known throughout all her neighbourhood, at any rate. Then, she had a large circle of friends, who all took sides, either for the disowned son or for the old lady's rigid and staunch principles of filial obedience.

"Directly, therefore, that the papers mentioned the sudden death of Mrs Yule, tongues began to wag, and, whilst some asserted 'Accident', others had already begun to whisper 'Murder'.

"For the moment nothing definite was known. Mr Bloggs had sent for Mr Statham, and the most persevering and most inquisitive persons of both sexes could glean no information from the cautious old lawyer.

"The inquest was to be held on the following day, and perforce curiosity had to be bridled until then. But you may imagine how that coroner's court at Kensington was packed on that day. I, of course, was at my usual place – well to the front, for I was already keenly interested in the tragedy, and knew that a palpitating mystery lurked behind the old lady's death.

"Annie, the housemaid at Dartmoor Terrace, was the first, and I may say the only really important, witness during the interesting inquest. The story she told amounted to this: Mrs Yule, it appears, was very religious, and, in spite of her advancing years and decided weakness of the heart, was in the habit of going to early morning service every day of her life at six o'clock. She would get up before anyone else in the house, and winter or summer, rain, snow, or fine, she would walk round to St Matthias' Church, coming home at about a quarter to seven, just when her servants were getting up.

"On this sad morning (28th March) Annie explained that she got up as usual and went downstairs (the servants slept at the top of the house) at seven o'clock. She noticed nothing wrong; her mistress's bedroom door was open as usual, Annie merely remarking to herself that the mistress was later than usual from church that morning. Then suddenly, in the hall at the foot of the stairs, she caught sight of Mrs Yule lying head downwards, her head on the mat, motionless.

"'I ran downstairs as quickly as I could,' continued Annie, 'and I suppose I must 'ave screamed, for cook came out of 'er room upstairs, and Mr Bloggs, too, shouted down to know what was the matter. At first we only thought Mrs Yule was unconscious-like. Me and Mr Bloggs carried 'er to 'er room, and then Mr Bloggs ran for the doctor.'

"The rest of Annie's story," continued the man in the corner, "was drowned in a deluge of tears. As for the doctor, he could add but little to what the public had already known and guessed. Mrs Yule undoubtedly suffered from a weak heart, although she had never been known to faint. In this instance, however, she undoubtedly must have turned giddy, as she was about to go downstairs, and fallen headlong. She was of course very much injured, the doctor explained, but she actually died of heart failure, brought on by the shock of the fall. She must have been on her way to church, for her prayer-book was found on the floor close by her, also a candle – which she must have carried, as it was a dark morning – had rolled along and extinguished itself as it rolled. From these facts, therefore, it was gathered that the poor old lady came by this tragic death at about six o'clock, the hour at which she regularly started out for morning service. Both the servants and also Mr Bloggs slept at the top of the house, and it is a known fact that sleep in most cases is always heaviest in the early morning hours; there was, therefore, nothing strange in the fact that no one heard either the fall or a scream, if Mrs Yule uttered one, which is doubtful.

"So far, you see," continued the man in the corner, after a slight pause, "there did not appear to be anything very out of the way or mysterious about Mrs Yule's tragic death. But the public had expected interesting developments, and I must say their expectations were more than fully realized.

"Jane, the cook, was the first witness to give the public an inkling of the sensations to come.

"She deposed that on Thursday, the 27th, she was alone in the kitchen in the evening after dinner, as it was the housemaid's evening out, when, at about nine o'clock, there was a ring at the bell.

"'I went to answer the door,' said Jane, 'and there was a lady, all dressed in black, as far as I could see – as the 'all gas always did burn very badly – still, I think she was dressed dark, and she 'ad on a big 'at and a veil with spots. She says to me: "Mrs Yule lives 'ere?" I says, "She do, 'm," though I don't think she was quite the lady, so I don't know why I said 'm, but –'

"'Yes, yes!' here interrupted the coroner somewhat impatiently, 'it doesn't matter what you said. Tell us what happened.'

"'Yes, sir,' continued Jane, quite undisturbed, 'as I was saying, I asked the lady her name, and she says: "Tell Mrs Yule I would wish to speak with 'er," then as she saw me 'esitating, for I didn't like leaving 'er all alone in the 'all, she said, "Tell Mrs Yule that Mrs William Yule wishes to speak with 'er."'

"Jane paused to take breath, for she talked fast and volubly, and all eyes were turned to a corner of the room, where William Yule, dressed in the careless fashion affected by artists, sat watching and listening eagerly to everything that was going on. At the mention of his wife's name he shrugged his shoulders, and I thought for the moment that he would jump up and say something; but he evidently thought better of it, and remained as before, silent and quietly watching.

"'You showed the lady upstairs?' asked the coroner, after an instant's most dramatic pause.

"'Yes, sir,' replied Jane; 'but I went to ask the mistress first. Mrs Yule was sitting in the drawing-room, reading. She says to me, "Show the lady up at once; and, Jane," she says, "ask Mr Bloggs to kindly come to the drawing-room." I showed the lady up, and I told Mr Bloggs, 'oo was smoking in the library, and 'e went to the drawing-room.

"'When Annie come in,' continued Jane with increased volubility, 'I told 'er 'oo 'ad come, and she and me was very astonished, because we 'ad often seen Mr William Yule come to see 'is mother, but we 'ad never seen 'is wife. "Did you see what she was like, cook?" says Annie to me. "No," I says, "the 'all gas was burnin' that badly, and she 'ad a veil on." Then Annie ups and says, "I must go up, cook," she says, "for my things is all wet. I never did see such rain in all my life. I tell you my boots and petticoats is all soaked through." Then up she runs, and I thought then that per'aps she meant to see if she couldn't 'ear anything that was goin' on upstairs. Presently she come down –'

"But at this point Jane's flow of eloquence received an unexpected check. The coroner preferred to hear from Annie herself whatever the latter may have overheard, and Jane, very wrathful and indignant, had to stand aside, while Annie, who was then recalled, completed the story.

"'I don't know what made me stop on the landing,' she explained timidly, 'and I'm sure I didn't mean to listen. I was going upstairs to change my things, and put on my cap and apron, in case the mistress wanted anything.

"'Then, I don't think I ever 'eard Mrs Yule's voice so loud and angry.'

"'You stopped to listen?' asked the coroner.

"'I couldn't 'elp it, sir. Mrs Yule was shouting at the top of 'er voice. "Out of my 'ouse," she says; "I never wish to see you or your precious husband inside my doors again."'

"'You are quite sure that you heard those very words?' asked the coroner earnestly.

"'I'll take my Bible oath on every one of them, sir,' said Annie emphatically. 'Then I could 'ear someone crying and moaning: "Oh! what 'ave I done? Oh! what 'ave I done?" I didn't like to stand on the landing then, for fear someone should come out, so I ran upstairs, and put on my cap and apron, for I was all in a tremble, what with what I'd 'eard, and the storm outside, which was coming down terrible.

"'When I went down again, I 'ardly durst stand on the landing, but the door of the drawing-room was ajar, and I 'eard Mr Bloggs say: "Surely you will not turn a human being, much less a woman, out on a night like this?" And the mistress said, still speaking very angry: "Very well, you may sleep here; but remember, I don't wish to see your face again. I go to church at six and come home again at seven; mind you are out of the house before then. There are plenty of trains after seven o'clock."'

"After that," continued the man in the corner, "Mrs Yule rang for the housemaid and gave orders that the spare room should be got ready, and that the visitor should have some tea and toast brought to her in the morning as soon as Annie was up.

"But Annie was rather late on that eventful morning of the 28th. She did not go downstairs till seven o'clock. When she did, she found her mistress lying dead at the foot of the stairs. It was not until after the doctor had been and gone that both the servants suddenly recollected the guest in the spare room. Annie knocked at her door, and, receiving no answer, she walked in; the bed had not been slept in, and the spare room was empty.

"'There, now!' was the housemaid's decisive comment, 'me and cook did 'ear someone cross the 'all, and the front door bang about an hour after everyone else was in bed.'

"Presumably, therefore, Mrs William Yule had braved the elements and left the house at about midnight, leaving no trace behind her, save, perhaps, the broken lock of the desk that had held the deed of gift in favour of young Bloggs."

### 3

"Some say there's a Providence that watches over us," said the man in the corner, when he had looked at me keenly, and assured himself that I was really interested in his narrative, "others use the less poetic and more direct formula, that 'the devil takes care of his own'. The impression of the general public during this interesting coroner's inquest was that the devil was taking special care of his own – ('his own' being in this instance represented by Mrs William Yule, who, by the way, was not present).

"What the Evil One had done for her was this: He caused the hall gas to burn so badly on that eventful Thursday night, 27th March, that Jane, the cook, had not been able to see Mrs William Yule at all distinctly. He, moreover, decreed that when Annie went into the drawing-room later on to take her mistress' orders with regard to the spare room,

Mrs William was apparently dissolved in tears, for she only presented the back of her head to the inquisitive glances of the young housemaid.

"After that the two servants went to bed, and heard someone cross the hall and leave the house about an hour or so later; but neither of them could swear positively that they would recognize the mysterious visitor if they set eyes on her again.

"Throughout all these proceedings, however, you may be sure that Mr William Yule did not remain a passive spectator. In fact, I, who watched him, could see quite clearly that he had the greatest possible difficulty in controlling himself. Mind you, I knew by then exactly where the hitch lay, and I could, and will presently, tell you exactly all that occurred on Thursday evening, 27th March, at No. 9 Dartmoor Terrace, just as if I had spent that memorable night there myself; and I can assure you that it gave me great pleasure to watch the faces of the two men most interested in the verdict of this coroner's jury.

"Everyone's sympathy had by now entirely veered round to young Bloggs, who for years had been brought up to expect a fortune, and had then, at the last moment, been defrauded of it, through what looked already much like a crime. The deed of gift had, of course, not been what the lawyers call 'completed'. It had rested in Mrs Yule's desk, and had never been 'delivered' by the donor to the donee, or even to another person on his behalf.

"Young Bloggs, therefore, saw himself suddenly destined to live his life as penniless as he had been when he was still the old gardener's son.

"No doubt the public felt that what lurked mostly in his mind was a desire for revenge, and I think everyone forgave him when he gave his evidence with a distinct tone of animosity against the woman who had apparently succeeded in robbing him of a fortune.

"He had only met Mrs William Yule once before, he explained, but he was ready to swear that it was she who called that night. As for the original motive of the quarrel between the two ladies, young Bloggs was inclined to think that it was mostly on the question of money.

"'Mrs William,' continued the young man, 'made certain peremptory demands on Mrs Yule, which the old lady bitterly resented.'

"But here there was an awful and sudden interruption. William Yule, now quite beside himself with rage, had with one bound reached the witness-box, and struck young Bloggs a violent blow in the face.

"'Liar and cheat!' he roared, 'take that!'

"And he prepared to deal the young man another even more vigorous blow, when he was overpowered and seized by the constables. Young Bloggs had become positively livid; his face looked grey and ashen, except there, where his powerful assailant's fist had left a deep purple mark.

"'You have done your wife's cause no good,' remarked the coroner dryly, as William Yule, sullen and defiant, was forcibly dragged back to his place. 'I shall adjourn the inquest until Monday, and will expect Mrs Yule to be present and explain exactly what happened after her quarrel with the deceased, and why she left the house so suddenly and mysteriously that night.'

"William Yule tried an explanation even then. His wife had never left the studio in Sheriff Road, West Hampstead, the whole of that Thursday evening. It was a fearfully stormy night, and she never went outside the door. But the Yules kept no servant at the cheap little rooms; a charwoman used to come in every morning only for an hour or two, to do the rough work; there was no one, therefore, except the husband himself to prove Mrs William Yule's alibi.

"At the adjourned inquest, on the Monday, Mrs William Yule duly appeared; she was a young, delicate-looking woman, with a patient and suffering face, that had not an atom of determination or vice in it.

"Her evidence was very simple; she merely swore solemnly that she had spent the whole evening indoors, she had never been to 9 Dartmoor Terrace in her life, and, as a matter of fact, would never have dared to call on her irreconcilable mother-in-law. Neither she nor her husband were specially in want of money either.

"'My husband had just sold a picture at the Watercolour Institute,' she explained, 'we were not hard up; and certainly I should never have attempted to make the slightest demand on Mrs Yule.'

"There the matter had to rest with regard to the theft of the document, for that was no business of the coroner's or of the jury. According to medical evidence the old lady's death had been due to a very natural and possible accident – a sudden feeling of giddiness – and the verdict had to be in accordance with this.

"There was no real proof against Mrs William Yule – only one man's word, that of young Bloggs; and it would no doubt always have been felt that his evidence might not be wholly unbiased. He was therefore well advised not to prosecute. The world was quite content to believe that the Yules had planned and executed the theft, but he never would have got a conviction against Mrs William Yule just on his own evidence."

4

"Then William Yule and his wife were left in full possession of their fortune?" I asked eagerly.

"Yes, they were," he replied; "but they had to go and travel abroad for a while, feeling was so high against them. The deed, of course, not having been 'delivered', could not be upheld in a court of law; that was the opinion of several eminent counsel whom Mr Statham, with a lofty sense of justice, consulted on behalf of young Bloggs."

"And young Bloggs was left penniless?"

"No," said the man in the corner, as, with a weird and satisfied smile, he pulled a piece of string out of his pocket; "the friends of the late Mrs Yule subscribed the sum of £1,000 for him, for they all thought he had been so terribly badly treated, and Mr Statham has taken him in his office as articled pupil. No! no! young Bloggs has not done so badly either –"

"What seems strange to me," I remarked, "is that, for all she knew, Mrs William Yule might have committed only a silly and purposeless theft. If Mrs Yule had not died suddenly and accidentally the next morning, she would, no doubt, have executed a fresh deed of gift, and all would have been *in statu quo.*"

"Exactly," he replied dryly, whilst his fingers fidgeted nervously with his bit of string.

"Of course," I suggested, for I felt that the funny creature wanted to be drawn out; "she may have reckoned on the old lady's weak heart, and the shock to her generally, but it was, after all, very problematical."

"Very," he said, "and surely you are not still under the impression that Mrs Yule's death was purely the result of an accident?"

"What else could it be?" I urged.

"The result of a slight push from the top of the stairs," he remarked placidly, whilst a complicated knot went to join a row of its fellows.

"But Mrs William Yule had left the house before midnight – or, at any rate, someone had. Do you think she had an accomplice?"

"I think," he said excitedly, "that the mysterious visitor who left the house that night had an instigator whose name was William Bloggs."

"I don't understand," I gasped in amazement.

"Point No. 1," he shrieked, while the row of knots followed each other in rapid succession. "Young Bloggs swore a lie when he swore that it was Mrs William Yule who called at Dartmoor Terrace that night."

"What makes you say that?" I retorted.

"One very simple fact," he replied, "so simple that it was, of course, overlooked. Do you remember that one of the things which Annie overheard was old Mrs Yule's irate words, 'Very well, you may sleep here; but, remember, I do not wish to see your face again. You can leave my house before I return

67

from church; you can get plenty of trains after seven o'clock.' Now what do you make of that?" he added triumphantly.

"Nothing in particular," I rejoined; "it was an awfully wet night, and –"

"And High Street Kensington Station within two minutes' walk of Dartmoor Terrace, with plenty of trains to West Hampstead, and Sheriff Road within two minutes of this latter station," he shrieked, getting more and more excited, "and the hour only about ten o'clock, when there are plenty of trains from one part of London to another? Old Mrs Yule, with her irascible temper and obstinate ways, would have said: 'There's the station, not two minutes' walk; get out of my house, and don't ever let me see your face again.' Wouldn't she, now?"

"It certainly seems more likely."

"Of course it does. She only allowed the woman to stay because the woman had either a very long way to go to get a train, or perhaps had missed her last train – a connection on a branch line presumably – and could not possibly get home at all that night."

"Yes, that sounds logical," I admitted.

"Point No. 2," he shrieked. "Young Bloggs having told a lie, had some object in telling it. That was my starting-point; from there I worked steadily until I had reconstructed the events of that Thursday night – nay, more, until I knew something more about young Bloggs' immediate future, in order that I might then imagine his past.

"And this is what I found.

"After the tragic death of Mrs Yule, young Bloggs went abroad at the expense of some kind friends, and came home with a wife, whom he is supposed to have met and married in Switzerland. From that point everything became clear to me. Young Bloggs had told a lie when he swore that it was Mrs William Yule who called that night – it was certainly not Mrs William Yule; therefore it was somebody who either represented herself as such, or who believed herself to be Mrs William Yule.

"The first supposition," continued the funny creature, "I soon dismissed as impossible; young Bloggs knew Mrs William Yule by sight – and since he had lied, he had done so deliberately. Therefore to my mind, the lady who called herself Mrs William Yule did so because she believed that she had a right to that name; that she had married a man, who, for purposes of his own, had chosen to call himself by that name. From this point to that of guessing who that man was was simple enough."

"Do you mean young Bloggs himself?" I asked in amazement.

"And whom else?" he replied. "Isn't that sort of thing done every day? Bloggs was a hideous name, and Yule was eventually to be his own. With William Yule's example before him, he must have known that it would be dangerous to broach the marriage question at all before the old lady, and probably only meant to wait for a favourable opportunity of doing so. But after a while the young wife would naturally become troubled and anxious, and, like most women under the same circumstances, would become jealous and inquisitive as well.

"She soon found out where he lived, and no doubt called there, thinking that old Mrs Yule was her husband's own fond mother.

"You can picture the rest. Mrs Yule, furious at having been deceived, herself destroys the deed of gift which she meant to present to her adopted son, and from that hour young Bloggs sees himself penniless.

"The false Mrs Yule left the house, and young Bloggs waited for his opportunity on the dark landing of a small London house. One push and the deed was done. With her weak heart, Mrs Yule was sure to die of the shock, if not of the fall.

"Before that, already the desk had been broken open and every appearance of a theft given to it. After the tragedy, then, young Bloggs retired quietly to his room. The whole thing looked so like an accident that, even had the servants heard the fall at once, there would still have been time enough for the young villain to sneak into his room, and then to reappear at his door, as if he, too, had been just awakened by the noise.

"The result turned out just as he expected. The William Yules have been and still are suspected of the theft; and young Bloggs is a hero of romance with whom everyone is in sympathy."

# *Who Stole the Black Diamonds?*

**1**

"Do you know who that is?" said the man in the corner, as he pushed a small packet of photos across the table.

The picture on the top represented an entrancingly beautiful woman, with bare arms and neck, and a profusion of pearl and diamond ornaments about her head and throat.

"Surely this is the Queen of –"

"Hush!" he broke in abruptly, with mock dismay; "you must mention no names."

"Why not?" I asked, laughing, for he looked so droll in his distress.

"Look closely at the photo," he replied, "and at the necklace and tiara that the lady is wearing."

"Yes," I said. "Well?"

"Do you mean to say you don't recognize them?"

I looked at the picture more closely, and then there suddenly came back to my mind that mysterious story of the Black Diamonds, which had not only bewildered the police of Europe, but also some of its diplomats.

"Ah! I see you do recognize the jewels!" said the funny creature, after a while. "No wonder! for their design is unique, and photographs of that necklace and tiara were circulated practically throughout all the world.

"Of course I am not going to mention names, for you know very well who the royal heroes of this mysterious adventure were. For the purposes of my narrative, suppose I call them the King and Queen of 'Bohemia'.

"The value of the stones was said to be fabulous, and it was only natural when the King of 'Bohemia' found himself somewhat in want of money – a want which has made itself felt before now with even the most powerful European monarchs – that he should decide to sell the precious trinkets, worth a small kingdom in themselves. In order to be in closer touch with the most likely customers, Their Majesties of 'Bohemia' came over to England during the season of 1902 – a season memorable alike for its deep sorrow and its great joy.

"After the sad postponement of the Coronation festivities, they rented Eton Chase, a beautiful mansion just outside Chislehurst, for the summer months. There they entertained right royally, for the queen was very gracious and the king a real sportsman – there also the rumour first got about that His Majesty had decided to sell the world-famous *parure* of Black Diamonds.

"Needless to say, they were not long in the market: quite a host of American millionaires had already coveted them for their wives, and brisk and sensational offers were made to His Majesty's business man both by letter and telegram.

"At last, however, Mr Wilson, the multimillionaire, was understood to have made an offer, for the necklace and tiara, of £500,000, which had been accepted.

"But a very few days later, that is to say, on the Sunday and Monday, 6th and 7th July, there appeared in the papers the short, but deeply sensational announcement that a burglary had occurred at Eton Chase, Chislehurst, the mansion inhabited by Their Majesties the King and Queen of 'Bohemia', and that among the objects stolen was the famous *parure* of Black Diamonds, for which a bid of half a million sterling had just been made and accepted.

"The burglary had been one of the most daring and most mysterious ones ever brought under the notice of the police authorities. The mansion was full of guests at the time, among whom were many diplomatic notabilities, and also Mr and Mrs Wilson, the future owners of the gems; there was also a very large staff of servants. The burglary must have occurred between the hours of 10 and 11.30 p.m., though the precise moment could not be ascertained.

"The house itself stands in the midst of a large garden, and has deep French windows opening out upon a terrace at the back. There are ornamental iron balconies to the windows of the upper floors, and it was to one of these, situated immediately above the dining-room, that a rope ladder was found to be attached.

"The burglar must have chosen a moment when the guests were dispersed in the smoking-, billiard-, and drawing-rooms; the servants were having their own meal, and the dining-room was deserted. He must have slung his rope ladder, and entered Her Majesty's own bedroom by the window which – as the night was very warm – had been left open. The jewels were locked up in a small iron box, which stood upon the dressing-table, and the burglar took the

73

box bodily away with him, and then, no doubt, returned the way he came.

"The wonderful point in this daring attempt was the fact that most of the windows on the ground floor were slightly open that night, that the rooms themselves were filled with guests, and that the dining-room was not empty for more than a few minutes at a time, as the servants were still busy clearing away after dinner.

"At nine o'clock some of the younger guests had strolled out on to the terrace, and the last of these returned to the drawing-room at ten o'clock; at half past eleven one of the servants caught sight of the rope ladder in front of one of the dining-room windows, and the alarm was given.

"All traces of the burglar, however, and of his princely booty had completely disappeared."

## 2

"Not only did this daring burglary cause a great deal of excitement," continued the man in the corner, "but it also roused a good deal of sympathy in the public mind for the King and Queen of 'Bohemia', who thus found their hope of raising half a million sterling suddenly dashed to the ground. The loss to them would, of course, be irreparable.

"Matters were, however, practically at a standstill, all enquiries from enterprising journalists only eliciting the vague information that the police 'held a clue'. We all know what that means. Then all at once a wonderful rumour got about.

"Goodness only knows how these rumours originate – sometimes solely in the imagination of the man in the street. In this instance, certainly, that worthy gentleman had a very sensational theory. It was, namely, rumoured all over London that the clue which the police held pointed to no less a person than Mr Wilson himself.

"What had happened was this: minute enquiries on the part of the most able detectives of Scotland Yard had brought to light the fact that the burglary at Eton Chase must have occurred precisely between ten minutes and a quarter past eleven; at every other moment of the entire evening somebody or other had observed either the terrace or the dining-room windows.

"I told you that until ten o'clock some of Their Majesties' guests were walking up and down the terrace; between ten and half past servants were clearing away in the dining-room, and here it was positively ascertained beyond any doubt that no burglar could have slung a rope ladder and climbed up it immediately outside those windows, for one or other of the six servants engaged in clearing away the dinner must of necessity have caught sight of him.

At half past ten John Lucas, the head gardener, was walking through the gardens with a dog at his heels, and did not get back to the lodge until just upon eleven. He certainly did not go as far as the terrace, and as that side of the house was in shadow he could not say positively whether the ladder was there or not, but he certainly did assert most emphatically that there was no burglar about the *grounds* then, for the dog was a good watchdog and would have barked if any stranger was about. Lucas took the dog in with him and gave him a bit of supper, and only fastened him to his kennel outside at a quarter past eleven.

"Surmising, therefore, that at half past ten, when John Lucas started on his round, the deed was not yet done, that quarter of an hour would give the burglar the only possible opportunity of entering the premises *from the outside*, without being barked at by the dog. Now, during most of that same quarter of an hour, His Majesty the King of 'Bohemia' himself had retired into a small library with his private secretary, in order to glance through certain despatches which had arrived earlier in the evening.

"The window of this library was immediately next to the one outside which the ladder was found, and both the secretary and His Majesty himself think that they would have seen something or heard a noise if the rope ladder had been slung while they were in the room. They both, however, returned to the drawing-room at ten minutes past eleven.

"And here," continued the man in the corner, rubbing his long, bony fingers together, "arose the neatest little complication I have ever come across in a case of this kind. His Majesty had, it appears, privately made up his mind to accept Mr Wilson's bid, but the transaction had not yet been completed. Mr Wilson and his wife came down to stay at Eton Chase on 29th June, and directly they arrived many of those present noticed that Mr Wilson was obviously repenting of his bargain. This impression had deepened day by day, Mrs Wilson herself often throwing out covert hints about 'fictitious value' and 'fancy prices for merely notorious trinkets'. In fact, it became very obvious that the Wilsons were really seeking a loophole for evading the conclusion of the bargain.

"On the memorable evening of 5th July Mrs Wilson had been forced to retire to her room early in the evening, owing, she said, to a bad headache; her room was in the west wing of the Chase, and opened out on the same corridor as the apartments of Her Majesty the Queen. At half past eleven Mrs Wilson rang for her maid – Mary Pritchard, who, on entering her mistress' room, met Mr Wilson just coming out of it, and the girl heard him say: 'Oh, don't worry! I'll have the whole reset when we get back.'

"The detectives, on the other hand, had obtained information that two or three days previously Mr Wilson had sustained a very severe loss on the 'Change, and that he had subsequently remarked to two or three business friends that the Black Diamonds had become a luxury which he had no right to afford.

"Be this as it may, certain it is that within a week of the notorious burglary the rumour was current in every club in London that James S. Wilson, the reputed American millionaire, having found himself unable to complete the purchase of the Black Diamonds, had found this other very much less legitimate means of gaining possession of the gems.

"You must admit that the case looked black enough against him – all circumstantial, of course, for there was absolutely nothing to prove that he had the jewels in his possession; in fact no trace of them whatever had been found, but the public argued that Mr Wilson would lie low with them for a while, and then have them reset when he returned to America.

"Of course, ugly rumours of that description don't become general about a man without his getting some inkling of them. Mr Wilson very soon found his position in London absolutely intolerable: his friends ignored him at the club, ladies ceased to call upon his wife, and one fine day he was openly cut by Lord Barnsdale, an MFH, in the hunting field.

"Then Mr Wilson thought it high time to take action. He placed the whole matter in the hands of an able, if not very scrupulous, solicitor, who promised within a given time to find him a defendant with plenty of means, against whom he could bring a sensational libel suit, with thundering damages.

"The solicitor was as good as his word. He bribed some of the waiters at the Carlton, and so laid his snares that within six months, Lord and Lady Barnsdale had been overheard to say in public what everybody now thought in private, namely, that Mr James S. Wilson, finding himself unable to purchase the celebrated Black Diamonds, had thought it more profitable to steal them.

"Two days later Mr James S. Wilson entered an action in the High Courts for slander against Lord and Lady Barnsdale, claiming damages to the tune of £50,000."

### 3

"Still the mystery of the lost jewels was no nearer to its solution. Their Majesties the King and Queen of 'Bohemia' had left England soon after the disastrous event which deprived them of what amounted to a small fortune.

"It was expected that the sensational slander case would come on in the autumn, or rather more than sixteen months after the mysterious disappearance of the Black Diamonds.

"This last season was not a very brilliant one, if you remember; the wet weather, I believe, had quite a good deal to do with the fact; nevertheless London, that great world centre, was, as usual, full of distinguished visitors, among whom Mrs Vanderdellen, who arrived the second week in July, was perhaps the most interesting.

"Her enormous wealth spread a positive halo round her, it being generally asserted that she was the richest woman in the world. Add to this that she was young, strikingly handsome, and a widow, and you will easily understand what a *furore* her appearance during this London season caused in all high social circles.

"Though she was still in slight mourning for her husband, she was asked everywhere, went everywhere, and was courted and admired by everybody, including some of the highest in the land; her dresses and jewellery were the talk of the ladies' papers, her style and charm the gossip of all the clubs. And no doubt that, although the July evening Court promised to be very brilliant, everyone thought that it would be doubly so, since Mrs Vanderdellen had been honoured with an invitation, and would presumably be present.

"I like to picture to myself that scene at Buckingham Palace," continued the man in the corner, as his fingers toyed lovingly with a beautiful and brand-new bit of string. "Of course, I was not present actually, but I can see it all before me: the lights, the crowds, the pretty women, the glistening diamonds; then, in the midst of the chatter, a sudden silence fell as 'Mrs Vanderdellen' was announced.

"All women turned to look at the beautiful American as she entered, because her dress – on this her first appearance at the English Court – was sure to be a vision of style and beauty. But for once nobody noticed the dress from Felix, nobody even gave a glance at the exquisitely lovely face of the wearer. Everyone's eyes had fastened on one thing only, and everyone's lips framed but one exclamation, and that an 'Oh!' half of amazement and half of awe.

"For round her neck and upon her head Mrs Vanderdellen was wearing a gorgeously magnificent *parure* composed of black diamonds."

### 4

"I don't know how the case of *Wilson* v. *Barnsdale* was settled, for it never came into court. There were many people in London who owed the Wilsons an apology, and it is to be hoped that these were tendered in full.

"As for Mrs Vanderdellen, she seemed quite unaware why her appearance at Their Majesties' Court had caused quite so much sensation. No one, of course, broached the subject of the diamonds to her, and she no doubt attributed those significant 'Oh's' to her own dazzling beauty.

"The next day, however, Detective Marsh, of Scotland Yard, had a very difficult task before him. He had to go and ask a beautiful, rich, and refined woman how she happened to be in possession of stolen jewellery.

"Luckily for Marsh, however, he had to deal with a woman who was also charming, and who met his polite enquiry with an equally pleasant reply:

"'My husband gave me the Black Diamonds,' she said, 'a year ago, on his return from Europe. I had them set in Vienna last spring, and wore them for the first time last night. Will you please tell me the reason of this strange enquiry?'

"'Your husband?' echoed Marsh, ignoring her question, 'Mr Vanderdellen?'

"'Oh yes,' she replied sweetly, 'I dare say you have never heard of him. His name is very well known in America, where they call him the "Petrol King". One of his hobbies was the collection of gems, which he was very fond of seeing me wear, and he gave me some magnificent jewels. The Black Diamonds certainly are very handsome. May I now request you to tell me,' she repeated, with a certain assumption of hauteur, 'the reason of all these enquiries?'

"'The reason is simple enough, madam,' replied the detective abruptly. 'Those diamonds were the property of Her Majesty the Queen of "Bohemia", and were stolen from Their Majesties' residence, Eton Chase, Chislehurst, on the 5th of July last year.'

"'Stolen!' she repeated, aghast and obviously incredulous.

"'Yes, stolen,' said old Marsh. 'I don't wish to distress you unnecessarily, madam, but you will see how imperative it is that you should place me in immediate communication with Mr Vanderdellen, as an explanation from him has become necessary.'

"'Unfortunately, that is impossible,' said Mrs Vanderdellen, who seemed under the spell of a strong emotion.

"'Impossible?'

"'Mr Vanderdellen has been dead just over a year. He died three days after his return to New York, and the Black Diamonds were the last present he ever made me.'

"There was a pause after that. Marsh – experienced detective though he was – was literally at his wits' ends what to do. He said afterwards that Mrs Vanderdellen, though very young and frivolous outwardly, seemed at the same time an exceedingly shrewd, far-seeing businesswoman. To begin with, she absolutely refused to have the matter hushed up, and to return the jewels until their rightful ownership had been properly proved.

"'It would be tantamount,' she said, 'to admitting that my husband had come by them unlawfully.'

"At the same time she offered the princely reward of £10,000 to anyone who found the true solution of the mystery: for, mind you, the late Mr Vanderdellen sailed from Havre for New York on July the 8th, 1902, that is to say, three clear days after the theft of the diamonds from Eton Chase, and he presented his wife with the loose gems immediately on his arrival in New York. Three days after that he died.

"It was difficult to suppose that Mr Vanderdellen purchased those diamonds not knowing that they must have been stolen, since directly after the burglary the English police telegraphed to all their Continental colleagues, and within four-and-twenty hours a description of the stolen jewels was circulated throughout Europe.

"It was, to say the least of it, very strange that an experienced businessman and shrewd collector like Mr

Vanderdellen should have purchased such priceless gems without making some enquiries as to their history, more especially as they must have been offered to him in a more or less 'hole-in-the-corner' way.

"Still, Mrs Vanderdellen stuck to her guns, and refused to give up the jewels pending certain enquiries she wished to make. She declared that she wished to be sued for the diamonds in open court, charged with wilfully detaining stolen goods if necessary, for the more publicity was given to the whole affair the better she would like it, so firmly did she believe in her husband's innocence.

"The matter was indeed brought to the High Courts, and the sensational action brought against Mrs Vanderdellen by the representative of His Majesty the King of 'Bohemia' for the recovery of the Black Diamonds is, no doubt, still fresh in your memory.

"No one was allowed to know what witnesses Mrs Vanderdellen would bring forward in her defence. She had engaged the services of Sir Arthur Inglewood, and of some of the most eminent counsel at the Bar. The court was packed with the most fashionable crowd ever seen inside the Law Courts; and both days that the action lasted Mrs Vanderdellen appeared in exquisite gowns and ideal hats.

"The evidence for the Royal plaintiff was simple enough. It all went to prove that the very day after the burglary not a jeweller, pawnbroker, or diamond merchant throughout the whole of Europe could have failed to know that a unique *parure* of black diamonds had been stolen, and would probably be offered for sale. The Black Diamonds in themselves, and out of their setting, were absolutely unique, and if the late Mr Vanderdellen purchased them in Paris from some private individual, he must at least have very strongly suspected that they were stolen.

"Throughout the whole of that first day Mrs Vanderdellen sat in court, absolutely calm and placid. She listened to the evidence, made little notes, and chatted with two or three American friends – elderly men – who were with her.

"Then came the turn of the defence.

"Everybody had expected something sensational, and listened more eagerly than ever as the name of Mr Albert V. B. Sedley was called. He was a tall, elderly man, the regular angular type of the American, with his nasal twang and reposeful manner.

"His story was brief and simple. He was a great friend of the late Mr Vanderdellen, and had gone on a European tour with him in the early spring of 1902. They were together in Vienna in the month of March, staying at the Hotel Imperial, when one day Vanderdellen came to his room with a remarkable story.

"'He told me,' continued Mr Albert V. B. Sedley, 'that he had just purchased some very beautiful diamonds, which he meant to present to his wife on his return to New York. He would not tell me where he bought them, nor would he show them to me, but he spoke about the beauty and rarity of the stones, which were that rarest of all things, beautiful black diamonds.

"'As the whole story sounded to me a little bit queer and mysterious, I gave him a word of caution, but he was quite confident as to the integrity of the vendor of the jewels, since the latter had made a somewhat curious bargain.

Vanderdellen was to have the diamonds in his keeping for three months without paying any money, merely giving a formal receipt for them; then, if after three months he was quite satisfied with his bargain, and there had been no suspicion or rumour of any kind that the diamonds were stolen, then only was the money, £500,000, to be paid.

"'Vanderdellen thought this very fair and above-board, and so it sounded to me. The only thing I didn't like about it all was that the vendor had given what I thought was a false name and no address; the money was to be paid over to him in French notes when the three months had expired, at an hotel in Paris where Vanderdellen would be staying at the time, and where he would call for it.

"'I heard nothing more about the mysterious diamonds and their still more mysterious vendor,' continued Mr Sedley, amidst intense excitement, 'for Vanderdellen and I soon parted company after that, he going one way and I another. But at the beginning of July I met him in Paris, and on the 4th I dined with him at the Élysée Palace Hotel, where he was staying.

"'Mr Cornelius R. Shee was there too, and Vanderdellen related to him during dinner the history of his mysterious purchase of the Black Diamonds, adding that the vendor had called upon him that very day as arranged, and that he (Vanderdellen) had had no hesitation in handing him over the agreed price of £500,000, which he thought a very low one. Both Mr Shee and I agreed that the whole thing must have been clear and above-board, for jewels of such fabulous value could not have been stolen since last spring without the hue and cry being in every paper in Europe.

"'It is my opinion, therefore,' said Mr Albert V. B. Sedley, at the conclusion of this remarkable evidence, 'that Mr Vanderdellen bought those diamonds in perfect good faith. He would never have wittingly subjected his wife to the indignity of being seen in public with stolen jewels round her neck. If after 5th July he did happen to hear that a *parure* of black diamonds had been stolen in England at the date, he could not possibly think that there could be the slightest connection between these and those he had purchased more than three months ago.'

"And, amidst indescribable excitement, Mr Albert V. B. Sedley stepped back into his place.

"That he had spoken the truth from beginning to end no one could doubt for a single moment. His own social position, wealth, and important commercial reputation placed him above any suspicion of committing perjury, even for the sake of a dead friend. Moreover, the story told by Vanderdellen at the dinner in Paris was corroborated by Mr Cornelius R. Shee in every point.

"But there! a dead man's words are *not* evidence in a court of law. Unfortunately, Mr Vanderdellen had not shown the diamonds to his friends at the time. He had certainly drawn enormous sums of money from his bank about the end of June and beginning of July, amounting in all to just over a million sterling; and there was nothing to prove which special day he had paid away a sum of £500,000, whether *before* or *after* the burglary at Eton Chase.

"He had made extensive purchases in Paris of pictures, furniture, and other works of art, all of priceless value, for the decoration of his new palace in Fifth Avenue, and no diary of private expenditure was produced in court. Mrs Vanderdellen herself had said that after her husband's death, as all his affairs were in perfect order, she had destroyed his personal and private diaries.

"Thus the counsel for the plaintiff was able to demolish the whole edifice of the defence bit by bit, for it rested on but very ephemeral foundations: a story related by a dead man.

"Judgment was entered for the plaintiff, although every-one's sympathy, including that of judge and of jury, was entirely for the defendant, who had so nobly determined to vindicate her husband's reputation.

"But Mrs Vanderdellen proved to the last that she was no ordinary everyday woman. She had kept one final sensation up her sleeve. Two days after she had legally been made to give up the Black Diamonds, she offered to purchase them back for £500,000. Her bid was accepted, and during last autumn, on the occasion of the last Royal visit to London and the consequent grand society functions, no one was more admired, more *fêted* and envied, than beautiful Mrs Vanderdellen as she entered a drawing-room exquisitely gowned, and adorned with the *parure*, of which an empress might have been proud."

The man in the corner had paused, and was idly tapping his fingers on the marble-topped table of the ABC shop.

"It was a curious story, wasn't it?" said the funny creature after a while. "More like a romance than a reality."

"It is absolutely bewildering," I said.

"What is your theory?" he asked.

"What about?" I retorted.

"Well, there are so many points, aren't there, of which only one is quite clear, namely, that the *parure* of Black Diamonds disappeared from Eton Chase, Chislehurst, on 5th July 1902, and that the next time they were seen they were on the neck and head of Mrs Vanderdellen, the widow of one of the richest men of modern times, whilst the story of how her husband came by them was, to all intents and purposes, *legally* disbelieved."

"Then," I argued, "the only logical conclusion to arrive at in all this is that the Black Diamonds, owned by His Majesty the King of 'Bohemia', were not unique, and that Mr Vanderdellen bought some duplicate ones."

"If you knew anything about diamonds," he said irritably, "you would also know that your statement is an absurdity. There are no such things as 'duplicate' diamonds."

"Then what *is* the only logical conclusion to arrive at?" I retorted, for he had given up playing with the photos and was twisting and twining that bit of string as if his brain was contained inside it and he feared it might escape.

"Well, to me," he said, "the only logical conclusion of the affair is that the Black Diamonds which Mrs Vanderdellen wore were the only and original ones belonging to the Crown of 'Bohemia'."

"Then you think that a man in Mr Vanderdellen's position would have been fool enough to buy gems worth £500,000 at the very moment when there was a hue and cry for them all over Europe?"

"No, I don't," he replied quietly.

"But then –" I began.

"No?" he repeated once again, as his long fingers

completed knot number one in that eternal piece of string. "The Black Diamonds which Mrs Vanderdellen wore were bought by her husband in all good faith from the mysterious vendor in Vienna in March 1902."

"Impossible!" I retorted. "Her Majesty the Queen of 'Bohemia' wore them regularly during the months of May and June, and they were stolen from Eton Chase on July the 5th."

"Her Majesty the Queen of 'Bohemia' wore a *parure* of Black Diamonds during those months, and those certainly were stolen on July the 5th," he said excitedly; "but what was there to prove that *those* were the genuine stones?"

"Why! –" I ejaculated.

"Point No. 2," he said, jumping about like a monkey on a stick; "although Mr Wilson was acknowledged to be innocent of the theft of the diamonds, isn't it strange that no one has ever been proved guilty of it?"

"But I don't understand –"

"Yet it is simple as daylight. I maintain that His Majesty the King of 'Bohemia' being short, very short, of money, decided to sell the celebrated Black Diamonds; to avoid all risks the stones were taken out of their settings, and a trusted and secret emissary is then deputed to find a possible purchaser; his choice falls on the multimillionaire Vanderdellen, who is travelling in Europe, is a noted collector of rare jewellery, and has a beautiful young wife – three attributes, you see, which make him a very likely purchaser.

"The emissary then seeks him out, and offers him the diamonds for sale. Mr Vanderdellen at first hesitates, wondering how such valuable gems had come in the vendor's possession, but the bargain suggested by the latter – the three months during which the gems are to be held on trust by the purchaser – seems so fair and above-board, that Mr Vanderdellen's objections fall to the ground; he accepts the bargain, and three months later completes the purchase."

"But I don't understand," I repeated again, more bewildered than before. "You say the King of 'Bohemia' sold the loose gems originally to Mr Vanderdellen; then, what about the *parure* worn by the queen and offered for sale to Mr and Mrs Wilson? What about the theft at Eton Chase?"

"Point No. 3," he shrieked excitedly, as another series of complicated knots went to join its fellows. "I told you that the King of 'Bohemia' was *very* short of money, everyone knows *that*. He sells the Black Diamonds to Mr Vanderdellen, but before he does it, he causes duplicates of them to be made, but this time in exquisite, beautiful, perfect Parisian imitation, and has these mounted into the original settings by some trusted man who, you may be sure, was well paid to hold his tongue. Then it is given out that the *parure* is for sale; a purchaser is found, and a few days later the false diamonds are stolen."

"By whom?"

"By the King of 'Bohemia's' valued and trusted friend, who has helped in the little piece of villainy throughout; it is he who drops a rope ladder through Her Majesty's bedroom window on to the terrace below, and then hands the imitation *parure* to his Royal master, who sees to its complete destruction and disappearance. Then there is a hue and cry for the *real* stones, and after a year or so they are found on the person of a lady, who is legally forced to give them up.

90

And thus His Majesty the King of 'Bohemia' got one solid million for the Black Diamonds, instead of half that sum, for if Mrs Vanderdellen had not purchased the jewels, someone else would have done so."

And he was gone, leaving me to gaze at the pictures of three lovely women, and wondering if indeed it was the Royal lady herself who could best solve the mystery of who stole the Black Diamonds.

# *The Murder of Miss Pebmarsh*

## 1

"You must admit," said the man in the corner to me one day, as I folded up and put aside my *Daily Telegraph*, which I had been reading with great care, "that it would be difficult to find a more interesting plot, or more thrilling situations, than occurred during the case of Miss Pamela Pebmarsh. As for downright cold-blooded villainy, commend me to some of the actors in that real drama.

"The facts were simple enough: Miss Lucy Ann Pebmarsh was an old maid who lived with her young niece Pamela and an elderly servant in one of the small, newly built houses not far from the railway station at Boreham Wood. The fact that she kept a servant at all, and that the little house always looked very spick and span, was taken by the neighbours to mean that Miss Pebmarsh was a lady of means; but she kept very much to herself, seldom went to church, and never attended any of the mothers' meetings, parochial teas, and other social gatherings for which that popular neighbourhood has long been famous.

"Very little, therefore, was known of the Pebmarsh household, save that the old lady had seen better days, that she had taken her niece to live with her recently, and that the latter had had a somewhat chequered career before she had found her present haven of refuge; some more venturesome gossips went so far as to hint – but only just above a whisper – that Miss Pamela Pebmarsh had been on the stage.

"Certain it is that that young lady seemed to chafe very much under the restraint imposed upon her by her aunt, who seldom allowed her out of her sight, and evidently kept her very short of money, for, in spite of Miss Pamela's obvious love of fine clothes, she had latterly been constrained to wear the plainest of frocks and most unbecoming of hats.

"All very commonplace and uninteresting, you see, until that memorable Wednesday in October, after which the little house in Boreham Wood became a nine-days' wonder throughout newspaper-reading England.

"On that day Miss Pebmarsh's servant, Jemima Gadd, went over to Luton to see a sick sister; she was not expected back until the next morning. On that same afternoon Miss Pamela – strangely enough – seems also to have elected to go up to town, leaving her aunt all alone in the house and not returning home until the late train, which reaches Boreham Wood a few minutes before one.

"It was about five minutes past one that the neighbours in the quiet little street were roused from their slumbers by most frantic and agonized shrieks. The next moment Miss Pamela was seen to rush out of her aunt's house and then to hammer violently at the door of one of her neighbours, still uttering piercing shrieks. You may imagine what a commotion such a scene at midnight would cause in a place like Boreham Wood. Heads were thrust out of the windows; one or two neighbours in hastily donned miscellaneous attire came running out; and very soon the news spread round like wildfire that Miss Pamela on coming home had found her aunt lying dead in the sitting-room.

"Mr Miller, the local greengrocer, was the first to pluck up sufficient courage to effect an entrance into the house. Miss Pamela dared not follow him; she had become quite hysterical, and was shrieking at the top of her voice that her aunt had been murdered. The sight that greeted Mr Miller and those who had been venturesome enough to follow him, was certainly calculated to unhinge any young girl's mind.

"In the small bow-window of the sitting-room stood a writing-table, with drawers open and papers scattered all over and around it; in a chair in front of it, half-sitting and half-lying across the table, face downwards, and with arms outstretched, was the dead body of Miss Pebmarsh. There was sufficient indications to show to the most casual observer that, undoubtedly, the unfortunate lady had been murdered.

"One of the neighbours, who possessed a bicycle, had in the meantime had the good sense to ride over to the police station. Very soon two constables were on the spot; they quickly cleared the room of gossiping neighbours, and then endeavoured to obtain from Miss Pamela some lucid information as to the terrible event.

"At first she seemed quite unable to answer coherently the many questions which were being put to her; however, with infinite patience and wonderful kindness, Sergeant Evans at last managed to obtain from her the following statement:

"'I had had an invitation to go to the theatre this evening; it was an old invitation, and my aunt had said long ago that I might accept it. When Jemima Gadd wanted to go to Luton, I didn't see why I should give up the theatre and offend my friend, just because of her. My aunt and I had some words about it, but I went... I came back by the last train, and walked straight home from the station. I had taken the latchkey with me, and went straight into the sitting-room; the lamp was alight, and – and –'

"The rest was chaos in the poor girl's mind; she was only conscious of having seen something awful and terrible, and of having rushed out screaming for help. Sergeant Evans asked her no further questions then; a kind neighbour had offered to take charge of Pamela for the night, and took her away with her, the constable remaining in charge of the body and the house until the arrival of higher authorities."

## 2

"Although, as you may well suppose," continued the man in the corner, after a pause, "the excitement was intense at Boreham Wood, it had not as yet reached the general newspaper-reading public. As the tragic event had occurred at one o'clock in the morning, the papers the following day only contained a brief announcement that an old lady had been found murdered at Boreham Wood under somewhat mysterious circumstances. Later on, the evening editions added that the police were extremely reticent, but that it was generally understood that they held an important clue.

"The following day had been fixed for the inquest, and I went down myself in the morning, for somehow I felt that this case was going to be an interesting one. A murder which at first seems absolutely purposeless always, in my experience, reveals, sooner or later, an interesting trait in human nature.

"As soon as I arrived at Boreham Wood, I found that the murder of Miss Pebmarsh and the forthcoming inquest seemed to be the sole subjects of gossip and conversation. After I had been in the place half an hour the news began to spread like wildfire that the murderer had been arrested. Five minutes later the name of the murderer was on everybody's lips.

"It was that of the murdered woman's niece, Miss Pamela Pebmarsh.

"'Oh, oh!' I said to myself, 'my instincts have not deceived me: this case is indeed going to be interesting.'

"It was about two o'clock in the afternoon when I at last managed to find my way to the little police station, where the inquest was to be held. There was scarcely standing room, I can tell you, and I had some difficulty in getting a front place from which I could see the principal actors in this village drama.

"Pamela Pebmarsh was there in the custody of two constables – she, a young girl scarcely five-and-twenty, stood there accused of having murdered, in a peculiarly brutal way, an old lady of seventy, her relative who had befriended her and given her a home."

The man in the corner paused for a moment, and from the capacious pocket of his magnificent ulster he drew two or three small photos, which he placed before me.

"This is Miss Pamela Pebmarsh," he said, pointing to one of these; "tall and good-looking, in spite of the shabby bit of mourning with which she had contrived to deck herself. Of course, this photo does not give you an idea of what she looked like that day at the inquest. Her face then was almost ashen in colour; her large eyes were staring before her with a look of horror and of fear; and her hands were twitching incessantly, with spasmodic and painful nervousness.

"It was pretty clear that public feeling went dead against her from the very first. A murmur of disapproval greeted her appearance, to which she seemed to reply with a look of defiance. I could hear many uncharitable remarks spoken all round me; Boreham Wood found it evidently hard to forgive Miss Pamela her good looks and her unavowed past.

"The medical evidence was brief and simple. Miss Pebmarsh had been stabbed in the back with some sharp instrument, the blade of which had pierced the left lung. She had evidently been sitting in the chair in front of her writing-table when the murderer had caught her unawares. Death had ensued within the next few seconds.

"The medical officer was very closely questioned upon this point by the coroner; it was evident that the latter had something very serious in his mind, to which the doctor's replies would give confirmation.

"'In your opinion,' he asked, 'would it have been possible for Miss Pebmarsh to do anything after she was stabbed? Could she have moved, for instance?'

"'Slightly, perhaps,' replied the doctor; 'but she did not attempt to rise from her chair.'

"'No; but could she have tried to reach the handbell, for instance, which was on the table, or – the pen and ink – and written a word or two?'

"'Well, yes,' said the doctor thoughtfully; 'she might have done that, if pen and ink, or the handbell, were *very* close to her hand. I doubt, though, if she could have written anything very clearly, but still it is impossible to say quite definitely – anyhow, it could only have been a matter of a few seconds.'

"Delightfully vague, you see," continued the man in the corner, "as these learned gentlemen's evidence usually is.

"Sergeant Evans then repeated the story which Pamela Pebmarsh had originally told him, and from which she had never departed in any detail. She had gone to the theatre, leaving her aunt all alone in the house; she had arrived home at one o'clock by the late Wednesday-night train, and had gone straight into the sitting-room, where she had found her aunt dead before her writing-table.

"That she travelled up to London in the afternoon was easily proved; the station-master and the porters had seen her go. Unfortunately for her alibi, however, those late 'theatre' trains on that line are always very crowded; the night had been dark and foggy, and no one at or near the station could swear positively to having seen her arrive home again by the train she named.

"There was one thing more; although the importance of it had been firmly impressed upon Pamela Pebmarsh, she absolutely refused to name the friends with whom she had been to the theatre that night, and who, presumably, might have helped her to prove at what hour she left London for home.

"Whilst all this was going on, I was watching Pamela's face intently. That the girl was frightened – nay more, terrified – there could be no doubt; the twitching of her hands, her eyes dilated with terror, spoke of some awful secret which she dare not reveal, but which she felt was being gradually brought to light. Was that secret the secret of a crime – a crime so horrible, so gruesome, that surely so young a girl would be incapable of committing?

"So far, however, what struck everyone mostly during this inquest was the seeming purposelessness of this cruel murder. The old lady, as far as could be ascertained, had no money to leave, so why should Pamela Pebmarsh have deliberately murdered the aunt who provided her, at any rate, with the comforts of a home? But the police, assisted by one of the most able detectives on the staff, had not effected so sensational an arrest without due cause; they had a formidable array of witnesses to prove their case up to the hilt. One of these was Jemima Gadd, the late Miss Pebmarsh's servant.

"She came forward attired in deep black, and wearing a monumental crape bonnet crowned with a quantity of glistening black beads. With her face the colour of yellow wax, and her thin lips pinched tightly together, she stood as the very personification of Puritanism and uncharitableness.

"She did not look once towards Pamela, who gazed at her like some wretched bird caught in a net, which sees the meshes tightening round it more and more.

"Replying to the coroner, Jemima Gadd explained that on the Wednesday morning she had had a letter from her sister at Luton, asking her to come over and see her some day.

"'As there was plenty of cold meat in the 'ouse,' she said, 'I asked the mistress if she could spare me until the next day, and she said yes, she could. Miss Pamela and she could manage quite well.'

"'She said nothing about her niece going out, too, on the same day?' asked the coroner.

"'No,' replied Jemima acidly, 'she did not. And later on, at breakfast, Miss Pebmarsh said to Miss Pamela before me: "Pamela," she says, "Jemima is going to Luton, and won't be back until tomorrow. You and I will be alone, in the 'ouse until then."'

"'And what did the accused say?'

"'She says, "All right, Aunt."'

"'Nothing more?'

"'No, nothing more.'

"'There was no question, then, of the accused going out also, and leaving Miss Pebmarsh all alone in the house?'

"'None at all,' said Jemima emphatically. 'If there 'ad been I'd 'ave 'eard of it. I needn't 'ave gone that day. Any day would 'ave done for me.'

"She closed her thin lips with a snap, and darted a vicious look at Pamela. There was obviously some old animosity lurking beneath that gigantic crape monument on the top of Jemima's wax-coloured head.

"'You know nothing, then, about any disagreement between the deceased and the accused on the subject of her going to the theatre that day?' asked the coroner, after a while.

"'No, not about *that*,' said Jemima curtly, 'but there was plenty of disagreements between those two, I can tell you.'

100

"'Ah? what about?'

"'Money, mostly. Miss Pamela was over-fond of fine clothes, but Miss Pebmarsh, who was giving 'er a 'ome and 'er daily bread, 'adn't much money to spare for fallalery. Miss Pebmarsh 'ad a small pension from a lady of the haristocracy, but it wasn't much – a pound a week it was. Miss Pebmarsh might 'ave 'ad a lot more if she'd wanted to.'

"'Oh?' queried the coroner, 'how was that?'

"'Well, you see, that fine lady 'ad not always been as good as she ought to be. She'd been Miss Pamela's friend when they were both on the stage together, and pretty goings on, I can tell you, those two were up to, and –'

"'That'll do,' interrupted the coroner sternly. 'Confine yourself, please, to telling the jury about the pension Miss Pebmarsh had from a lady.'

"'I was speaking about that,' said Jemima, with another snap of her thin lips. 'Miss Pebmarsh knew a thing or two about this fine lady, and she 'ad some letters which she often told me that fine lady would not care for 'er 'usband or 'er fine friends to read. Miss Pamela got to know about these letters, and she worried 'er poor aunt to death, for she wanted to get those letters and sell them to the fine lady for 'undreds of pounds. I 'ave 'eard 'er ask for those letters times and again, but Miss Pebmarsh wouldn't give them to 'er, and they was locked up in the writing-table drawer, and Miss Pamela wanted those letters, for she wanted to get 'undreds of pounds from the fine lady, and my poor mistress was murdered for those letters – and she was murdered by that wicked girl 'oo eat 'er bread and 'oo would 'ave starved but for 'er. And so I tell you, and I don't care 'oo 'ears me say it."

101

"No one had attempted to interrupt Jemima Gadd as she delivered herself of this extraordinary tale, which so suddenly threw an unexpected and lurid light upon the mystery of poor Miss Pebmarsh's death.

"That the tale was a true one, no one doubted for a single instant. One look at the face of the accused was sufficient to prove it beyond question. Pamela Pebmarsh had become absolutely livid; she tottered almost as if she would fall, and the constable had to support her until a chair was brought forward for her.

"As for Jemima Gadd, she remained absolutely impassive. Having given her evidence, she stepped aside automatically like a yellow waxen image, which had been wound up and had now run down. There was silence for a while. Pamela Pebmarsh, more dead than alive, was sipping a glass of brandy and water, which alone prevented her from falling in a dead faint.

"Detective Inspector Robinson now stepped forward. All the spectators there could read on his face the consciousness that his evidence would be of the most supreme import.

"'I was telegraphed for from the Yard,' he said, in reply to the coroner, 'and came down here by the first train on the Thursday morning. Beyond the short medical examination the body had not been touched: as the constables know, we don't like things interfered with in cases of this kind. When I went up to look at deceased, the first thing I saw was a piece of paper just under her right hand. Sergeant Evans had seen it before, and pointed it out to me. Deceased had a pen in her hand, and the ink bottle was close by. This is the paper I found, sir.'

"And amidst a deadly silence, during which nothing could be heard but the scarcely perceptible rustle of the paper, the inspector handed a small note across to the coroner. The latter glanced at it for a moment, and his face became very grave and solemn as he turned towards the jury.

"'Gentlemen of the jury,' he said, 'these are the contents of the paper which the inspector found under the hand of the deceased.'

"He paused once more before he began to read, whilst we all in that crowded court held our breath to listen:

"'*I am dying. My murderess is my niece, Pam –*'

"'That is all, gentlemen,' added the coroner, as he folded up the note. 'Death overtook the unfortunate woman in the very act of writing down the name of her murderess.'

"Then there was a wild and agonized shriek of horror. Pamela Pebmarsh, with hair dishevelled and eyes in which the light of madness had begun to gleam, threw up her hands, and without a word, and without a groan, fell down senseless upon the floor."

### 3

"Yes," said the man in the corner with a chuckle, "there was enough evidence there to hang twenty people, let alone that one fool of a girl who had run her neck so madly into a noose. I don't suppose that anyone left the court that day with the slightest doubt in their minds as to what the verdict would be; for the coroner had adjourned the inquest, much to the annoyance of the jury, who had fully made up their minds and had their verdict pat on the tips of their tongues: 'Wilful murder against Pamela Pebmarsh.'

"But this was a case which to the last kept up its reputation for surprises. By the next morning rumour had got about that 'the lady of the aristocracy' referred to by Jemima Gadd, and who was supposed to have paid a regular pension to Miss Pebmarsh, was none other than Lady de Chavasse.

"When the name was first mentioned, everyone – especially the fair sex – shrugged their shoulders, and said: 'Of course what else *could* one expect?'

"As a matter of fact, Lady de Chavasse, *née* Birdie Fay, was one of the most fashionable women in society; she was at the head of a dozen benevolent institutions, was a generous patron of hospitals, and her house was one of the most exclusive ones in London. True, she had been on the stage in her younger days, and when Sir Percival de Chavasse married her, his own relations looked somewhat askance at the showy, handsome girl who had so daringly entered the ancient county family.

"Sir Percival himself was an extraordinarily proud man – proud of his lineage, of his social status, of the honour of his name. His very pride had forced his relations, had forced society, to accept his beautiful young wife, and to Lady de Chavasse's credit be it said, not one breath of scandal as to her past life had ever become public gossip. No one could assert that they *knew* anything derogatory to Birdie Fay before she became the proud baronet's wife. As a matter of fact, all society asserted that Sir Percival would never have married her and introduced her to his own family circle if there had been any gossip about her.

"Now suddenly the name of Lady de Chavasse was on everybody's tongue. People at first spoke it under their breath, for everyone felt great sympathy with her. She was so rich, and entertained so lavishly. She was very charming, too; most fascinating in her ways; deferential to her austere mother-in-law; not a little afraid of her proud husband; very careful lest by word or look she betrayed her early connection with the stage before him.

"On the following day, however, we had further surprises in store for us. Pamela Pebmarsh, advised by a shrewd and clear-headed solicitor, had at last made up her mind to view her danger a little more coolly, and to speak rather more of the truth than she had done hitherto.

"Still looking very haggard, but perhaps a little less scared, she now made a statement which, when it was fully substantiated, as she stated it could be, would go far towards clearing her of the terrible imputation against her. Her story was this: on the memorable day in question, she did go up to town, intending to go to the theatre. At the station she purchased an evening paper, which she began to read. This paper in its fashionable columns contained an announcement which arrested her attention; this was that Sir Percival and Lady de Chavasse had returned to their flat in town at 51 Marsden Mansions, Belgravia, from 'The Chase', Melton Mowbray.

"'De Chavasse,' continued Pamela, was the name of the lady who paid my aunt the small pension on which she lived. I knew her years ago, when she was on the stage, and I suddenly thought I would like to go and see her, just to have a chat over old times. Instead of going to the theatre I went and had some dinner at Slater's, in Piccadilly, and then I thought I would take my chance, and go and see if Lady de Chavasse was at home. I got to 51 Marsden Mansions about eight o'clock, and was fortunate enough to see Lady de Chavasse at once. She kept me talking some considerable time; so much so, in fact, that I missed the 11 train from St Pancras. I only left Marsden Mansions at a quarter to eleven, and had to wait at St Pancras until twenty minutes past midnight.'

"This was all reasonable and clear enough, and, as her legal adviser had subpoenaed Lady de Chavasse as a witness, Pamela Pebmarsh seemed to have found an excellent way out of her terrible difficulties, the only question being whether Lady de Chavasse's testimony alone would, in view of her being Pamela's friend, be sufficient to weigh against the terribly overwhelming evidence of Miss Pebmarsh's dying accusation.

"But Lady de Chavasse settled this doubtful point in the way least expected by anyone. Exquisitely dressed, golden-haired, and brilliant-complexioned, she looked strangely out of place in this fusty little village court, amidst the local dames in their plain gowns and antiquated bonnets. She was, moreover, extremely self-possessed, and only cast a short, very haughty, look at the unfortunate girl whose life probably hung upon that fashionable woman's word.

"'Yes,' she said sweetly, in reply to the coroner, 'she was the wife of Sir Percival de Chavasse, and resided at 51 Marsden Mansions, Belgravia.'

"'The accused, I understand, has been known to you for some time?' continued the coroner.

"'Pardon me,' rejoined Lady de Chavasse, speaking in a beautifully modulated voice, 'I did know this young – hem – person, years ago, when I was on the stage, but, of course, I had not seen her for years.'

"'She called on you on Wednesday last at about nine o'clock?'

"'Yes, she did, for the purpose of levying blackmail upon me.'

"There was no mistaking the look of profound aversion and contempt which the fashionable lady now threw upon the poor girl before her.

"'She had some preposterous story about some letters which she alleged would be compromising to my reputation,' continued Lady de Chavasse quietly. 'These she had the kindness to offer me for sale for a few hundred pounds. At first her impudence staggered me, as, of course, I had no knowledge of any such letters. She threatened to take them to my husband, however, and I then – rather foolishly, perhaps – suggested that she should bring them to me first. I forget how the conversation went on, but she left me with the understanding that she would get the letters from her aunt, Miss Pebmarsh, who, by the way, had been my governess when I was a child, and to whom I paid a small pension in consideration of her having been left absolutely without means.'

"And Lady de Chavasse, conscious of her own disinterested benevolence, pressed a highly scented bit of cambric to her delicate nose.

"'Then the accused did spend the evening with you on that Wednesday?' asked the coroner, while a great sigh of relief seemed to come from poor Pamela's breast.

"'Pardon me,' said Lady de Chavasse, 'she spent a little time with me. She came about nine o'clock.'

"'Yes. And when did she leave?'

"'I really couldn't tell you – about ten o'clock, I think.'

"'You are not sure?' persisted the coroner. 'Think, Lady de Chavasse,' he added earnestly, 'try to think – the life of a fellow-creature may, perhaps, depend upon your memory.'

"'I am indeed sorry,' she replied in the same musical voice. 'I could not swear without being positive, could I? And I am not quite positive.'

"'But your servants?'

"'They were at the back of the flat – the girl let herself out.'

"'But your husband?'

"'Oh! when he saw me engaged with the girl, he went out to his club, and was not yet home when she left.'

"'Birdie! Birdie! won't you try and remember?' here came in an agonized cry from the unfortunate girl, who thus saw her last hope vanish before her eyes.

"But Lady de Chavasse only lifted a little higher a pair of very prettily arched eyebrows, and having finished her evidence she stepped on one side and presently left the court, leaving behind her a faint aroma of violet sachet powder, and taking away with her, perhaps, the last hope of an innocent fellow-creature."

4

"But Pamela Pebmarsh?" I asked after a while, for he had paused and was gazing attentively at the photograph of a very beautiful and exquisitely gowned woman.

"Ah yes, Pamela Pebmarsh," he said with a smile. "There was yet another act in that palpitating drama of her life – one act – the *dénouement* as unexpected as it was thrilling. Salvation came where it was least expected – from Jemima Gadd, who seemed to have made up her mind that Pamela had killed her aunt, and yet who was the first to prove her innocence.

"She had been shown the few words which the murdered woman was alleged to have written after she had been stabbed. Jemima, not a very good scholar, found it difficult to decipher the words herself.

"'Ah, well, poor dear,' she said after a while, with a deep sigh, ''er 'andwriting was always peculiar, seein' as 'ow she wrote always with 'er left 'and.'

"'*Her left hand!!!*' gasped the coroner, while public and jury alike, hardly liking to credit their ears, hung upon the woman's thin lips, amazed, aghast, puzzled.

"'Why, yes,' said Jemima placidly. 'Didn't you know she 'ad a bad accident to 'er right 'and when she was a child, and never could 'old anything in it? 'Er fingers were like para-lysed; the inkpot was always on the left of 'er writing-table. Oh! she couldn't write with 'er right 'and at all.'

"Then a strange revulsion of feeling came over everyone there.

"Stabbed in the back, with her lung pierced through and through, how could she have done, dying, what she never did in life?

"Impossible!

"The murderer, whoever it was, had placed pen and paper to her hand, and had written on it the cruel words which were intended to delude justice and to send an innocent fellow-creature – a young girl not five-and-twenty – to an unjust and ignominious death. But, fortunately for that innocent girl, the cowardly miscreant had ignored the fact that Miss Pebmarsh's right hand had been paralysed for years.

"The inquest was adjourned for a week," continued the man in the corner, "which enabled Pamela's solicitor to obtain further evidence of her innocence. Fortunately for her, he was enabled to find two witnesses who had seen her in an omnibus going towards St Pancras at about 11.15 p.m., and a passenger on the 12.25 train, who had travelled down with her as far as Hendon. Thus, when the inquest was resumed, Pamela Pebmarsh left the court without a stain upon her character.

"But the murder of Miss Pebmarsh has remained a mystery to this day – as has also the secret history of the compromising letters. Did they exist or not? is a question the interested spectators at that memorable inquest have often asked themselves. Certain is it that failing Pamela Pebmarsh, who might have wanted them for purposes of blackmail, no one else could be interested in them except Lady de Chavasse."

"Lady de Chavasse!" I ejaculated in surprise. "Surely you are not going to pretend that that elegant lady went down to Boreham Wood in the middle of the night in order to murder Miss Pebmarsh, and then to lay the crime at another woman's door?"

"I only pretend what's logic," replied the man in the corner with inimitable conceit; "and in Pamela Pebmarsh's own statement, she was with Lady de Chavasse at 51 Marsden

Mansions until eleven o'clock, and there is no train from St Pancras to Boreham Wood between eleven and twenty-five minutes past midnight. Pamela's alibi becomes that of Lady de Chavasse, and is quite conclusive. Besides, that elegant lady was not one to do that sort of work for herself."

"What do you mean?" I asked.

"Do you mean to say you never thought of the real solution of this mystery?" he retorted sarcastically.

"I confess –" I began a little irritably.

"Confess that I have not yet taught you to think logically, and to look at the beginning of things."

"What do you call the beginning of this case, then?"

"Why! the compromising letters, of course."

"But –" I argued.

"Wait a minute!" he shrieked excitedly, whilst with frantic haste he began fidgeting, fidgeting again at that eternal bit of string. "These did exist, otherwise why did Lady de Chavasse parley with Pamela Pebmarsh? Why did she not order her out of the house then and there, if she had nothing to fear from her?"

"I admit that," I said.

"Very well; then, as she was too fine, too delicate to commit the villainous murder of which she afterwards accused poor Miss Pamela, who was there sufficiently interested in those letters to try and gain possession of them for her?"

"Who, indeed?" I queried, still puzzled, still not understanding.

"Ay! who but her husband?" shrieked the funny creature, as with a sharp snap he broke his beloved string in two.

"Her husband!" I gasped.

"Why not? He had plenty of time, plenty of pluck. In a flat it is easy enough to overhear conversations that take place in the next room – he was in the house at the time, remember, for Lady de Chavasse said herself that he went out afterwards. No doubt he overheard everything – the compromising letters, and Pamela's attempt at levying blackmail. What the effect of such a discovery must have been upon the proud man I leave you to imagine – his wife's social position ruined, a stain upon his ancient name, his relations pointing the finger of scorn at his folly.

"Can't you picture him, hearing the two women's talk in the next room, and then resolving at all costs to possess himself of those compromising letters? He had just time to catch the 10 train to Boreham Wood.

"Mind you, I don't suppose that he went down there with any evil intent. Most likely he only meant to buy those letters from Miss Pebmarsh. What happened, however, nobody can say but the murderer himself.

"Who knows? But the deed done, imagine the horror of a refined, aristocratic man, face to face with such a crime as that.

"Was it this terror, or merely rage at the girl who had been the original cause of all this, that prompted him to commit the final villainy of writing out a false accusation and placing it under the dead woman's hand? Who can tell?

"Then, the deed done, and the *mise-en-scène* complete, he is able to catch the last train – 11.23 – back to town. A man travelling alone would pass practically unperceived.

"Pamela's innocence was proved, and the murder of Miss Pebmarsh has remained a mystery, but if you will reflect on my conclusions, you will admit that no one else – *no one else* – could have committed that murder, for no one else had a greater interest in the destruction of those letters."

# The Lisson Grove Mystery

## 1

The man in the corner ordered another glass of milk, and timidly asked for a second cheesecake at the same time.

"I am going down to the Marylebone Police Court, to see those people brought up before the 'beak'," he remarked.

"What people?" I queried.

"What people!" he exclaimed, in the greatest excitement. "You don't mean to say that you have not studied the Lisson Grove Mystery?"

I had to confess that my knowledge on that subject was of the most superficial character.

"One of the most interesting cases that has cropped up in recent years," he said, with an indescribable look of reproach.

"Perhaps. I did not study it in the papers because I preferred to hear *you* tell me all about it," I said.

"Oh, if that's it," he replied, as he settled himself down in his corner like a great bird after the rain, "then you showed more sense than lady journalists usually possess. I can, of course, give you a far clearer account than the newspapers have done; as for the police – well! I never saw such a muddle as they are making of this case."

"I dare say it is a peculiarly difficult one," I retorted, for I am ever a champion of that hardworking department.

"H'm!" he said, "so, so – it is a tragedy in a prologue and three acts. I am going down this afternoon to see the curtain fall for the third time on what, if I mistake not, will prove a good burlesque; but it all began dramatically enough. It was last Saturday, 21st November, that two boys, playing in the little spinney just outside Wembley Park Station, came across three large parcels done up in American cloth.

"With the curiosity natural to their age, they at once proceeded to undo these parcels, and what they found so upset the little beggars that they ran howling through the spinney and the polo ground, straight as a dart to Wembley Park Station. Half-frantic with excitement, they told their tale to one of the porters off duty, who walked back to the spinney with them. The three parcels, in point of fact, contained the remains of a dismembered human body. The porter sent one of the boys for the local police, and the remains were duly conveyed to the mortuary, where they were kept for identification.

"Three days later – that is to say, on Tuesday, 24th November – Miss Amelia Dyke, residing at Lisson Grove Crescent, returned from Edinburgh, where she had spent three or four days with a friend. She drove up from St Pancras in a cab, and carried her small box up herself to the door of the flat, at which she knocked loudly and repeatedly – so loudly and so persistently, in fact, that the inhabitants of the neighbouring flats came out on to their respective landings to see what the noise was about.

"Miss Amelia Dyke was getting anxious. Her father, she

said, must be seriously ill, or else why did he not come and open the door to her? Her anxiety, however, reached its culminating point when Mr and Mrs Pitt, who reside in the flat immediately beneath that occupied by the Dykes, came forward with the alarming statement that, as a matter of fact, they had themselves been wondering if anything were wrong with old Mr Dyke, as they had not heard any sound overhead for the last few days.

"Miss Amelia, now absolutely terrified, begged one of the neighbours to fetch either the police or a locksmith, or both. Mr Pitt ran out at once, both police and locksmith were brought upon the scene, the door was forcibly opened, and amidst indescribable excitement Constable Turner, followed by Miss Dyke, who was faint and trembling with apprehension, effected an entrance into the flat.

"Everything in it was tidy and neat to a degree, all the fires were laid, the beds made, the floors were clean and washed, the brasses polished, only a slight, very slight layer of dust lay over everything, dust that could not have accumulated for more than a few days. The flat consisted of four rooms and a bathroom; in not one of them was there the faintest trace of old Mr Dyke.

"In order fully to comprehend the consternation which all the neighbours felt at this discovery," continued the man in the corner, "you must understand that old Mr Dyke was a helpless cripple; he had been a mining engineer in his young days, and a terrible blasting accident deprived him, at the age of forty, of both legs. They had been amputated just above the knee, and the unfortunate man – then a widower with one little girl – had spent the remainder of his life on crutches. He had a small – a very small – pension, which, as soon as his daughter Amelia was grown up, had enabled him to live in comparative comfort in the small flat in Lisson Grove Crescent.

"His misfortune, however, had left him terribly sensitive; he never could bear the looks of compassion thrown upon him, whenever he ventured out on his crutches, and even the kindliest sympathy was positive torture to him. Gradually, therefore, as he got on in life, he took to staying more and more at home, and after a while gave up going out altogether. By the time he was sixty-five years old and Miss Amelia a fine young woman of seven-and-twenty, old Dyke had not been outside the door of his flat for at least five years.

"And yet, when Constable Turner aided by the locksmith entered the flat on that memorable 24th November, there was not a trace anywhere of the old man.

"Miss Amelia was in the last stages of despair, and at first she seemed far too upset and hysterical to give the police any coherent and definite information. At last, however, from amid the chaos of tears and of ejaculations, Constable Turner gathered the following facts:

"Miss Amelia had some great friends in Edinburgh whom she had long wished to visit, her father's crippled condition making this extremely difficult. A fortnight ago, however, in response to a very urgent invitation, she at last decided to accept it, but in order to leave her father altogether comfortable, she advertised in the local paper for a respectable woman who would come to the flat every day and see to all the work, cook his dinner, make the bed, and so on.

"She had several applications in reply to this advertisement, and ultimately selected a very worthy looking elderly person, who, for seven shillings a week, undertook to come daily from seven in the morning until about six in the afternoon, to see to all Mr Dyke's comforts.

"Miss Amelia was very favourably impressed with this person's respectable and motherly appearance, and she left for Edinburgh by the 5.15 a.m. train on the morning of Thursday, 19th November, feeling confident that her father would be well looked after. She certainly had not heard from the old man while she was away, but she had not expected to hear unless, indeed, something had been wrong.

"Miss Amelia was quite sure that something dreadful had happened to her father, as he could not possibly have walked downstairs and out of the house alone; certainly his crutches were nowhere to be found, but this only helped to deepen the mystery of the old man's disappearance.

"The constable, having got thus far with his notes, thought it best to refer the whole matter at this stage to higher authority. He got from Miss Amelia the name and address of the charwoman, and then went back to the station.

"There, the very first news that greeted him was that the medical officer of the district had just sent round to the various police stations his report on the human remains found in Wembley Park the previous Saturday. They had proved to be the dismembered body of an old man between sixty and seventy years of age, the immediate cause of whose death had undoubtedly been a violent blow on the back of the head with a heavy instrument, which had shattered the cranium. Expert examination further revealed the fact that deceased had had in early life both legs removed by a surgical operation just above the knee.

"That was the end of the prologue in the Lisson Grove tragedy," continued the man in the corner, after a slight and dramatic pause, "as far as the public was concerned. When the curtain was subsequently raised upon the first act, the situation had been considerably changed.

"The remains had been positively identified as those of old Mr Dyke, and a charge of wilful murder had been brought against Alfred Wyatt, of no occupation, residing in Warlock Road, Lisson Grove, and against Amelia Dyke for complicity in the crime. They are the two people whom I am going to see this afternoon brought before the 'beak' at the Marylebone Police Court."

## 2

"Two very important bits of evidence, I must tell you, had come to light, on the first day of the inquest and had decided the police to make this double arrest.

"In the first place, according to one or two of the neighbours, who happened to know something of the Dyke household, Miss Amelia had kept company for some time with a young man named Alfred Wyatt; he was an electrical engineer, resided in the neighbourhood, and was some years younger than Miss Dyke. As he was known not to be very steady, it was generally supposed that the old man did not altogether approve of his daughter's engagement.

"Mrs Pitt, residing in the flat immediately below the one occupied by the Dykes, had stated, moreover, that on

Wednesday the 18th, at about midday, she heard very loud and angry voices proceeding from above, Miss Amelia's shrill tones being specially audible. Shortly afterwards she saw Wyatt go out of the house; but the quarrel continued for some little time without him, for the neighbours could still hear Miss Amelia's high-pitched voice, speaking very excitedly and volubly.

"'An hour later,' further explained Mrs Pitt, 'I met Miss Dyke on the stairs; she seemed very flushed and looked as if she had been crying. I suppose she saw that I noticed this, for she stopped and said to me:

"''All this fuss, you know, Mrs Pitt, because Alfred asked me to go for a drive with him this afternoon, but I am going all the same.'''

"'Later in the afternoon – it must have been quite half past four, for it was getting dark – young Wyatt drove up in a motor car, and presently I heard Miss Dyke's voice on the stairs saying very pleasantly and cheerfully: "All right, Daddy, we shan't be long." Then Mr Dyke must have said something which I didn't hear, for she added, "Oh, that's all right; I am well wrapped up, and we have plenty of rugs."'

"Mrs Pitt then went to her window and saw Wyatt and Amelia Dyke start off in a motor. She concluded that the old man had been mollified, for both Amelia and Wyatt waved their hands affectionately up towards the window. They returned from their drive about six o'clock; Wyatt saw Amelia to the door, and then went off again. The next day Miss Dyke went to Scotland.

"As you see," continued the man in the corner, "Alfred Wyatt had become a very important personality in this case;

he was Amelia's sweetheart, and it was strange – to say the least of it – that she had never as yet even mentioned his name. Therefore, when she was recalled in order to give further evidence, you may be sure that she was pretty sharply questioned on the subject of Alfred Wyatt.

"In her evidence before the coroner, she adhered fairly closely to her original statement:

"'I did not mention Mr Wyatt's name,' she explained, 'because I did not think it was of any importance; if he knew anything about my dear father's mysterious fate he would have come forward at once, of course, and helped me to find out who the cowardly murderer was who could attack a poor, crippled old man. Mr Wyatt was devoted to my father, and it is perfectly ridiculous to say that daddy objected to my engagement; on the contrary, he gave us his full consent, and we were going to be married directly after the New Year, and continue to live with father in the flat.'

"'But,' questioned the coroner, who had not by any means departed from his severity, 'what about this quarrel which the last witness overheard on the subject of your going out driving with Mr Wyatt?'

"'Oh, that was nothing,' replied Miss Dyke very quietly. 'Daddy only objected because he thought that it was rather too late to start at four o'clock, and that I should be cold. When he saw that we had plenty of rugs he was quite pleased for me to go.'

"'Isn't it rather astonishing, then,' asked the coroner, 'seeing that Mr Wyatt was on such good terms with your father, that he did not go to see him while you were away?'

"'Not at all,' she replied unconcernedly; 'Alfred went down to Edinburgh on the Thursday evening. He couldn't travel with me in the morning, for he had some business to see to in town that day; but he joined me at my friends' house on the Friday morning, having travelled all night.'

"'Ah!' remarked the coroner dryly, 'then he had not seen your father since you left.'

"'Oh yes,' said Miss Amelia; 'he called round to see dad during the day, and found him looking well and cheerful.'

"Miss Amelia Dyke, as she gave this evidence, seemed absolutely unconscious of saying anything that might in any way incriminate her lover. She is a handsome, though somewhat coarse-looking, woman, nearer thirty I should say, than she would care to own. I was present at the inquest, mind you, for that case had too many mysteries about it from the first for it to have eluded my observation, and I watched her closely throughout. Her voice struck me as fine and rich, with – in this instance also – a shade of coarseness in it; certainly, it was very far from being high-pitched, as Mrs Pitt had described it.

"When she had finished her evidence she went back to her seat, looking neither flustered nor uncomfortable, although many looks of contempt and even of suspicion were darted at her from every corner of the crowded court.

"Nor did she lose her composure in the slightest degree when Mr Parlett, clerk to Messrs Snow and Patterson, solicitors, of Bedford Row, in his turn came forward and gave evidence; only while the little man spoke her full red lips curled and parted with a look of complete contempt.

"Mr Parlett's story was indeed a remarkable one, inasmuch as it suddenly seemed to tear asunder the veil of mystery which so far had surrounded the murder of old Dyke by supplying it with a motive – a strong motive, too: the eternal greed of gain.

"In June last, namely, it appears that Messrs Snow and Patterson received intimation from a firm of Melbourne solicitors that a man of the name of Dyke had died there recently, leaving a legacy of £4,000 to his only brother, James Arthur Dyke, a mining engineer, who in 1890 was residing at Lisson Grove Crescent. The Melbourne solicitors in their communication asked for Messrs Snow and Patterson's kind assistance in helping them to find the legatee.

"The search was easy enough, since James Arthur Dyke, mining engineer, had never ceased to reside at Lisson Grove Crescent. Armed, therefore, with full instructions from their Melbourne correspondent, Messrs Snow and Patterson communicated with Dyke, and after a little preliminary correspondence, the sum of £4,000 in Bank of Australia notes and various securities were handed over by Mr Parlett to the old cripple.

"The money and securities were – so Mr Parlett understood – subsequently deposited by Mr Dyke at the Portland Road Branch of the London and South-western Bank: as the old man apparently died intestate, the whole of the £4,000 would naturally devolve upon his only daughter and natural legatee.

"Mind you, all through the proceedings the public had instinctively felt that money was somewhere at the bottom of this gruesome and mysterious crime. There is not much object in murdering an old cripple except for purposes of gain, but now Mr Parlett's evidence had indeed furnished a damning motive for the appalling murder.

"What more likely than that Alfred Wyatt, wanting to finger that £4,000, had done away with the old man? And if Amelia Dyke did not turn away from him in horror, after such a cowardly crime, then she must have known of it and had perhaps connived in it.

"As for Nicholson, the charwoman, her evidence had certainly done more to puzzle everybody all round than any other detail in this strange and mysterious crime.

"She deposed that on Friday, 13th November, in answer to an advertisement in the *Marylebone Star*, she had called on Miss Dyke at Lisson Grove, when it was arranged that she should do a week's work at the flat, beginning Thursday, the 19th, from seven in the morning until six in the afternoon. She was to keep the place clean, get Mr Dyke – who, she understood, was an invalid – all his meals, and make herself generally useful to him.

"Accordingly, Nicholson turned up on the Thursday morning. She let herself into the flat, as Miss Dyke had entrusted the latchkey to her, and went on with the work. Mr Dyke was in bed, and she got him all his meals that day. She thought she was giving him satisfaction, and was very astonished when, at six o'clock, having cleared away his tea, he told her that he would not require her again. He gave her no explanation, asked her for the latchkey, and gave her her full week's money – seven shillings in full. Nicholson then put on her bonnet, and went away.

"Now," continued the man in the corner, leaning excitedly forward, and marking each sentence he uttered with an exquisitely complicated knot in his bit of string, "an hour later, another neighbour, Mrs Marsh, who lived on the same floor as the Dykes, on starting to go out, met Alfred Wyatt on the landing. He took off his hat to her, and then knocked at the door of the Dykes' flat.

"When she came home at eight o'clock, she again passed him on the stairs; he was then going out. She stopped to ask him how Mr Dyke was, and Wyatt replied: 'Oh, fairly well, but he misses his daughter, you know.'

"Mrs Marsh, now closely questioned, said that she thought Wyatt was carrying a large parcel under his arm, but she could not distinguish the shape of the parcel as the angle of the stairs, where she met him, was very dark. She stated, though, that he was running down the stairs very fast.

"It was on all that evidence that the police felt justified in arresting Alfred Wyatt for the murder of James Arthur Dyke, and Amelia Dyke for connivance in the crime. And now this very morning, those two young people have been brought before the magistrate, and at this moment evidence – circumstantial, mind you, but positively damning – is being heaped upon them by the prosecution. The police did their work quickly. The very evening after the first day of the inquest, the warrant was out for their arrest."

He looked at a huge silver watch which he always carried in his waistcoat pocket.

"I don't want to miss the defence," he said, "for I know that it will be sensational. But I did not want to hear the police and medical evidence all over again. You'll excuse me, won't you? I shall be back here for five o'clock tea. I know you will be glad to hear all about it."

<h2 style="text-align:center">3</h2>

When I returned to the ABC shop for my tea at five minutes past five, there he sat in his accustomed corner, with a cup of tea before him, another placed opposite to him, presumably for me, and a long piece of string between his bony fingers.

"What will you have with your tea?" he asked politely, the moment I was seated.

"A roll and butter and the end of the story," I replied.

"Oh, the story has no end," he said with a chuckle; "at least, not for the public. As for me, why, I never met a more simple 'mystery'. Perhaps that is why the police were so completely at sea."

"Well, and what happened?" I queried, with some impatience.

"Why, the usual thing," he said, as he once more began to fidget nervously with his bit of string. "The prisoners had pleaded not guilty, and the evidence for the prosecution was gone into in full. Mr Parlett repeated his story of the £4,000 legacy, and all the neighbours had some story or other to tell about Alfred Wyatt, who, according to them, was altogether a most undesirable young man.

"I heard the fag end of Mrs Marsh's evidence. When I reached the court she was repeating the story she had already told to the police.

"Someone else in the house had also heard Wyatt running helter-skelter downstairs at eight o'clock on the Thursday evening; this was a point, though a small one, in favour of the accused. A man cannot run downstairs when he is carrying the whole weight of a dead body, and the theory of the prosecution was that Wyatt had murdered old Dyke on that Thursday evening, got into his motor car somewhere, scorched down to Wembley with the dismembered body of his victim, deposited it in the spinney where it was subsequently found, and finally had driven back to town, stabled his motor car, and reached King's Cross in time for the 11.30 night express to Edinburgh. He would have time for all that, remember, for he would have three hours and a half to do it in.

"Besides which the prosecution had unearthed one more witness, who was able to add another tiny link to the already damning chain of evidence built up against the accused.

"Wilfred Poad, namely, manager of a large cycle and motor-car depot in Euston Road, stated that on Thursday afternoon, 19th November, at about half past six o'clock, Alfred Wyatt, with whom he had had some business dealings before, had hired a small car from him, with the understanding that he need not bring it back until after 11 p.m. This was agreed to, Poad keeping the place open until just before eleven, when Wyatt drove up in the car, paid for the hire of it, and then walked away from the shop in the direction of the Great Northern terminus.

"That was pretty strong against the male prisoner, wasn't it? For, mind you, Wyatt had given no satisfactory account whatever of his time between 8 p.m., when Mrs Marsh had met him going out of Lisson Grove Crescent, and 11 p.m., when he brought back the car to the Euston Road shop. 'He had been driving about aimlessly,' so he said. Now, one doesn't go out motoring for hours on a cold, drizzly night in November for no purpose whatever.

"As for the female prisoner, the charge against her was merely one of complicity.

"This closed the case for the prosecution," continued the funny creature, with one of his inimitable chuckles, "leaving but one tiny point obscure, and that was, the murdered man's strange conduct in dismissing the woman Nicholson.

"Yes, the case was strong enough, and yet there stood both prisoners in the dock, with that sublime air of indifference and contempt which only complete innocence or hardened guilt could give.

"Then when the prosecution had had their say, Alfred Wyatt chose to enter the witness-box and make a statement in his own defence. Quietly, and as if he were making the most casual observation he said:

"'I am not guilty of the murder of Mr Dyke, and in proof of this I solemnly assert that on Thursday, 19th November, the day I am supposed to have committed the crime, the old man was still alive at half past ten o'clock in the evening.'

"He paused a moment, like a born actor, watching the effect he had produced. I tell you, it was astounding.

"'I have three separate and independent witnesses here,' continued Wyatt, with the same deliberate calm, who heard and saw Mr Dyke as late as half past ten that night. Now, I understand that the dismembered body of the old man was found close to Wembley Park. How could I, between half past ten and eleven o'clock, have killed Dyke, cut him up, cleaned and put the flat all tidy, carried the body to the car, driven on to Wembley, hidden the corpse in the spinney, and be back in Euston Road, all in the space of half an hour? I am absolutely innocent of this crime, and, fortunately, it is easy for me now to prove my innocence.'

"Alfred Wyatt had made no idle boast. Mrs Marsh had seen him running downstairs at 8 p.m. An hour after that, the Pitts in the flat beneath heard the old man moving about overhead.

"'Just as usual,' observed Mrs Pitt. 'He always went to bed about nine, and we could always hear him most distinctly.'

"John Pitt, the husband, corroborated this statement; the old man's movements were quite unmistakable because of his crutches.

"Henry Ogden, on the other hand, who lived in the house facing the block of flats, saw the light in Dyke's window that evening, and the old man's silhouette upon the blind from time to time. The light was put out at half past ten. This statement again was corroborated by Mrs Ogden, who also had noticed the silhouette and the light being extinguished at half past ten.

"But this was not all; both Mr and Mrs Ogden had seen old Dyke at his window, sitting in his accustomed armchair, between half past eight and nine o'clock. He was gesticulating, and apparently talking to someone else in the room whom they could not see.

"Alfred Wyatt, therefore, was quite right when he said that he would have no difficulty in proving his innocence. The man whom he was supposed to have murdered was, according to the testimony, alive at six o'clock; according to Mr and Mrs Ogden he was alive and sitting in his window until nine; again, he was heard to move about until ten o'clock by both the Pitts, and at half past ten only was the light put out in his flat. Obviously, therefore, as his dead body was found twelve miles away, Wyatt, who was out of the Crescent at eight, and in Euston Road at eleven, could not have done the deed.

"He was discharged, of course, the magistrate adding a very severe remark on the subject of 'carelessly collected evidence'. As for Miss Amelia she sailed out of the court like a queen after her coronation, for with Wyatt's discharge the case against her naturally collapsed. As for me, I walked out too, with an elated feeling at the thought that the intelligence of the British race had not yet sunk so low as our friends on the Continent would have us believe."

## 4

"But then, who murdered the old man?" I asked, for I confess the matter was puzzling me in an irritating kind of a way.

"Ah! who indeed?" he rejoined sarcastically, while an artistic knot went to join its fellows along that never-ending bit of string.

"I wish you'd tell me what's in your mind," I said, feeling peculiarly irritated with him just at that moment.

"What's in my mind?" he replied, with shrug of his thin shoulders. "Oh, only a certain degree of admiration!"

"Admiration at what?"

"At a pair of exceedingly clever criminals."

"Then you do think that Wyatt murdered Dyke?"

"I don't think – I am sure."

"But when did they do it?"

"Ah, that's more to the point. Personally, I should say between them on Wednesday morning, 18th November."

"The day they went for that motor-car ride?" I gasped.

"And carried away the old man's remains beneath a multiplicity of rugs," he added.

"But he was *alive* long after that!" I urged. "The woman Nicholson –"

"The woman Nicholson saw and spoke to a man in bed, whom she *supposed* was old Mr Dyke. Among the many questions put to her by those clever detectives, no one thought, of course, of asking her to describe the old man. But even if she had done so, Wyatt was far too great an artist in crime not to have contrived a make-up which, described by a witness who had never before seen Dyke, would easily pass as a description of the old man himself."

"Impossible!" I said, struck in spite of myself by the simplicity of his logic.

"Impossible, you say?" he shrieked excitedly.

"Why, I call that crime a masterpiece from beginning to end; a display of ingenuity which, fortunately, the criminal classes seldom possess, or where would society be? Here was a crime committed, where everything was most beautifully stage-managed, nothing left unforeseen. Shall I reconstruct it for you?"

"Do!" I said, handing across the table to him a brand-new, beautiful bit of string, on which his talon-like fingers fastened as upon a prey.

"Very well," he said, marking each point with a scientific knot. "Here, it is, scene by scene. There was Alfred Wyatt and Amelia Dyke – a pair of blackguards, eager to obtain that £4,000 which only the old man's death could secure for them. They decide upon killing him, and: Scene 1 – Miss Amelia makes her arrangements. She advertises for a charwoman, and engages one, who is to be a very useful witness presently.

"Scene 2 – The murder, brutal, horrible, on the person of an old cripple, whilst his own daughter stands by, and the dismembering of the body.

"Scene 3 – The ride in the motor car – after dark, remember, and with plenty of rugs, beneath which the gruesome burden is concealed. The scene is accompanied by the comedy of Miss Dyke speaking to her father, and waving her hand affectionately at him from below. I tell you, that woman must have had some nerve!

"Then, Scene 4 – The arrival at Wembley, and the hiding of the remains.

"Scene 5 – Amelia goes to Edinburgh by the 5.15 a.m. train, and thus secures her own alibi. After that, the comedy begins in earnest. The impersonation of the dead man by Wyatt during the whole of that memorable Thursday. Mind you, that was not very difficult; it only needed the brain to invent, and the nerve to carry it through. The charwoman had never seen old Dyke before; she only knew that he was an invalid. What more natural than that she should accept as her new master the man who lay in bed all day, and only spoke a few words to her? A very slight make-up of hair and beard would complete the illusion.

"Then, at six o'clock, the woman gone, Wyatt steals out of the house, bespeaks the motor car, leaves it in the street in a convenient spot, and is back in time to be seen by Mrs Marsh at seven.

"The rest is simplicity itself. The silhouette at the window was easy enough to arrange; the sound of a man walking on crutches is easily imitated with a couple of umbrellas – the actual crutches were, no doubt, burned directly after the murder. Lastly, the putting out of the light at half past ten was the crowning stroke of genius.

"One little thing might have upset the whole wonderful plan, but that one thing only; and that was if the body had been found *before* the great comedy scene of Thursday had been fully played. But that spinney near Wembley was well chosen. People don't go wandering under trees and in woods on cold November days, and the remains were not found until the Saturday.

"Ah, it was cleverly stage-managed, and no mistake. I couldn't have done it better myself. Won't you have another cup of tea? No? Don't look so upset. The world does not contain many such clever criminals as Alfred Wyatt and Amelia Dyke."

## VII

# The Tremarn Case

1

"Well, it certainly is most amazing!" I said that day, when I had finished reading about it all in *The Daily Telegraph*.

"Yet the most natural thing in the world," retorted the man in the corner, as soon as he had ordered his lunch. "Crime invariably begets crime. No sooner is a murder, theft, or fraud committed in a novel or striking way, than this method is aged – probably within the next few days – by some other less imaginative scoundrel.

"Take this case, for instance," he continued, as he slowly began sipping his glass of milk, "which seems to amaze you so much. It was less than a year ago, was it not? that in Paris a man was found dead in a cab, stabbed in a most peculiar way – right through the neck, from ear to ear – with, presumably, a long, sharp instrument of the type of an Italian stiletto.

"No one in England took much count of the crime, beyond a contemptuous shrug of the shoulders at the want of safety of the Paris streets, and the incapacity of the French detectives, who not only never discovered the murderer, who had managed to slip out of the cab unperceived, but who did not even succeed in establishing the identity of the victim.

"But this case," he added, pointing once more to my daily paper, "strikes nearer home. Less than a year has passed, and last week, in the very midst of our much vaunted London streets, a crime of a similar nature has been committed. I do not know if your paper gives full details, but this is what happened: last Monday evening two gentlemen, both in evening dress and wearing opera hats, hailed a hansom in Shaftesbury Avenue. It was about a quarter past eleven, and the night, if you remember, was a typical November one – dark, drizzly, and foggy. The various theatres in the immediate neighbourhood were disgorging a continuous stream of people after the evening performance.

"The cabman did not take special notice of his fares. They jumped in very quickly, and one of them, through the little trap above, gave him an address in Cromwell Road. He drove there as quickly as the fog would permit him, and pulled up at the number given. One of the gentlemen then handed him up a very liberal fare – again through the little trap – and told him to drive his friend on to Westminster Chambers, Victoria Street.

"Cabby noticed that the 'swell', when he got out of the hansom, stopped for a moment to say a few words to his friend, who had remained inside; then he crossed over the road and walked quickly in the direction of the Natural History Museum.

"When the cabman pulled up at Westminster Chambers, he waited for the second fare to get out; the latter seemingly making no movement that way, cabby looked down at him through the trap.

"'I thought 'e was asleep,' he explained to the police later on. ''E was leaning back in 'is corner, and 'is 'ead was turned towards the window. I gets down and calls to 'im, but 'e don't move. Then I gets on to the step and give 'im a shake... There! – I'll say no more... We was near a lamppost, the mare took a step forward, and the light fell full on the gent's face. 'E was dead and no mistake. I saw the wound just underneath 'is ear, and "Murder!" I says to myself at once.'

"Cabby lost no time in whistling for the nearest point-policeman, then he called the night porter of the Westminster Chambers. The latter looked at the murdered man, and declared that he knew nothing of him; certainly he was not a tenant of the Chambers.

"By the time a couple of policemen arrived upon the scene, quite a crowd had gathered around the cab, in spite of the lateness of the hour and the darkness of the night. The matter was such an important one that one of the constables thought it best at once to jump into the hansom beside the murdered man and to order the cabman to drive to the nearest police station.

"There the cause of death was soon ascertained; the victim of this daring outrage had been stabbed through the neck from ear to ear with a long, sharp, instrument, in shape like an antique stiletto, which, I may tell you, was subsequently found under the cushions of the hansom. The murderer must have watched his opportunity, when his victim's head was turned away from him, and then dealt the blow, just below the left ear, with amazing swiftness and precision.

"Of course the papers were full of it the next day; this was such a lovely opportunity for driving home a moral lesson, of how one crime engenders another, and how – but for that murder in Paris a year ago – we should not now have to deplore a crime committed in the very centre of fashionable London, the detection of which seems likely to completely baffle the police.

"Plenty more in that strain, of course, from which the reading public quickly jumped to the conclusion that the police held absolutely no clue as to the identity of the daring and mysterious miscreant.

"A most usual and natural thing had happened; cabby could only give a very vague description of his other 'fare', of the 'swell' who had got out at Cromwell Road, and been lost to sight after having committed so dastardly and so daring a crime.

"This was scarcely to be wondered at, for the night had been very foggy, and the murderer had been careful to pull his opera hat well over his face, thus hiding the whole of his forehead and eyes; moreover, he had always taken the additional precaution of only communicating with the cabman through the little trapdoor.

"All cabby had seen of him was a clean-shaven chin. As to the murdered man, it was not until about noon, when the early editions of the evening papers came out with a fuller account of the crime and a description of the victim, that his identity was at last established.

"Then the news spread like wildfire, and the evening papers came out with some of the most sensational headlines it had ever been their good fortune to print. The man who had been so mysteriously murdered in the cab was none other than Mr Philip Le Cheminant, the nephew and heir-presumptive of the Earl of Tremarn."

"In order fully to realize the interest created by this extra-ordinary news, you must be acquainted with the various details of that remarkable case, popularly known as the 'Tremarn Peerage Case'," continued the man in the corner, as he placidly munched his cheesecake. "I do not know if you followed it in its earlier stages, when its many details – which read like a romance – were first made public."

I looked so interested and so eager that he did not wait for my reply.

"I must try and put it all clearly before you," he said; "I was interested in it all from the beginning, and from the numerous wild stories afloat I have sifted only what was undeniably true. Some points of the case are still in dispute, and will, perhaps, now for ever remain a mystery. But I must take you back some five-and-twenty years. The Hon. Arthur Le Cheminant, second son of the late Earl of Tremarn, was then travelling round the world for health and pleasure.

"In the course of his wanderings he touched at Martinique, one of the French West Indian islands, which was devastated by volcanic eruptions about two years ago. There he met and fell in love with a beautiful half-caste girl named Lucie Legrand, who had French blood in her veins, and was a Christian, but who, otherwise, was only partially civilized, and not at all educated.

"How it all came about it is difficult to conjecture, but one thing is absolutely certain, and that is that the Hon. Arthur Le Cheminant, the son of one of our English peers, married this half-caste girl at the parish church of St Pierre, in Martinique, according to the forms prescribed by French laws, both parties being of the same religion.

"I suppose now no one will ever know whether that marriage was absolutely and undisputably a legal one – but, in view of subsequent events, we must presume that it was. The Hon. Arthur, however, in any case, behaved like a young scoundrel. He only spent a very little time with his wife, quickly tired of her, and within two years of his marriage callously abandoned her and his child, then a boy about a year old.

"He lodged a sum of £2,000 in the local bank in the name of Mme Le Cheminant, the interest of which was to be paid to her regularly for the maintenance of herself and child, then he calmly sailed for England, with the intention never to return. This intention fate itself helped him to carry out, for he died very shortly afterwards, taking the secret of his incongruous marriage with him to his grave.

"Mme Le Cheminant, as she was called out there, seems to have accepted her own fate with perfect equanimity. She had never known anything about her husband's social position in his own country, and he had left her what, in Martinique amongst the coloured population, was considered a very fair competence for herself and child.

"The grandson of an English earl was taught to read and write by the worthy *curé* of St Pierre, and during the whole of her life, Lucie never once tried to find out who her husband was, and what had become of him.

"But here the dramatic scene comes in this strange story," continued the man in the corner, with growing excitement; "two years ago St Pierre, if you remember, was completely destroyed by volcanic eruptions. Nearly the entire population perished, and every house and building was in ruins. Among those who fell a victim to the awful catastrophe was Mme Le Cheminant, otherwise the Hon. Mrs Arthur Le Cheminant, whilst amongst those who managed to escape and ultimately found refuge in the English colony of St Vincent, was her son, Philip.

"Well, you can easily guess what happened, can't you? In that English-speaking colony the name of Le Cheminant was, of course, well known, and Philip had not been in St Vincent many weeks, before he learned that his father was none other than a younger brother of the present Earl of Tremarn, and that he himself – seeing that the present peer was over fifty and still unmarried – was heir-presumptive to the title and estates.

"You know the rest. Within two or three months of the memorable St Pierre catastrophe Philip Le Cheminant had written to his uncle, Lord Tremarn, demanding his rights. Then he took passage on board a French liner and crossed over to Havre *en route* for Paris and London.

"He and his mother – both brought up as French subjects – had, mind you, all the respect which French people have for their papers of identification; and when the house in which they had lived for twenty years was tumbling about the young man's ears, when his mother had already perished in the flames, he made a final and successful effort to rescue the papers which proved him to be a French citizen, the son of Lucie Legrand by her lawful marriage with Arthur Le Cheminant at the church of the Immaculate Conception of St Pierre.

"What happened immediately afterwards it is difficult to conjecture. Certain it is, however, that over here the newspapers soon were full of vague allusions about the newly found heir to the Earldom of Tremarn, and within a few weeks the whole of the story of the secret marriage at St Pierre was in everybody's mouth.

"It created an immense sensation; the Hon. Arthur Le Cheminant had lived a few years in England after his return from abroad, and no one, not even his brother, seemed to have had the slightest inkling of his marriage.

"The late Lord Tremarn, you must remember, had three sons, the eldest of whom is the present peer, the second was the romantic Arthur, and the third, the Hon. Reginald, who also died some years ago, leaving four sons, the eldest of whom, Harold, was just twenty-three, and had always been styled heir-presumptive to the Earldom.

"Lord Tremarn had brought up these four nephews of his, who had lost both father and mother, just as if they had been his own children, and his affection for them, and notably for the eldest boy, was a very beautiful trait in his otherwise unattractive character.

"The news of the existence and claim of this unknown nephew must have come upon Lord Tremarn as a thunderbolt. His attitude, however, was one of uncompromising incredulity. He refused to believe the story of the marriage, called the whole tale a tissue of falsehoods, and denounced the claimant as a bare-faced and impudent impostor.

"Two or three months more went by; the public were eagerly awaiting the arrival of this semi-exotic claimant to an English peerage, and sensations, surpassing those of the Tichborne case, were looked forward to with palpitating interest.

"But in the romances of real life, it is always the unexpected that happens. The claimant did arrive in London about a year ago. He was alone, friendless, and moneyless, since the £2,000 lay buried somewhere beneath the ruins of the St Pierre bank. However, he called upon a well-known London solicitor, who advanced him some money and took charge of all the papers relating to his claim.

"Philip Le Cheminant then seems to have made up his mind to make a personal appeal to his uncle, trusting apparently in the old adage that 'blood is thicker than water'.

"As was only to be expected, Lord Tremarn flatly refused to see the claimant, whom he was still denouncing as an impostor. It was by stealth, and by bribing the servants at the Grosvenor Square mansion, that the young man at last obtained an interview with his uncle.

"Last New Year's Day he gave James Tovey, Lord Tremarn's butler, a five-pound note, to introduce him, surreptitiously, into his master's study. There uncle and nephew at last met face to face.

"What happened at that interview nobody knows; was the cry of blood and of justice so convincing that Lord Tremarn dare not resist it? Perhaps.

"Anyway, from that moment the new heir-presumptive was installed within his rights. After a single interview with Philip Le Cheminant's solicitor, Lord Tremarn openly acknowledged the claimant to be his brother Arthur's only son, and therefore his own nephew and heir.

"Nay, more, everyone noticed that the proud, bad-tempered old man was as wax in the hands of this newly found nephew. He seemed even to have withdrawn his affection from the four other young nephews, whom hitherto he had brought up as his own children, and bestowed it all upon his brother Arthur's son – some people said in compensation for all the wrong that had been done to the boy in the past.

"But the scandal around his dead brother's name had wounded the old man's pride very deeply, and from this he never recovered. He shut himself away from all his friends, living alone with his newly found nephew in his gloomy house in Grosvenor Square. The other boys, the eldest of whom, Harold, was just twenty-three, decided very soon to leave a house where they were no longer welcome. They had a small private fortune of their own from their father and mother; the youngest boy was still at college, two others had made a start in their respective professions.

"Harold had been brought up as an idle young man about town, and on him the sudden change of fortune fell most heavily. He was undecided what to do in the future, but, in the meanwhile, partly from a spirit of independence, and partly from a desire to keep a home for his younger brothers, he took and furnished a small flat, which, it is interesting to note, is just off Exhibition Road, not far from the Natural History Museum in Kensington.

"This was less than a year ago. Ten months later the newly found heir to the peerage of Tremarn was found murdered in a hansom cab, and Harold Le Cheminant is once more the future Earl."

## 3

"The papers, as you know, talked of nothing else but the mysterious murder in the hansom cab. Everyone's sympathy went out at once to Lord Tremarn, who, on hearing the terrible news, had completely broken down, and was now lying on a bed of sickness, from which they say he may never recover.

"From the first there had been many rumours of the terrible enmity which existed between Harold Le Cheminant and the man who had so easily captured Lord Tremarn's heart, as well as the foremost place in the Grosvenor Square household.

"The servants in the great and gloomy mansion told the detectives in charge of the case many stories of terrible rows which occurred at first between the cousins. And now everyone's eyes were already turned with suspicion on the one man who could most benefit by the death of Philip Le Cheminant.

"However careful and reticent the police may be, details in connection with so interesting a case have a wonderful way of leaking out. Already one other most important fact had found its way into the papers. It appears that in their endeavours to reconstruct the last day spent by the murdered man the detectives had come upon most important evidence.

"It was Thomas Sawyer, hall porter of the Junior Grosvenor Club, who first told the following interesting story. He stated that deceased was a member of the club, and had dined there on the evening preceding his death.

"'Mr Le Cheminant was just coming downstairs after his dinner,' explained Thomas Sawyer to the detectives, 'when a stranger comes into the hall of the club; Mr Le Cheminant saw him as soon as I did, and appeared very astonished. "What do you want?" he says rather sharply. "A word with you," replies the stranger. Mr Le Cheminant seemed to hesitate for a moment. He lights a cigar, whilst the stranger stands there glaring at him with a look in his eye I certainly didn't like.

"'Mind you,' added Thomas Sawyer, 'the stranger was a gentleman in evening dress, and all that. Presently Mr Le Cheminant says to him: "This way, then," and takes him along into one of the club rooms. Half an hour later the stranger comes out again. He looked flushed and excited. Soon after Mr Le Cheminant comes out too; but he was quite calm and smoking a cigar. He asks for a cab, and tells the driver to take him to the Lyric Theatre.'

"This was all that the hall porter had to say, but his evidence was corroborated by one of the waiters of the club who saw Mr Le Cheminant and the stranger subsequently enter the dining-room, which was quite deserted at the time.

"'They 'adn't been in the room a minute,' said the waiter, 'when I 'eard loud voices, as if they was quarrelling frightful. I couldn't 'ear what they said, though I tried, but they was shouting so, and drowning each other's voices. Presently there's a ring at my bell, and I goes into the room. Mr Le Cheminant was sitting beside one of the tables, quietly lighting a cigar. "Show this – er – gentleman out of the club," 'e says to me. The stranger looked as if 'e would strike 'im. "You'll pay for this," 'e says, then 'e picks up 'is 'at, and dashes out of the club helter-skelter. "One is always pestered by these beggars," says Mr Le Cheminant to me, as 'e stalks out of the room.'

"Later on it was arranged that both Thomas Sawyer and the waiter should catch sight of Harold Le Cheminant, as he went out of his house in Exhibition Road. Neither of them had the slightest hesitation in recognizing in him the stranger who had called at the club that night.

"Now that they held this definite clue, the detectives continued their work with a will. They made enquiries at the Lyric Theatre, but there they only obtained very vague testimony; one point, however, was of great value, the commissionaire outside one of the neighbouring theatres stated that, some time after the performance had begun, he noticed a gentleman in evening dress walking rapidly past him.

"He seemed strangely excited, for as he went by he muttered quite audibly to himself: 'I can stand it no longer, it must be he or I.' Then he disappeared in the fog, walking away towards Shaftesbury Avenue. Unfortunately the commissionaire, just like the cabman, was not prepared to swear to the identity of this man, whom he had only seen momentarily through the fog.

"But add to all this testimony the very strong motive there was for the crime, and you will not wonder that, within twenty-four hours of the murder, the strongest suspicions had already fastened on Harold Le Cheminant, and it was generally understood that, even before the inquest, the police already had in readiness a warrant for his arrest on the capital charge."

## 4

"It would be difficult, I think, for anyone who was not present at that memorable inquest to have the least idea of the sensation which its varied and dramatic incidents caused among the crowd of spectators there.

"At first the proceedings were of the usual kind. The medical officer gave his testimony as to the cause of death; this was, of course, not in dispute. The stiletto was produced; it was of an antique and foreign pattern, probably of Eastern or else Spanish origin. In England, it could only have been purchased at some *bric-à-brac* shop.

"Then it was the turn of the servants at Grosvenor Square, of the cabman, and of the commissionaire. Lord Tremarn's evidence, which he had sworn to on his sickbed, was also read. It added nothing to the known facts of the case, for he had last seen his favourite nephew alive in the course of the afternoon preceding the latter's tragic end.

"After that the *employés* of the Junior Grosvenor Club retold their story, and they were the first to strike the note of sensation which was afterwards raised to its highest possible pitch.

"Both of them, namely, were asked each in their turn to look round the court and see if they could recognize the stranger who had called at the club that memorable evening. Without the slightest hesitation, both the hall porter and the waiter pointed to Harold Le Cheminant, who sat with his solicitor in the body of the court.

"But already an inkling of what was to come had gradually spread through that crowded court – instinctively everyone felt that behind the apparent simplicity of this tragic case there lurked another mystery, more strange even than that murder in the hansom cab.

"Evidence was being taken as to the previous history of the deceased, his first appearance in London, his relationship with his uncle, and subsequently his enmity with his cousin Harold. At this point a man was brought forward as a witness, who it was understood had communicated with the police at the very last moment, offering to make a statement which he thought would throw considerable light upon the mysterious affair.

"He was a man of about fifty years of age, who looked like a very seedy, superannuated clerk of some insurance office.

"He gave his name as Charles Collins, and said that he resided in Caxton Road, Clapham.

"In a perfectly level tone of voice, he then explained that some three years ago, his son William, who had always been idle and good for nothing, had suddenly disappeared from home.

"'We heard nothing of him for over two years,' continued Charles Collins, in that same cheerless and even voice which spoke of a monotonous existence of ceaseless, patient grind, 'but some few weeks ago my daughter went up to the West End to see about an engagement – she plays dance music at parties sometimes – when, in Regent Street, she came face to face with her brother William. He was no longer wretched, as we all are,' added the old man pathetically, 'he was dressed like a swell, and when his sister spoke to him, he pretended not to know her. But she's a sharp girl, and guessed at once that there was something strange there which William wished to hide. She followed him from a distance, and never lost sight of him that day, until she saw him about six o'clock in the evening go into one of the fine houses in Grosvenor Square. Then she came home and told her mother and me all about it.'

"I can assure you," continued the man in the corner, "that you might have heard a pin drop in that crowded court whilst the old man spoke. That he was stating the truth no one doubted for a moment. The very fact that he was brought forward as a witness showed that his story had been proved, at any rate, to the satisfaction of the police.

"The Collinses seem to have been very simple, good-natured people. It never struck any of them to interfere with William, who appeared, in their own words, to have 'bettered himself'. They concluded that he had obtained some sort of position in a rich family and was now ashamed of his poor relations at Clapham.

"Then one morning they read in the papers the story of the mysterious murder in the hansom cab, together with a description of the victim, who had not yet been identified. 'William,' they said with one accord. Michael Collins, one of the younger sons, went up to London to view the murdered man at the mortuary. There was no doubt whatever that it was William, and yet all the papers persisted in saying that the deceased was the heir to some grand peerage.

"'So I wrote to the police,' concluded Charles Collins, 'and my wife and children were all allowed to view the body, and we are all prepared to swear that it is that of my son,

William Collins, who was no more heir to a peerage than your worship.'

"And mopping his forehead with a large coloured hand-kerchief, the old man stepped down from the box.

"Well, you may imagine what this bombshell was in the midst of that coroner's court. Everyone looked at his neighbour, wondering if this was real life, or some romantic play being acted upon a stage. Amidst indescribable excitement, various other members of the Collins family corroborated the old man's testimony, as did also one or two friends from Clapham. All those who had been allowed to view the body of the murdered man pronounced it without hesitation to be that of William Collins, who had disappeared from home three years ago.

"You see, it was like a repetition of the Tichborne case, only with this strange difference: this claimant was dead, but all his papers were in perfect order, the certificate of marriage between Lucie Legrand and Arthur Le Cheminant at Martinique, as well as the birth and baptismal certificate of Philip Le Cheminant, their son. Yet there were all those simple, honest folk swearing that the deceased had been born in Clapham, and the mother, surely, could not have been mistaken.

"That is where the difference with the other noteworthy case came in, for in this instance, as far as the general public is concerned, the actual identity of the murdered man will always remain a matter of doubt – Philip Le Cheminant or William Collins took that part of his secret, at any rate, with him to his grave."

## 5

"But the murder?" I asked eagerly, for the man in the corner had paused, intent upon the manufacture of innumerable knots in a long piece of string.

"Ah, yes, the murder, of course," he replied, with a chuckle, "the second mystery in this extraordinary case. Well, of course, whatever the identity of the deceased really was, there was no doubt in the minds of the police that Harold Le Cheminant had murdered him. To him, at any rate, the Collins family were unknown; he only knew the man who had supplanted him in his uncle's affections, and snatched a rich inheritance away from him. The charge brought against him at the Westminster Court was also one of the greatest sensations of this truly remarkable case.

"It looked, indeed, as if the unfortunate young man had committed a crime which was as appalling as it was useless. Instead of murdering the impostor – if impostor he was – how much more simple it would have been to have tried to unmask him. But, strange to say, this he never seems to have done, at any rate, as far as the public knew.

"But here again mystery stepped in. When brought before the magistrate, Harold Le Cheminant was able to refute the terrible charge brought against him by the simple means of a complete alibi. After the stormy episode at the Junior Grosvenor Club, he had gone to his own club in Pall Mall, and fortunately for him, did not leave until twenty minutes past eleven, some few minutes *after* the two men in evening dress got into the hansom in Shaftesbury Avenue.

"But for this lucky fact, for which he had one or two witnesses, it might have fared ill with him, for feeling unduly excited, he walked all the way home afterwards; and had he left his club earlier, he might have found it difficult to account for his time. As it was, he was of course discharged.

"But one more strange fact came out during the course of the magisterial investigation, and that was that Harold Le Cheminant, on the very day preceding the murder, had booked a passage for St Vincent. He admitted in court that he meant to conduct certain investigations there, with regard to the identity of the supposed heir to the Tremarn peerage.

"And thus the curtain came down on the last act of that extraordinary drama, leaving two great mysteries unsolved: the real identity of the murdered man, and that of the man who killed him. Some people still persist in thinking it was Harold Le Cheminant. Well, we may easily dismiss that supposition. Harold had decided to investigate the matter for himself; he was on his way to St Vincent.

"Surely common sense would assert that, having gone so far, he would assure himself first whether the man was an impostor or not, before he resorted to crime, in order to rid himself of him. Moreover, the witnesses who saw him leave his own club at twenty minutes past eleven were quite independent and very emphatic.

"Another theory is that the Collins gang tried to blackmail Philip Le Cheminant – or William Collins, whichever we like to call him – and that it was one of them who murdered him out of spite, when he refused to submit to the blackmailing process.

"Against that theory, however, there are two unanswerable arguments – firstly, the weapon used, which certainly was not one that would commend itself to the average British middle-class man on murder intent – a razor or knife would be more in his line; secondly, there is no doubt whatever that the murderer wore evening dress and an opera hat, a costume not likely to have been worn by any member of the Collins family, or their friends. We may, therefore, dismiss that theory also with equal certainty."

And he surveyed placidly the row of fine knots in his bit of string.

"But then, according to you, who was the man in evening dress, and who but Harold Le Cheminant had any interest in getting rid of the claimant?" I asked at last.

"Who, indeed?" he replied with a chuckle, "who but the man who was as wax in the hands of that impostor?"

"Whom do you mean?" I gasped.

"Let us take things from the beginning," he said with ever-growing excitement, "and take the one thing which is absolutely beyond dispute, and that is the authenticity of the *papers* – the marriage certificate of Lucie Legrand, etc. – as against the authenticity of the *man*. Let us admit that the real Philip Le Cheminant was a refugee at St Vincent, that he found out about his parentage, and determined to go to England. He writes to his uncle, then sails for Europe, lands at Havre, and arrives in Paris."

"Why Paris?" I asked.

"Because you, like the police and like the public, have persistently shut your eyes to an event which, to my mind, has bearing upon the whole of this mysterious case, and that is the original murder committed in Paris a year ago, also in a cab, also with a stiletto – which that time was *not* found – in fact, in the self-same manner as this murder a week ago.

"Well, that crime was never brought home to its perpetrator any more than this one will be. But my contention is, that the man who committed that murder a year ago, repeated this crime last week – that the man who was murdered in Paris was the real Philip Le Cheminant, whilst the man who was murdered in London was some friend to whom he had confided his story, and probably his papers, and who then hit upon the bold plan of assuming the personality of the Martinique creole, heir to an English peerage."

"But what in the world makes you imagine such a preposterous thing?" I gasped.

"One tiny unanswerable fact," he replied quietly. "William Collins, the impostor, when he came to London, called upon a solicitor, and deposited with him the valuable papers; *after that* he obtained his interview with Lord Tremarn. Then mark what happens. Without any question, immediately after that interview, and, therefore, without even having seen the papers of identification, Lord Tremarn accepts the claimant as his newly found nephew.

"And why?

"Only because that claimant has a tremendous hold over the Earl, which makes the old man as wax in his hands, and it is only logical to conclude that that hold was none other than that Lord Tremarn had met his real nephew in Paris, and had killed him, sooner than to see him supplant his beloved heir, Harold.

"I followed up the subsequent history of that Paris crime, and found that the Paris police had never established the identity of the murdered man. Being a stranger, and moneyless, he had apparently lodged in one of those innumerable ill-famed little hotels that abound in Paris, the proprietors of which have very good cause to shun the police, and therefore would not even venture so far as to go and identify the body when it lay in the Morgue.

"But William Collins knew who the murdered man was; no doubt he lodged at the same hotel, and could lay his hands on the all-important papers. I imagine that the two young men originally met in St Vincent, or perhaps on board ship. He assumed the personality of the deceased, crossed over to England, and confronted Lord Tremarn with the threat to bring the murder home to him if he ventured to dispute his claim.

"Think of it all, and you will see that I am right. When Lord Tremarn first heard from his brother Arthur's son, he went to Paris in order to assure himself of the validity of his claim. Seeing that there was no doubt of that, he assumed a friendly attitude towards the young man, and one evening took him out for a drive in a cab and murdered him on the way.

"Then came Nemesis in the shape of William Collins, whom he dared not denounce, lest his crime be brought home to him. How could he come forward and say: 'I know that this man is an impostor, as I happened to have murdered my nephew myself'?

"No; he preferred to temporize, and bide his time until, perhaps, chance would give him his opportunity. It took a year in coming. The yoke had become too heavy. 'It must be he or I!' he said to himself that very night. Apparently he was on the best of terms with his tormentor, but in his heart of hearts he had always meant to be even with him at the last.

"Everything favoured him; the foggy night, even the dispute between Harold and the impostor at the club. Can you not picture him meeting William Collins outside the theatre, hearing from him the story of the quarrel, and then saying, 'Come with me to Harold's; I'll soon make the young jackanapes apologize to you'?

"Mind you, a year had passed by since the original crime. William Collins, no doubt, never thought he had anything to fear from the old man. He got into the cab with him, and thus this remarkable story has closed, and Harold Le Cheminant is once more heir to the Earldom of Tremarn.

"Think it all over, and bear in mind that Lord Tremarn *never* made the slightest attempt to prove the rights or wrongs of the impostor's claim. On this base your own conclusions, and then see if they do not inevitably lead you to admit mine as the only possible solution of this double mystery."

He was gone, leaving me bewildered and amazed staring at my *Daily Telegraph*, where, side by side with a long recapitulation of the mysterious claimant to the Earldom, there was the following brief announcement:

We regret to say that the condition of Lord Tremarn is decidedly worse today, and that but little hope is entertained of his recovery. Mr Harold Le Cheminant has been his uncle's constant and devoted companion during the noble Earl's illness.

# VIII

# *The Fate of the Artemis*

## 1

"Well, I'm ——!" was my inelegant mental comment upon the news in that morning's paper.

"So are most people," rejoined the man in the corner, with that eerie way he had of reading my thoughts. "The *Artemis* has come home, having safely delivered her dangerous cargo, and Captain Jutland's explanations only serve to deepen the mystery."

"Then you admit there is one in this case?" I said.

"Only to the public. Not to me. But I do admit that the puzzle is a hard one. Do you remember the earlier details of the case? It was towards the end of 1903. Negotiations between Russia and Japan were just reaching a point of uncomfortable tension, and the man in the street guessed that war in the Far East was imminent.

"Messrs Mills and Co. had just completed an order for a number of their celebrated quick-firing guns for the Russian Government, and these – according to the terms of the contract – were to be delivered at Port Arthur on or about 1st February 1904. Effectively, then, on 1st December last, the *Artemis*, under the command of Captain Jutland, sailed from Goole, with her valuable cargo on board, and with orders to proceed along as fast as possible, in view of the probable outbreak of hostilities.

"Less than two hours after she had started, Messrs Mills received intimation from the highest official quarters, that in all probability before the *Artemis* could reach Port Arthur, and in view of coming eventualities, the submarine mines would have been laid at the entrance to the harbour. A secret plan of the port was therefore sent to the firm for Captain Jutland's use, showing the only way through which he could possibly hope to navigate the *Artemis* safely into the harbour, and without which she would inevitably come in contact with one of those terrible engines of wholesale destruction, which have since worked such awful havoc in this war.

"But *there* was the trouble. This official intimation, together with the plan, reached Messrs Mills just two hours too late; it is a way peculiar to many official intimations. Fortunately, however, the *Artemis* was to touch at Portsmouth on private business of the firm's, and, therefore, it only meant finding a trustworthy messenger to meet Captain Jutland there, and to hand him over that all-important plan.

"Of course, there was no time to be lost, but, above all, someone of extreme trustworthiness must be found for so important a mission. You must remember that the great European Power in question is beset by many foes in the shape of her own disaffected children, who desire her downfall even more keenly than does her Asiatic opponent. Also, in times like these, when every method is fair which gives one adversary an advantage over the other, we must remember that our plucky little allies of the Far East are past masters in that art which is politely known as secret intelligence.

"All this, you see, made it an absolute necessity to keep the mission to Captain Jutland a profound secret. I need not impress upon you the fact, I think, that it is not expedient for the plans of an important harbour to fall under prying eyes.

"Finally, the choice fell on Captain Markham, RNR, lately of the mercantile marine, and at the time in the employ of our own Secret Intelligence Department, to which he has rendered frequent and valuable services. This choice was determined also mainly through the fact that Captain Markham's wife had relatives living in Portsmouth, and that, therefore, his journey thither could easily be supposed to have an unofficial and quite ordinary character – especially if he took his wife with him, which he did.

"Captain and Mrs Markham left Waterloo for Portsmouth at ten minutes past twelve on Wednesday, 2nd December, the secret plan lying safely concealed at the bottom of Mrs Markham's jewel case.

"As the *Artemis* would not touch at Portsmouth until the following morning, Captain Markham thought it best not to spend the night at an hotel, but to go into rooms; his choice fell on a place, highly recommended by his wife's relations, and which was situated in a quiet street on the Southsea side of the town. There he and his wife stayed the night, pending the arrival of the *Artemis*.

"But at twelve o'clock on the following morning the police were hastily called in by Mrs Bowden, the landlady of 49 Gastle Street, where the Markhams had been staying.

Captain Markham had been found lying half-insensible, gagged and bound, on the floor of the sitting-room, his hands and feet tightly pinioned, and a woollen comforter wound closely round his mouth and neck; whilst Mrs Markham's jewel case, containing valuable jewellery and the secret plans of Port Arthur, had disappeared."

## 2

"Mind you," continued the man in the corner, after he had assured himself of my undivided attention, "all these details were unknown to the public at first. I have merely co-ordinated them, and told them to you in the actual sequence in which they occurred, so that you may be able to understand the subsequent events.

"At the time – that is to say, on 3rd December 1903 – the evening papers only contained an account of what was then called 'the mysterious outrage at Gastle Street, Portsmouth'. A private gentleman was presumably assaulted and robbed in broad daylight, and inside a highly respectable house in a busy part of the city.

"Mrs Bowden, the landlady, was, as you may imagine, most excited and indignant. Her house and herself had been grossly insulted by this abominable outrage, and she did her level best to throw what light she could on this mysterious occurrence.

"The story she told the police was indeed extraordinary, and as she repeated it to all her friends, and subsequently to one or two journalists, it roused public excitement to its highest pitch.

"What she related at great length to the detective in charge of the case, was briefly this:

"Captain and Mrs Markham, it appears, arrived at 49 Gastle Street, on Wednesday afternoon, 2nd December, and Mrs Bowden accommodated them with a sitting-room and bedroom, both on the ground floor. In the evening Mrs Markham went out to dine with her brother, a Mr Paulton, who is a well-known Portsmouth resident, but Captain Markham stayed in and had dinner alone in his sitting-room.

"According to Mrs Bowden's version of the story, at about nine o'clock a stranger called to see Captain Markham. This stranger was obviously a foreigner, for he spoke broken English. Unfortunately, the hall at 49 Gastle Street was very dark, and, moreover, the foreigner was attired in a magnificent fur coat, the collar of which hid the lower part of his face. All Mrs Bowden could see of him was that he was very tall, and wore gold-rimmed spectacles.

"'He was so very peremptory in his manner,' continued Mrs Bowden, 'that I had to show him in at once. The Captain seemed surprised to see him – in fact he looked decidedly annoyed, I might say; but just as I was closing the door I heard the stranger laugh, and say quite pleasantly: "You gave me the slip, my friend, but you see I have found you out all right."'

"Mrs Bowden, after the manner of her class, seems to have made vigorous efforts to hear what went on in the sitting-room after that," continued the man in the corner, "but she was not successful. Later on, however, the Captain rang and ordered whiskies and sodas. Both gentlemen were then sitting by the fire, looking quite friendly.

161

"'I took a look round the room,' explained the worthy landlady, 'and took particular notice that the jewel case was on the table, with the lid open. Captain Markham, as soon as he saw me, closed it very quickly.'

"The stranger seems to have gone away again at about half past ten, and subsequently Mrs Markham came home, accompanied by her brother, Mr Paulton. The next morning she went out at a quarter past eleven o'clock, and about half an hour later the mysterious stranger called again.

"This time he pushed his way straight into the sitting-room; but the very next moment he uttered a cry of intense horror and astonishment, and rushed back into the hall, gesticulating wildly, and shrieking: 'A robbery! – a murder! – I go for the police!' And before Mrs Bowden could stop him or even could realize what had occurred, he had dashed out of the house.

"'I called to Meggie,' continued Mrs Bowden, 'I was so frightened, I didn't dare go into the parlour alone. But she was more frightened than I was, and we stood trembling in the hall waiting for the police. At last I began to have my suspicions, and I got Meggie to run out into the street and see if she could bring in a policeman.'

"When the police at last arrived upon the scene, they pushed open the sitting-room door, and there found Captain Markham in a most helpless condition, his hands tied behind his back and himself half-choked by the scarf over his mouth. As soon as he recovered his breath, he explained that he had no idea who his assailant was; he was standing with his back to the door, when he was suddenly dealt a blow on the head from behind, and he remembered nothing more.

"In the meantime Mrs Markham had come home, and of course was horrified beyond measure at the outrage which had been committed. She declared that her jewel case was in the sitting-room when she went out in the morning – a fact confirmed by Captain Markham himself.

"But here, at once, the police were seriously puzzled. Mrs Bowden, of course, told her story of the foreigner – a story which was corroborated by her daughter, Meggie. Captain Markham, pressed by the police, and by his wife, admitted that a friend had visited him the evening before.

"'He is an old friend I met years ago abroad, who happened to be in Portsmouth yesterday, and quite accidentally caught sight of me as I drove up to this door, and naturally came in to see me,' was the Captain's somewhat lame explanation.

"Nothing more was to be got out of him that day; he was still feeling very bewildered, he said, and certainly he looked very ill. Mrs Markham then put the whole matter in the hands of the police.

"Captain Markham had given a description of 'the old friend he had met years ago abroad'. This description vaguely coincided with that given by Mrs Bowden of the mysterious foreigner. But the Captain's replies to the cross-questionings of the detectives in charge of the case were always singularly reticent and lame. 'I had lost sight of him for nearly twenty years,' he explained, 'and do not know what his present abode and occupation might be. When I knew him years ago, he was a man of independent means, without a fixed abode, and a great traveller. I believe that he is a German by nationality, but I don't think that I ever knew this as a fact. His name was Johann Schmidt.'

"I may as well tell you here, at once, that the mysterious foreigner managed to make good his escape. He was traced as far as the South-western Railway Station, where he was seen to rush through the barrier, just in time to catch the express up to town. At Waterloo he was lost sight of in the crowd.

"The police were keenly on the alert; no trace of the missing jewels had as yet been found. Then it was that, gradually, the story of the secret plan of Port Arthur reached the ears of the general public. Who first told it and to whom, it is difficult to conjecture, but you know what a way things of that sort have of leaking out.

"The secret of Captain Markham's mission had of necessity been known to several people, and a secret shared by many soon ceases to be one at all; anyway, within a week of the so-called 'Portsmouth outrage', it began to be loudly whispered that the robbery of Mrs Markham's jewels was only a mask that covered the deliberate theft of the plans of Port Arthur.

"And then the inevitable happened. Already Captain Markham's strange attitude had been severely commented upon, and now the public, backed by the crowd of amateur detectives who read penny novelettes and form conclusions of their own, had made up its mind that Captain Markham was a party to the theft – that he was either the tool or the accomplice of the mysterious foreigner, and that, in fact, he had been either bribed or terrorized into giving up the plan of Port Arthur to an enemy of the Russian Government. The crime was all the more heinous as by this act of treachery a British ship, manned by a British crew, had been sent to certain destruction.

"What rendered the whole case doubly mysterious was that Messrs Mills and Co. seemed to take the matter with complete indifference. They refused to be interviewed, or to give any information about the *Artemis* at all, and seemed callously willing to await events.

"The public was furious; the newspapers stormed; everyone felt that the *Artemis* should be stopped at any cost at her next port of call, and not allowed to continue her perilous journey.

"And yet the days went by; the public read with horror at Lloyd's that the *Artemis* had called at Malta, at Port Said, at Aden, and was now well on her way to the Far East. Feeling ran so high throughout England, that, if the mysterious stranger had been discovered by the police, no protection from them would have saved him from being lynched.

"As for Captain Markham, public opinion reserved its final judgment. A cloud hung over him, of that there was no doubt; many said openly that he had sold the secret plans of Port Arthur, either to the Japanese or to the Nihilists, either through fear or intimidation, if not through greed.

"Then the inevitable climax came: a certain Mr Carleton constituted himself the spokesman of the general public; he met Captain Markham one day at one of the clubs in London. There were hot words between them; Mr Carleton did not mince matters; he openly accused Captain Markham of that which public opinion had already whispered, and finally, completely losing his temper, he struck the Captain in the face, calling him every opprobrious name he could think of.

"But for the timely interference of friends, there would have been murder committed then and there; as it was, Captain Markham was induced by his own friends to bring a criminal charge of slander and of assault against Mr Carleton, as the only means of making the whole story public, and possibly vindicating his character."

### 3

"A criminal action for slander and assault is always an interesting one," continued the man in the corner, after a while, "as it always argues an unusual amount of personal animosity on the part of the plaintiff.

"In this case, of course, public interest was roused to its highest pitch. Practically, though Captain Markham was the prosecutor, he would stand before his fellow-citizens after this action either as an innocent man, or as one of the most dastardly scoundrels this nation has ever known.

"The case for the Captain was briefly stated by his counsel. For the defence Sir Arthur Inglewood, on behalf of Mr Carleton, pleaded justification. With wonderful eloquence Sir Arthur related the whole story of the secret plan of Port Arthur confided to the honour of Captain Markham, and which involved the safety of the British ship and the lives of a whole British crew.

"The first witnesses called for the defence were Mrs Bowden and her daughter, Meggie. Both related the story I have already told you. When they came to the point of having seen the jewel case open on the table during that interview between Captain Markham and the mysterious stranger, there was a regular murmur of indignation throughout the whole crowd, so much so, that the judge threatened to clear the court, for Sir Arthur argued this to be a proof that Captain Markham had been a willing accomplice in the theft of the secret plans, and had merely played the comedy of being assaulted, bound, and gagged.

"But there was more to come.

"It appears that on the morning of 2nd December – that is to say, before going to Portsmouth – Captain Markham, directly after breakfast, and while his wife was up in her own room, received a message, which seemed greatly to disturb him. It was Jane Mason, the parlour-maid at the Markhams' town house, who told the story.

"A letter bearing no stamp had been dropped into the letterbox; she had taken it to her master, who, on reading it, became greatly agitated; he tore up the letter, stuffed it into his pocket, and presently took up his hat and rushed out of the house.

"'When the master was gone,' continued Jane, 'I found a scrap of paper, which had fallen out of his pocket.'

"This scrap of paper Jane Mason had carefully put away. She was a shrewd girl, and scented some mystery. It was now produced in court, and the few fragmentary words were read out by Sir Arthur Inglewood, amidst boundless excitement:

"'… if you lend a hand… Port Arthur safely… hold my tongue…'

"And at the end there were four letters in large capitals, 'STOW'.

"In view of all the evidence taken, there was momentous significance to be attached to those few words, of which only the last four letters seemed mysterious, but these probably were part of the confederate's signature, who had – no one doubted it now – some hold upon Captain Markham, and had by a process of blackmail induced him to send the *Artemis* to her doom.

"After that, according to a statement made by the head clerk of Messrs Mills and Co., Captain Markham came round to the office, begging that someone else should be sent to meet Captain Jutland at Portsmouth. 'This,' explained the head clerk, who had been subpoenaed for the defence, 'was quite impossible at this eleventh hour, and in the absence of the heads of the firm, I had, on Mr Mills' behalf, to hold Captain Markham to his promise.'

"This closed the case for the defence, and, in view of the lateness of the hour, counsel's speeches were reserved for the following day. There was not a doubt in anybody's mind that Captain Markham was guilty, and but for the presence of a large body of police, I assure you he would have been torn to pieces by the crowd."

The man in the corner paused in his narrative and blinked at me over his bone-rimmed spectacles, like some lean and frowzy tom-cat eager for a fight.

"Well?" I said eagerly.

"Well, surely you remember what happened the following day?" he replied, with a dry chuckle. "Personally, I don't think that there ever was quite so much sensation in any English court of law.

"It was crowded, of course, when counsel for the plaintiff rose to speak. He made, however, only a short statement, briefly and to the point; but this statement caused everyone to look at his neighbour, wondering if he were awake or dreaming.

"Counsel began by saying that Messrs Mills and Co., in view of the obvious conspiracy that had existed against the

*Artemis*, had decided, in conjunction with Captain Markham himself, to say nothing about the safety of the ship until she was in port; but now counsel had much pleasure in informing the court and public that the *Artemis* had safely arrived at Port Arthur, had landed her guns, and was on her way home again by now. A cablegram via St Petersburg had been received by Messrs Mills and Co. from Captain Jutland that very morning.

"That cablegram was read by counsel in court, and was received with loud and prolonged cheering which could not be suppressed.

"With heroic fortitude – explained counsel – Captain Markham had borne the gross suspicions against his integrity, only hoping that news of the safety of the *Artemis* would reach England in time to allow him to vindicate his character. But until Captain Jutland was safe in port, he had sworn to hold his tongue, and to bear insult and violence, sooner than once more jeopardize the safety of the British ship by openly avowing that she carried the plans of the important port with her.

"Well, you know the rest. The parties, at the suggestion of the judge, arranged the case amicably, and, Captain Markham being fully satisfied, Mr Carleton was nominally ordered to come up for trial when called upon.

"Captain Markham was the hero of the hour; but presently, after the first excitement had subsided, sensible people began to ponder. Everyone, of course, appreciated the fact that Messrs Mills and Co., prompted by the highest authorities, had insisted on not jeopardizing the safety of the *Artemis* by shouting on the housetops that she was carrying the plans of Port Arthur on board. Hostilities in the Far East were on the point of breaking out, and I need not insist, I think, on the obvious fact that silence in such matters and at such a time was absolutely imperative.

"But what sensible people wanted to know was, what part had Captain Markham played in all this?

"In the evening of that memorable 2nd December, he was sitting amicably by the fire with the mysterious stranger, who was evidently blackmailing him, and with the jewel case, which contained the plans of Port Arthur, open between them. What, then, had caused Captain Markham to change his attitude? What dispelled the fear of the stranger? Was he really assaulted? Was the jewel case really stolen?

"Captain Jutland, of the *Artemis*, has explained that he was only on shore for one hour at Portsmouth on the memorable morning of 3rd December, namely, between 10.30 and 11.30 a.m. On landing at the Hard from his gig, he was met by a gentleman whom he did not know, and who, without a word of comment, handed him some papers, which proved to be plans of Port Arthur.

"Now, at that very hour Captain Markham was lying helpless in his bedroom, and the question now is, who abstracted the plans from the jewel case, and then mysteriously handed them to Captain Jutland? Why was it not done openly? Why? – why? and, above all, by whom? –"

4

"Indeed, why?" I retorted, for he had paused, and was peering at me through his bone-rimmed spectacles. "You must have a theory," I added, as I quietly handed him a beautiful bit of string across the table.

"Of course I have a theory," he replied placidly; "nay, more, the only explanation of those mysterious events. But for this I must refer you to the scrap of paper found by Jane Mason, and containing the four fragmentary sentences which have puzzled everyone, and which Captain Markham always refused to explain.

"Do you remember," he went on, as he began feverishly to construct knot upon knot on that piece of string, "the wreck of the *Ridstow* some twenty years ago? She was a pleasure boat belonging to Mr Eyres, the great millionaire financier, and was supposed to have been wrecked in the South Seas, with nearly all hands. Five of her crew, however, were picked up by HMS *Pomona*, on a bit of rocky island to which they had managed to swim.

"I looked up the files of the newspapers relating to the rescue of these five shipwrecked mariners, who told a most pitiable tale of the loss of the yacht and their subsequent escape to, and sufferings on, the island. Fire had broken out in the hull of the *Ridstow*, and all her crew were drowned, with the exception of three sailors, a Russian friend, or rather secretary, of Mr Eyres, and a young petty officer named Markham.

"You see, the letters 'STOW' had given me the clue. Clearly Markham, on receiving the message in the morning of 2nd December, was frightened, and when we analyse the fragments of that message and try to reconstruct the missing fragments, do we not get something like this:

"'*If you lend a hand* in allowing the *Artemis* to reach *Port Arthur safely*, and to land her cargo there, I will no longer *hold my tongue* about the events which occurred on board the *Rid*STOW.'

"Clearly the mysterious stranger had a great hold over Captain Markham, for every scrap of evidence, if you think it over, points to his having been *frightened*. Did he not beg the clerk to find someone else to meet Captain Jutland in Portsmouth? He did not wish *to lend a hand* in allowing the *Artemis* to reach *Port Arthur safely*.

"We must, therefore, take it that on board the *Ridstow* some such tragedy was enacted as, alas! is not of unfrequent occurrence. The tragedy of a mutiny, a wholesale murder, the robbery of the rich financier, the burning of the yacht. Markham, then barely twenty, was no doubt an unwilling, perhaps passive, accomplice; one can trace the hand of a cunning, daring Russian in the whole of this mysterious tragedy.

"Since then, Markham, through twenty years' faithful service of his country, had tried to redeem the passive crime of his early years. But then came the crisis: the cunning leader of that bygone tragedy no doubt kept a strong hand over his weaker accomplices.

"What happened to the other three we do not know, but we have seen how terrified Markham is of him, how he dare not resist him, and when the mysterious Russian – some Nihilist, no doubt, at war with his own government – wishes to deal his country a terrible blow by possessing himself of the plan of her most important harbour, so that he might sell it to her enemies, Markham dare not say him nay.

"But mark what happens. Captain Markham terrorized, confronted with a past crime, threatened with exposure, is as wax in the hands of his unscrupulous tormentor. But beside him there is the saving presence of his wife."

"His wife?" I gasped.

"Yes, the woman! Did you think this was a crime without the inevitable woman? I sought her, and found her in Captain Markham's wife. To save her husband both from falling a victim to his implacable accomplice, and from committing another even more heinous crime, she suggests the comedy which was so cleverly enacted in the morning of 3rd December.

"When the landlady and her daughter saw the jewel case open on the table the evening before, Markham was playing the first act of the comedy invented by his wife. She had the plan safely in her own keeping by then. He pretended to agree to the Russian's demands, but showed him that he had not then the plan in his possession, promising, however, to deliver it up on the morrow.

"Then in the morning, Mrs Markham helps to gag and strap her husband down; he pretends to lie unconscious, and she goes out, carrying the jewel case. Her brother, Mr Paulton, of course, helps them both; without him it would have been more difficult; as it is, he takes charge of the jewel case, abstracts the plan and papers, and finally meets Captain Jutland at the Hard, and hands him over the plan of Port Arthur.

"Thus through the wits of a clever and devoted woman, not only are the *Artemis* and her British crew saved, but Captain Markham is effectually rid of the blackmailer, who otherwise would have poisoned his life, and probably out of revenge at being foiled, have ruined his victim altogether.

"To my mind, that was the neatest thing in the whole plan. The general public believed that Captain Markham (who obviously at the instigation of his wife had confided in Messrs Mills and Co.) held his tongue as to the safety of the *Artemis* merely out of heroism, in order not to run her into any further danger. Now, I maintain that this was the master-stroke of that clever woman's plan.

"By holding his tongue, by letting the public fear for the safety of the British crew and British ship, public feeling was stirred to such a pitch of excitement that the Russian now would never *dare* show himself. Not only – by denouncing Captain Markham now – would he never be even listened to for a moment, but, if he came forward at all, if he even showed himself, he would stand before the British public self-convicted as the man who had tried through the criminal process of blackmail to terrorize an Englishman into sending a British ship and thirty British sailors to certain annihilation.

"No; I think we may take it for granted that the Russian will not dare to show his face in England again."

And the funny creature was gone before I could say another word.

# IX

# *The Disappearance of Count Collini*

## 1

He was very argumentative that morning; whatever I said he invariably contradicted flatly and at once, and we both had finally succeeded in losing our temper.

The man in the corner was riding one of his favourite hobbyhorses.

"It is *impossible* for any person to completely disappear in a civilized country," he said emphatically, "provided that person has either friends or enemies of means and substance, who are interested in finding his or her whereabouts."

"Impossible is a sweeping word," I rejoined.

"None too big for the argument," he concluded, as he surveyed with evident pride and pleasure a gigantic and complicated knot, which his bony fingers had just fashioned.

"I think that, nevertheless, you should not use it," I said placidly. "It is not *impossible*, though it may be very difficult to disappear without leaving the slightest clue or trace behind you."

"Prove it," he said, with a snap of his thin lips.

"I can, quite easily."

"Now I know what is going on in your mind," said the uncanny creature; "you are thinking of that case last autumn."

"Well, I was," I admitted. "And you cannot deny that Count Collini has disappeared as effectually as if the sea had swallowed him up – many people think it did."

"Many idiots, you mean," he rejoined dryly. "Yes, I knew you would quote that case. It certainly was a curious one; all the more so, perhaps, as there was no inquest, no sensational police-court proceedings, nothing dramatic, in fact, save that strange and wonderful disappearance.

"I don't know if you call to mind the whole plot of that weird drama. There was Thomas Checkfield, a retired biscuit-baker of Reading, who died leaving a comfortable fortune, mostly invested in freehold property, and amounting to about £80,000, to his only child, Alice.

"At the time of her father's death Alice Checkfield was just eighteen, and at school in Switzerland, where she had spent most of her life. Old Checkfield had been a widower ever since the birth of his daughter, and seems to have led a very lonely and eccentric life, leaving the girl at school abroad for years, only going very occasionally to see her, and seemingly having but little affection for her.

"The girl herself had not been home in England since she was eight years old, and even when old Checkfield was dying he would not allow the girl to be apprised of his impending death, and to be brought home to a house of loneliness and mourning.

"'What's the good of upsetting a young girl, not eighteen,' he said to his friend, Mr Turnour, 'by letting her see all the sad paraphernalia of death? She hasn't seen much of her old father anyway, and will soon get over her loss, with young company round her, to help her bear up.'

"But though Thomas Checkfield cared little enough for his daughter, when he died he left his entire fortune to her, amounting altogether to £80,000; and he appointed his friend, Reginald Turnour, to be her trustee and guardian until her marriage or until she should attain her majority.

"It was generally understood that the words 'until her marriage' were put in because it had all along been arranged that Alice should marry Hubert Turnour, Reginald's younger brother.

"Hubert was old Checkfield's godson, and if the old man had any affection for anybody, it certainly was for Hubert. The latter had been a great deal in his godfather's house, when he and Alice were both small children, and had called each other 'hubby' and 'wifey' in play, when they were still in the nursery. Later on, whenever old Checkfield went abroad to see his daughter, he always took Hubert with him, and a boy-and-girl flirtation sprang up between the two young people; a flirtation which had old Checkfield's complete approval, and no doubt he looked upon their marriage as a *fait accompli*, merely desiring the elder Mr Turnour to administer the girl's fortune until then.

"Hubert Turnour, at the time of the subsequent tragedy, was a good-looking young fellow, and by profession what is vaguely known as a 'commission agent'. He lived in London, where he had an office in a huge block of buildings close to Cannon Street Station.

"There is no doubt that at the time of old Checkfield's death, Alice looked upon herself as the young man's *fiancée*. When the girl reached her nineteenth year, it was at last decided that she should leave school and come to England.

The question as to what should be done with her until her majority, or until she married Hubert, was a great puzzle to Mr Turnour. He was a bachelor, who lived in comfortable furnished rooms in Reading, and he did not at all relish the idea of starting housekeeping for the sake of his young ward, whom he had not seen since she was out of the nursery, and whom he looked upon as an intolerable nuisance.

"Fortunately for him this vexed question was most satisfactorily and unexpectedly settled by Alice herself. She wrote to her guardian, from Geneva, that a Mrs Brackenbury, the mother of her dearest school-fellow, had asked her to come and live with them, at any rate for a time, as this would be a more becoming arrangement than that of a young girl sharing a bachelor's establishment.

"Mr Turnour seems to have hesitated for some time: he was a conscientious sort of man, who took his duties of guardianship very seriously. What ultimately decided him, however, was that his brother Hubert added the weight of his eloquent letters of appeal to those of Alice herself. Hubert naturally was delighted at the idea of having his rich *fiancée* under his eye in London, and after a good deal of correspondence, Mr Turnour finally gave his consent, and Alice Checkfield duly arrived from Switzerland in order to make a prolonged stay in Mrs Brackenbury's house."

## 2

"All seems to have gone on happily and smoothly for a time in Mrs Brackenbury's pretty house in Kensington," continued the man in the corner. "Hubert Turnour was a constant visitor there, and the two young people seem to have had all the freedom of an engaged couple.

"Alice Checkfield was in no sense of the word an attractive girl; she was not good-looking, and no effort on Mrs Brackenbury's part could succeed in making her look stylish. Still, Hubert Turnour seemed quite satisfied, and the girl herself ready enough at first to continue the boy-and-girl flirtation as of old.

"Soon, however, as time went on, things began to change. Now that Alice had become mistress of a comfortable fortune there were plenty of people ready to persuade her that a 'commission agent', with but vague business prospects, was not half-good enough for her, and that her £80,000 entitled her to more ambitious matrimonial hopes. Needless to say that in these counsels Mrs Brackenbury was very much to the fore.

"She lived in Kensington, and had social ambitions, foremost among which was to see her daughter's bosom friend married to, at least, a baronet, if not a peer.

"A young girl's head is quickly turned. Within six months of her stay in London, Alice was giving Hubert Turnour the cold shoulder, and the young man had soon realized that she was trying to get out of her engagement.

"Scarcely had Alice reached her twentieth birthday, than she gave her erstwhile *fiancée* his formal *congé*.

"At first Hubert seems to have taken his discomfiture very much to heart. £80,000 were not likely to come his way again in a hurry. According to Mrs Brackenbury's servants, there were one or two violent scenes between him and Alice, until finally Mrs Brackenbury herself was forced to ask the young man to discontinue his visits.

"It was soon after that that Alice Checkfield first met Count Collini at one of the brilliant subscription dances given by the Italian colony in London, the winter before last. Mrs Brackenbury was charmed with him, Alice Checkfield was enchanted! The Count, having danced with Alice half the evening, was allowed to pay his respects at the house in Kensington.

"He seemed to be extremely well off, for he was staying at the Carlton, and, after one or two calls on Mrs Brackenbury, he began taking the ladies to theatres and concerts, always presenting them with the choicest and most expensive flowers, and paying them various other equally costly attentions.

"Mrs and Miss Brackenbury welcomed the Count with open arms (figuratively speaking). Alice was shy, but apparently over head and ears in love at first sight.

"At first Mrs Brackenbury did her best to keep this new acquaintanceship a secret from Hubert Turnour. I suppose that the old matchmaker feared another unpleasant scene. But the inevitable soon happened. Hubert, contrite, perhaps still hopeful, called at the house one day, when the Count was there, and, according to the story subsequently told by Miss Brackenbury herself, there was a violent scene between him and Alice. As soon as the fascinating foreigner had gone, Hubert reproached his *fiancée* for her fickleness in no measured language, and there was a good deal of evidence to prove that he then and there swore to be even with the man who had supplanted him in her affections. There was nothing to do then but for Mrs Brackenbury to 'burn her boats'. She peremptorily ordered Hubert out of her house, and admitted that Count Collini was a suitor, favoured by herself, for the hand of Alice Checkfield.

"You see, I am bound to give you all these details of the situation," continued the man in the corner, with his bland smile, "so that you may better form a judgment as to the subsequent fate of Count Collini. From the description which Mrs Brackenbury herself subsequently gave to the police, the Count was then in the prime of life; of a dark olive complexion, dark eyes, extremely black hair and moustache. He had a very slight limp, owing to an accident he had had in early youth, which made his walk and general carriage unusual and distinctly noticeable. His was certainly not a personality that could pass unperceived in a crowd.

"Hubert Turnour, furious and heartsick, wrote letter after letter to his brother, to ask him to interfere on his behalf; this Mr Turnour did, to the best of his ability, but he had to deal with an ambitious matchmaker and with a girl in love, and it is small wonder that he signally failed. Alice Checkfield by now had become deeply enamoured of her Count, his gallantries flattered her vanity, his title and the accounts he gave of his riches and his estates in Italy fascinated her, and she declared that she would marry him, either with or without her guardian's consent, either at once, or as soon as she had attained her majority, and was mistress of herself and of her fortune.

"Mr Turnour did all he could to prevent this absurd marriage. Being a sensible, middle-class Britisher, he had no respect for foreign titles, and little belief in foreign wealth. He wrote the most urgent letters to Alice, warning her against a man whom he firmly believed to be an impostor: finally he flatly refused to give his consent to the marriage.

"Thus a few months went by. The Count had been away in Italy all through the winter and spring, and returned to London for the season, apparently more enamoured with the Reading biscuit-baker's daughter than ever. Alice Checkfield was then within nine months of her twenty-first birthday, and determined to marry the Count. She openly defied her guardian.

"'Nothing,' she wrote to him, 'would ever induce me to marry Hubert.'

"I suppose it was this which finally induced Mr Turnour to give up all opposition to the marriage. Seeing that his brother's chances were absolutely nil, and that Alice was within nine months of her majority he no doubt thought all further argument useless, and with great reluctance finally gave his consent.

"The marriage, owing to the difference of religion, was to be performed before a registrar, and was finally fixed to take place on 22nd October 1903, which was just a week after Alice's twenty-first birthday.

"Of course the question of Alice's fortune immediately cropped up: she desired her money in cash, as her husband was taking her over to live in Italy where she desired to make all further investments. She, therefore, asked Mr Turnour to dispose of her freehold property for her. There again Mr Turnour hesitated, and argued, but once he had given his consent to the marriage, all opposition was useless, more especially as Mrs Brackenbury's solicitors had drawn up a very satisfactory marriage settlement, which the Count himself had suggested, by which Alice was to retain sole use and control of her own private fortune.

"The marriage was then duly performed before a registrar on that 22nd of October, and Alice Checkfield could henceforth style herself Countess Collini. The young couple were to start for Italy almost directly but meant to spend a day or two at Dover quietly together. There were, however, one or two tiresome legal formalities to go through. Mr Turnour had, by Alice's desire, handed over the sum of £80,000 in notes to her solicitor, Mr R. W. Stanford. Mr Stanford had gone down to Reading two days before the marriage, had received the money from Mr Turnour, and then called upon the new Countess, and formally handed her over her fortune in Bank of England notes.

"Then it was necessary, in view of immediate and future arrangements, to change the English money into foreign, which the Count and his young wife did themselves that afternoon.

"At 5 o'clock p.m. they started for Dover, accompanied by Mrs Brackenbury, who desired to see the last of her young friend, prior to the latter's departure for abroad. The Count had engaged a magnificent suite of rooms at the Lord Warden Hotel, and thither the party proceeded.

"So far, you see," added the man in the corner, "the story is of the utmost simplicity. You might even call it commonplace. A foreign count, an ambitious matchmaker, and a credulous girl; these form the ingredients of many a domestic drama that culminates at the police courts. But at this point this particular drama becomes more complicated, and, if you remember, ends in one of the strangest mysteries that has ever baffled the detective forces on both sides of the Channel."

3

The man in the corner paused in his narrative. I could see that he was coming to the palpitating part of the story, for his fingers fidgeted incessantly with that bit of string.

"Hubert Turnour, as you may imagine," he continued after a while, "did not take his final discomfiture very quietly. He was a very violent-tempered young man, and it was certainly enough to make anyone cross. According to Mrs Brackenbury's servants he used most threatening language in reference to Count Collini; and on one occasion was with difficulty prevented from personally assaulting the Count in the hall of Mrs Brackenbury's pretty Kensington house.

"Count Collini finally had to threaten Hubert Turnour with the police court: this seemed to have calmed the young man's nerves somewhat, for he kept quite quiet after that, ceased to call on Mrs Brackenbury, and subsequently sent the future Countess a wedding present.

"When the Count and Countess Collini, accompanied by Mrs Brackenbury, arrived at the Lord Warden, Alice found a letter awaiting her there. It was from Hubert Turnour. In it he begged her forgiveness for all the annoyance he had caused her, hoped that she would always look upon him as a friend, and finally expressed a strong desire to see her once more before her departure for abroad, saying that he would be in Dover either this same day or the next, and would give himself the pleasure of calling upon her and her husband.

"Effectively at about eight o'clock, when the wedding party was just sitting down to dinner, Hubert Turnour was announced. Everyone was most cordial to him, agreeing to let bygones be bygones: the Count, especially, was most genial and pleasant towards his former rival, and insisted upon his staying and dining with them.

"Later on in the evening, Hubert Turnour took an affectionate leave of the ladies, Count Collini offering to walk back with him to the Grand Hotel, where he was staying. The two men went out together, and – well! you know the rest! – for that was the last the young Countess Collini ever saw of her husband. He disappeared as effectively, as completely, as if the sea had swallowed him up.

"'And so it had,' say the public," continued the man in the corner, after a slight pause, "that delicious, short-sighted, irresponsible public is wondering, to this day, why Hubert Turnour was not hung for the murder of that Count Collini."

"Well! and why wasn't he?" I retorted.

"For the very simple reason," he replied, "that in this country you cannot hang a man for murder unless there is proof positive that a murder has been committed. Now, there was absolutely no proof that the Count was murdered at all. What happened was this: the Countess Collini and Mrs Brackenbury became anxious as time went on and the Count did not return. One o'clock, then two in the morning, and their anxiety became positive alarm. At last, as Alice was verging on hysterics, Mrs Brackenbury, in spite of the lateness of the hour, went round to the police station.

"It was, of course, too late to do anything in the middle of the night; the constable on duty tried to reassure the unfortunate lady, and promised to send word round to the Lord Warden at the earliest possible opportunity in the morning.

"Mrs Brackenbury went back with a heavy heart. No doubt Mr Turnour's sensible letters from Reading recurred to her mind. She had already ascertained from the distracted bride that the Count had taken the strange precaution to keep in his own pocketbook the £80,000 now converted into French and Italian banknotes, and Mrs Brackenbury feared not so much that he had met with some accident, but that he had absconded with the whole of his girl-wife's fortune.

"The next morning brought but scanty news. No one answering to the Count's description had met with an accident during the night, or been conveyed to a hospital, and no one answering his description had crossed over to Calais or Ostend by the night boats. Moreover, Hubert Turnour, who presumably had last been in Count Collini's company, had left Dover for town by the boat-train at 1.50 a.m.

"Then the search began in earnest after the missing man, and primarily Hubert Turnour was subjected to the closest and most searching cross-examination, by one of the most able men on our detective staff, Inspector Macpherson.

"Hubert Turnour's story was briefly this: He had strolled about on the parade with Count Collini for awhile. It was a very blustery night, the wind blowing a regular gale, and the sea was rolling gigantic waves, which looked magnificent, as there was brilliant moonlight. 'Soon after ten o'clock,' he continued, 'the Count and I went back to the Grand Hotel, and we had whiskies and sodas up in my room, and a bit of a chat until past eleven o'clock. Then he said good night and went off.'

"'You saw him down to the hall, of course?' asked the detective.

"'No, I did not,' replied Hubert Turnour. 'I had a few letters to write, and meant to catch the 1.50 a.m. back to town.'

"'How long were you in Dover altogether?' asked Macpherson carelessly.

"'Only a few hours. I came down in the afternoon.'

"'Strange, is it not, that you should have taken a room with a private sitting-room, at an expensive hotel, just for those few hours?'

"'Not at all. I originally meant to stay longer. And my expenses are nobody's business, I take it,' replied Hubert Turnour, with some show of temper. 'Anyway,' he added impatiently, after a while, 'if you choose to disbelieve me, you can make inquiries at the hotel, and ascertain if I have told the truth.'

"Undoubtedly he had spoken the truth; at any rate, to that extent. Inquiries at the Grand Hotel went to prove that he had arrived there in the early part of the afternoon, had engaged a couple of rooms, and then gone out. Soon after ten o'clock in the evening he came in, accompanied by a gentleman, whose description, as given by three witnesses, *employés* of the hotel, who saw him, corresponded exactly with that of the Count.

"Together the two gentlemen went up to Mr Hubert Turnour's rooms, and at half past ten they ordered whisky to be taken up to them. But at this point all trace of Count Collini had completely vanished. The passengers arriving by the 10.49 boat-train, and who had elected to spend the night in Dover, owing to the gale, had crowded up and filled the hall.

"No one saw Count Collini leave the Grand Hotel. But Mr Hubert Turnour came down into the hall at about half past eleven. He said he would be leaving by the 1.50 a.m. boat-train for town, but would walk round to the station as he only had a small bag with him. He paid his account, then waited in the coffee-room until it was time to go.

"And there the matter has remained. Mrs Brackenbury has spent half her own fortune in trying to trace the missing man. She has remained perfectly convinced that he slipped across the Channel, taking Alice Checkfield's money with him. But, as you know, at all ports of call on the South Coast, detectives are perpetually on the watch. The Count was a man of peculiar appearance, and there is no doubt that no one answering to his description crossed over to France or Belgium that night. By the following morning the detectives on both sides of the Channel were on the alert. There is no disguise that would have held good. If the Count had tried to cross over, he would have been spotted either on board or on landing; and we may take it as an absolute and positive certainty that he did not cross the Channel.

"He remained in England, but in that case, where is he? You would be the first to admit that, with the whole of our detective staff at his heels, it seems incredible that a man of the Count's singular appearance could hide himself so completely as to baffle detection. Moreover, the question at once arises, that if he did not cross over to France or

Belgium, what in the world did he do with the money? What was the use of disappearing and living the life of a hunted beast hiding for his life, with £80,000 worth of foreign money, which was practically useless to him?

"Now, I told you, from the first," concluded the man in the corner, with a dry chuckle, "that this strange episode contained no sensational incident, nor dramatic inquest or criminal procedure. Merely the complete, total disappearance, one may almost call it extinction, of a striking-looking man, in the midst of our vaunted civilization, and in spite of the untiring energy and constant watch of a whole staff of able men."

## 4

"Very well, then," I retorted in triumph, "that proves that Hubert Turnour murdered Count Collini out of revenge, not for greed of money, and probably threw the body of his victim, together with the foreign banknotes, into the sea."

"But where? When? How?" he asked, smiling good-humouredly at me over his great bone-rimmed spectacles.

"Ah! that I don't know."

"No, I thought not," he rejoined placidly. "You had, I think, forgotten one incident, namely, that Hubert Turnour, accompanied by the Count, was in the former's room at the Grand Hotel drinking whisky at half past ten o'clock. You must admit that, even though the hall of the hotel was very crowded later on, a man would nevertheless find it somewhat difficult to convey the body of his murdered enemy through a whole concourse of people."

189

"He did not murder the Count in the hotel," I argued. "The two men walked out again, when the hall was crowded, and they passed unnoticed. Hubert Turnour led the Count to a lonely part of the cliffs, then threw him into the sea."

"The nearest point at which the cliffs might be called 'lonely' for purposes of a murder, is at least twenty minutes' walk from the Grand Hotel," he said, with a smile, "always supposing that the Count walked quickly and willingly to such a lonely spot at eleven o'clock at night, and with a man who had already, more than once, threatened his life. Mr Hubert Turnour, remember, was seen in the hall of the hotel at half past eleven, after which hour he only left the hotel to go to the station after 1 o'clock a.m.

"The hall was crowded by the passengers from the boat-train a little after eleven. There was no time between that and half past to lead even a willing enemy to the slaughter, throw him into the sea, and come back again, all in the space of five-and-twenty minutes."

"Then what is your explanation of that extraordinary disappearance?" I retorted, beginning to feel very cross about it all.

"A simple one," he rejoined quietly, as he once more began to fidget with his bit of string. "A very simple one indeed; namely, that Count Collini, at the present moment, is living comfortably in England, calmly awaiting a favourable opportunity of changing his foreign money back into English notes."

"But you say yourself that that is impossible, as the most able detectives in England are on the watch for him."

"They are on the watch for a certain Count Collini," he said dryly, "who might disguise himself, perhaps, but whose hidden identity would sooner or later be discovered by one of these intelligent human bloodhounds."

"Yes? Well?" I asked.

"Well, that Count Collini never existed. It was *his* personality that was the disguise. Now it is thrown off. The Count is not dead, he is not hiding, he has merely ceased to exist. There is no fear that he will ever come to life again. Mr Turnour senior will see to that."

"Mr Turnour!" I ejaculated.

"Why, yes," he rejoined excitedly; "do you mean to tell me you never saw through it all? The money lying in his hands; his brother about to wed the rich heiress; then Mrs Brackenbury's matrimonial ambitions, Alice Checkfield's coldness to Hubert Turnour, the golden prize slipping away right out of the family for ever. Then the scheme was evolved by those two scoundrels, who deserve to be called geniuses in their criminal way. It could not be managed, except by collaboration, but as it was, the scheme was perfect in conception, and easy of execution.

"Remember that disguise *previous* to a crime is always fairly safe from detection, for then it has no suspicion to contend against, it merely deceives those who have no cause to be otherwise *but* deceived. Mrs Brackenbury lived in London, Reginald Turnour in Reading; they did not know each other personally, nor did they know each other's friends, of course; whilst Alice Checkfield had not seen her guardian since she was quite a child.

"Then the disguise was so perfect, I went down to Reading, some little time ago, and Reginald Turnour was pointed out to me: he is a Scotchman, with very light, sandy hair. That face clean-shaved, made swarthy, the hair, eyebrows, and lashes dyed a jet black, would render him absolutely unrecognizable. Add to this the fact that a foreign accent completely changes the voice, and that the slight limp was a master-stroke of genius to hide the general carriage.

"Then the winter came round; it was, perhaps, important that Mr Turnour should not be absent too long from Reading, for fear of exciting suspicion there; and the scoundrel played his part with marvellous skill. Can't you see him yourself leaving the Carlton Hotel, ostensibly going abroad, driving to Charing Cross, but only booking to Cannon Street?

"Then getting out at that crowded station and slipping round to his brother's office in one of those huge blocks of buildings where there is perpetual coming and going, and where any individual would easily pass unperceived?

"There, with the aid of a little soap and water, Mr Turnour resumed his Scotch appearance, went on to Reading, and spent winter and spring there, only returning to London to make a formal proposal, as Count Collini, for Alice Checkfield's hand. Hubert Turnour's office was undoubtedly the place where he changed his identity, from that of the British middle-class man, to the interesting personality of the Italian nobleman.

"He had, of course, to repeat the journey to Reading a day or two before his wedding, in order to hand over his ward's fortune to Mrs Brackenbury's solicitor. Then there were the supposed rows between Hubert Turnour and his rival; the letters of warning from the guardian, for which

Hubert no doubt journeyed down to Reading, in order to post them there: all this was dust thrown into the eyes of two credulous ladies.

"After that came the wedding, the meeting with Hubert Turnour, who, you see, was obliged to take a room in one of the big hotels, wherein, with more soap and water, the Italian Count could finally disappear. When the hall of the hotel was crowded, the sandy-haired Scotchman slipped out of it quite quietly: he was not remarkable, and no one specially noticed him. Since then the hue and cry has been after a dark Italian, who limps, and speaks broken English; and it has never struck anyone that such a person never existed.

"Mr Turnour is fairly safe by now; and we may take it for granted that he will not seek the acquaintanceship of the Brackenburys, whilst Alice Checkfield is no longer his ward. He will wait a year or two longer perhaps, then he and Hubert will begin quietly to reconvert their foreign money into English notes – they will take frequent little trips abroad, and gradually change the money at the various *bureaux de change* on the Continent.

"Think of it all, it is so simple – not even dramatic, only the work of a genius from first to last, worthy of a better cause, perhaps, but undoubtedly worthy of success."

He was gone, leaving me quite bewildered. Yet his disappearance had always puzzled me, and now I felt that that animated scarecrow had found the true explanation of it after all.

## X

# The Ayrsham Mystery

## 1

"I have never had a great opinion of our detective force here in England," said the man in the corner, in his funny, gentle, apologetic manner, "but the way that department mismanaged the affair at Ayrsham simply passes comprehension."

"Indeed?" I said, with all the quiet dignity I could command. "It is a pity they did not consult you in the matter, isn't it?"

"It is a pity," he retorted with aggravating meekness, "that they do not use a little common sense. The case resembles that of Columbus' egg, and is every bit as simple.

"It was one evening last October, wasn't it? that two labourers walking home from Ayrsham village turned down a lane, which, it appears, is a short cut to the block of cottages some distance off, where they lodged.

"The night was very dark, and there was a nasty drizzle in the air. In the picturesque vernacular of the two labourers, 'You couldn't see your 'and before your eyes.' Suddenly they stumbled over the body of a man lying right across the path.

"'At first we thought 'e was drunk,' explained one of them subsequently, 'but when we took a look at 'im, we soon saw there was something very wrong. Me and my mate turned 'im over, and "foul play" we both says at once. Then we see that it was Old Man Newton. Poor chap, 'e was dead, and no mistake.'

"Old Man Newton, as he was universally called by his large circle of acquaintances, was very well known throughout the entire neighbourhood, most particularly at every inn and public bar for some miles round.

"He also kept a local sweet-stuff shop at Ayrsham. No wonder that the men were horrified at finding him in such a terrible condition; even in their uneducated minds there could be no doubt that the old man had been murdered, for his skull had been literally shattered by a fearful blow, dealt him from behind by some powerful assailant.

"Whilst the labourers were cogitating as to what they had better do next, they heard footsteps also turning into the lane, and the next moment Samuel Holder, a well-known inhabitant of Ayrsham, arrived upon the scene.

"'Hello! is that you, Mat Newton?' shouted Samuel, as he came near.

"'Ay! 'tis Old Man Newton, right enough,' replied one of the labourers, 'but 'e won't answer you no more.'

"Samuel Holder seemed absolutely horrified when he saw the body of Old Man Newton; he uttered various ejaculations, which the two labourers, however, did not take special notice of at the time.

"Then the three men held a brief consultation together, with the result that one of them ran back to Ayrsham village to fetch the local police, whilst the two others remained in the lane to guard the body.

"The mystery – for it seemed one from the first – created a great deal of sensation in Ayrsham and all round the neighbourhood, and much sympathy was felt for, and shown to, Mary Newton, the murdered man's only child, a young girl about two- or three-and-twenty, who, moreover, was in ill health.

"True, Old Man Newton was not a satisfactory protector for a young girl. He was very much addicted to drink; he neglected the little bit of local business he had; and, moreover, had recently shamefully ill-treated his daughter, the neighbours testifying to the many and loud quarrels that occurred in the small back parlour behind the sweet-stuff shop.

"A case of murder – the moment an element of mystery hovers around it – immediately excites the attention of the newspaper-reading public, who is always seeking for new sensations.

"Very soon the history of Old Man Newton and of his daughter found its way into the London and provincial dailies, and the Ayrsham murder became a topic of all-absorbing interest.

"It appears that Old Man Newton was at one time a highly respectable local tradesman, always in a very small way, as there is not much business doing at Ayrsham. It is a poor and straggling village, although its railway station is an important junction on the Midland system.

"There is some very good shooting in the neighbourhood, and about four or five years ago some of it, together with The Limes, a pretty house just outside the village, was rented for the autumn by Mr Ledbury and his brother.

"You know the firm of Ledbury and Co., do you not – the great small-arms manufacturers? The elder Mr Ledbury was the recipient of birthday honours last year, and is the present Lord Walterton. His younger brother, Mervin, was in those days, and is still, a handsome young fellow in the Hussars.

"At the time – I mean about five years ago – Mary Newton was the local beauty of Ayrsham; she did a little dressmaking in her odd moments, but it appears that she spent most of her time in flirting. She was nominally engaged to be married to Samuel Holder, a young carpenter, but there was a good deal of scandal talked about her, for she was thought to be very fast; village gossip coupled her name with that of several young men in the neighbourhood, who were known to have paid the village beauty marked attention, and among these admirers of Mary Newton during the autumn of which I am speaking, young Mr Mervin Ledbury figured conspicuously.

"Be that as it may, certain it is that Mary Newton had a very bad reputation among the scandalmongers of Ayrsham, and though everybody was shocked, no one was astonished when one fine day in the winter following she suddenly left her father and her home, and went no one knew whither. She left, it appears, a very pathetic letter behind, begging for her father's forgiveness, and that of Samuel Holder, whom she was jilting, but she was going to marry a gentleman above them all in station, and was going to be a real lady; then only would she return home.

"A very usual village tragedy, as you see. Four years went by, and Mary Newton did not return home. As time went by

197

and with it no news of his daughter, Old Man Newton took her disappearance very much to heart. He began to neglect his business, and then his house, which became dirty and ill-kept by an occasional charwoman who would do a bit of promiscuous tidying for him from time to time. He was ill-tempered, sullen, and morose, and very soon became hopelessly addicted to drink.

"Then suddenly, as unexpectedly as she had gone, Mary Newton returned to her home one fine day, after an absence of four years. What had become of her in the interim no one in the village ever knew; she was generally supposed to have earned a living by dressmaking, until her failing health had driven her well-nigh to starvation, and then back to the home and her father she had so heedlessly left.

"Needless to say that all talk of her 'marriage with a gentleman above her in station' was entirely at an end. As for Old Man Newton, he seems, after his daughter's return, to have become more sullen and morose than ever, and the neighbours now busied themselves with talk of the fearful rows which frequently occurred in the back parlour of the little sweet-stuff shop.

"Father and daughter seemed to be leading a veritable cat-and-dog life together. Old Man Newton was hardly ever sober, and at the village inns he threw out weird and strange hints about 'breach of promise actions with £5,000 damages, which his daughter should get, if only he knew where to lay hands upon the scoundrel'.

"He also made vague and wholly useless enquiries about young Mervin Ledbury, but in a sleepy, out-of-the-way village like Ayrsham, no one knows anything about what goes on beyond a narrow five-mile radius at most. The Limes and the shooting were let to different tenants year after year, and neither Lord Walterton nor Mr Mervin Ledbury had ever rented them again."

2

"That was the past history of old Newton," continued the man in the corner, after a brief pause; "that is to say, of the man who on a dark night last October was found murdered in a lonely lane, not far from Ayrsham. The public, as you may well imagine, took a very keen interest in the case from the outset; the story of Mark Newton, of the threatened breach of promise, of the £5,000 damages, roused masses of conjecture to which no one as yet dared to give definite shape.

"One name, however, had already been whispered significantly, that of Mr Mervin Ledbury, the young Hussar, one of Mary Newton's admirers at the very time she left home in order, as she said, to be married to someone above her in station.

"Many thinking people, too, wanted to know what Samuel Holder, Mary's jilted *fiancée*, was doing close to the scene of the murder that night, and how he came to make the remark: 'Hello! is that you, Mat Newton?' when the old man lived nearly half a mile away, and really had no cause for being in that particular lane, at that hour of the night in the drizzling rain.

"The inquest, which, for want of other accommodation, was held at the local police station, was, as you imagine, very largely attended.

"I had read a brief statement of the case in the London papers, and had hurried down to Ayrsham Junction as I scented a mystery, and knew I should enjoy myself.

"When I got there, the room was already packed, and the medical evidence was being gone through.

"Old Man Newton, it appears, had been knocked on the head by a heavily leaded cane, which was found in the ditch close to the murdered man's body.

"The cane was produced in court; it was as stout as an old-fashioned club, and of terrific weight. The man who wielded it must have been very powerful, for he had only dealt one blow, but that blow had cracked the old man's skull. The cane was undoubtedly of foreign make, for it had a solid silver ferrule at one end, which was not English hallmarked.

"In the opinion of the medical expert, death was the result of the blow, and must have been almost instantaneous.

"The labourers who first came across the body of the murdered man then repeated their story; they had nothing new to add, and their evidence was of no importance. But after that there was some stir in the court. Samuel Holder had been called and sworn to tell the whole truth, and nothing but the truth.

"He was a youngish, heavily built man of about five-and-thirty, with a nervous, not altogether prepossessing, expression of face. Pressed by the coroner, he gave us a few details of Old Man Newton's earlier history, such as I have already told you.

"'Old Mat,' he explained, with some hesitation, 'was for ever wanting to find out who the gentleman was who had promised marriage to Mary four years ago. But Mary was that obstinate, and wouldn't tell him, and this exasperated the old man terribly, so that they had many rows on the subject.'

"'I suppose,' said the coroner tentatively, 'that you never knew who that gentleman was?'

"Samuel Holder seemed to hesitate for a moment. His manner became even more nervous than before; he shifted his position from one foot to the other; finally he said:

"'I don't know as I ought to say, but –'

"'I am quite sure that you must tell us everything you know which might throw light upon this extraordinary and terrible murder,' retorted the coroner sternly.

"'Well,' replied Samuel Holder, whilst great beads of perspiration stood out upon his forehead, 'Mary never would give up the letters she had had from him, and she would not hear anything about a breach of promise case and £5,000 damages; but old Mat 'e often says to me, says 'e, "It's young Mr Ledbury," 'e says, "she's told me that once. I got it out of 'er, and if I only knew where to find 'im –"'

"'You are quite sure of this?' asked the coroner, for Holder had paused, and seemed quite horrified at the enormity of what he had said.

"'Yes – yes – your worship – your honour –' stammered Holder. "E's told me 'twas young Mr Ledbury times out of count, and –'

"But Samuel Holder here completely broke down; he seemed unable to speak, his lips twitched convulsively, and the coroner, fearing that the man would faint, had him conveyed into the next room to recover himself, whilst another witness was brought forward.

"This was Michael Pitkin, landlord of the Fernhead Arms,

at Ayrsham, who had been on very intimate terms with old Newton during the four years which elapsed after Mary's disappearance. He had a very curious story to tell, which aroused public excitement to its highest pitch.

"It appears that to him also the old man had often confided the fact that it was Mr Ledbury who had promised to marry Mary, and then had shamefully left her stranded and moneyless in London.

"'But of course,' added the jovial and pleasant-looking landlord of the Fernhead Arms, 'the likes of us down here didn't know what became of Mr Ledbury after he left The Limes, until one day I reads in the local paper that Sir John Fernhead's daughter is going to be married to Captain Mervin Ledbury. Of course, your honour and me, and all of us know Sir John, our squire, down at Fernhead Towers, and I says to old Mat: "It strikes me," I says, "that you've got your man." Sure enough it was the same Mr Ledbury who rented The Limes years ago, who was engaged to the young lady up at The Towers, and last week there was grand doings there – lords and ladies and lots of quality staying there, and also the Captain.'

"'Well?' asked the coroner eagerly, whilst everyone held their breath, wondering what was to come.

"'Well,' continued Michael Pitkin, 'Old Man Newton went down to The Towers one day. 'E was determined to see young Mr Ledbury, and went. What 'appened I don't know, for old Mat wouldn't tell me, but 'e came back mighty furious from 'is visit, and swore 'e would ruin the young man and make no end of a scandal, and he would bring the law agin' 'im and get £5,000 damages.'

202

"This story, embellished, of course, by many details, was the gist of what the worthy landlord of the Fernhead Arms had to say, but you may imagine how everyone's excitement and curiosity was aroused; in the meanwhile Samuel Holder was getting over his nervousness, and was more ready to give a clear account of what happened on the fatal night itself.

"'It was about nine o'clock,' he explained, in answer to the coroner, 'and I was hurrying back to Ayrsham, through the fields; it was dark and raining, and I was about to strike across the hedge into the lane when I heard voices – a woman's, then a man's. Of course, I could see nothing, and the man spoke in a whisper, but I had recognized Mary's voice quite plainly. She kept on saying: "'Tisn't my fault!" she says, "it's father's, 'e 'as made up 'is mind. I held out as long as I could, but 'e worried me, and now 'e's got your letters, and it's too late."'

"Samuel Holder again paused a moment, then continued:

"They talked together for a long time: Mary seemed very upset and the man very angry. Presently 'e says to 'er: "Well, tell your father to come out here and speak to me for a moment. I'll see what I can do." Mary seemed to 'esitate for a time, then she went away, and the man waited there in the drizzling rain, with me the other side of the 'edge watchin' 'im. I waited for a long time, for I wanted to know what was goin' to 'appen; then time went on. I thought perhaps that old Mat was at the Fernhead Arms, and that Mary couldn't find 'im, so I went back to Ayrsham by the fields, 'oping to find the old man. The stranger didn't budge. 'E seemed inclined to wait – so I left 'im there – and – and – that's all. I went to the Fernhead Arms, saw old Mat wasn't there – then

I went back to the lane – and – Old Man Newton was dead, and the stranger was gone.'

"There was a moment or two of dead silence in the court when Samuel Holder had given his evidence, then the coroner asked quietly:

"'You do not know who the stranger was?'

"'Well, I couldn't be sure, your honour,' replied Samuel nervously, 'it was pitch-dark. I wouldn't like to swear a fellow-creature's life and character away.'

"'No, no, quite so,' rejoined the coroner; 'but do you happen to know what time it was when all this occurred?'

"'Oh yes, your honour,' said Samuel decisively, 'as I walked away from the Fernhead Arms I 'eard Ayrsham church clock strike ten o'clock.'

"'Ah that's always something,' said the coroner, with a sigh of satisfaction. 'Call Mary Newton, please.'"

### 3

"You may imagine," continued the man in the corner, after a slight pause, "with what palpitating interest we all watched the pathetic little figure, clad in deep black, who now stepped forward to give evidence.

"It was difficult to imagine that Mary Newton could ever have been pretty; trouble had obviously wrought havoc with her good looks. She was now a wizened little thing, with dark rings under her eyes, and a pale, anaemic complexion. She stood perfectly listlessly before the coroner, waiting to be questioned, but otherwise not seeming to take the slightest interest in the proceedings. In an even, toneless voice she told her name, age, and status, then waited for further questions.

"'Your father went out a little before ten o'clock on Tuesday night last, did he not?' asked the coroner very kindly.

"'Yes, sir, he did,' replied Mary quietly.

"'You had brought him a message from a gentleman whom you had met in the lane, and who wished to speak with your father?'

"'No, sir,' replied Mary, in the same even and toneless voice; 'I brought no message to father, and he went out on his own.'

"'But the gentleman you met in the lane?' insisted the coroner with some impatience.

"'I didn't meet anyone in the lane, sir. I never went out of the house that Tuesday night, it rained so.'

"'But the last witness, Samuel Holder, heard you talking in the lane at nine o'clock.'

"'Samuel Holder was mistaken,' she replied imperturbably; 'I wasn't out of the house the whole of that night.'

"It would be useless for me," continued the man in the corner, "to attempt to convey to you the intense feeling of excitement which pervaded that crowded court, as that wizened little figure stood there for over half an hour, quietly and obstinately parrying the most rigid cross-examination.

"That she was lying – lying to shield the very man who perhaps had murdered her father – no one doubted for a single instant. Yet there she stood, sullen, apathetic, and defiant, flatly denying Samuel Holder's story from end to end, strictly adhering and swearing to her first statement, that her father went out 'on his own', that she did not know where he was going to, and that she herself had never left the house that fatal Tuesday night.

"It did not seem to occur to her that by these statements she was hopelessly incriminating Samuel Holder, whom she was thus openly accusing of deliberate lies; on the contrary, many noticed a distinct touch of bitter animosity in the young girl against her former sweetheart, which was singularly emphasized when the coroner asked her whether she approved of the idea of a breach of promise action being brought against Mr Ledbury.

"'No,' she said; 'all that talk about damages and breach of promise was between father and Sam Holder, because Sam had told father that he wouldn't mind marrying me if I had £5,000 of my own.'

"It would be impossible to render the tone of hatred and contempt with which the young girl uttered these words. One seemed to live through the whole tragedy of the past few months – the girl, pestered by the greed of her father, yet refusing obstinately to aid in causing a scandal, perhaps disgrace, to the man whom she had once loved and trusted.

"As nothing more could be got out of her, and as circumstances now seemed to demand it, the coroner adjourned the inquest. The police, as you may well imagine, wanted to make certain enquiries. Mind you, Mary Newton flatly refused to mention Mr Ledbury's name; she was questioned and cross-questioned, yet her answer uniformly was:

"'I don't know what you're talking about. The person I was going to marry four years ago has gone out of my life – I have never seen him since. I saw no one on that Tuesday night.'

"Against that, when she was asked to swear that it was *not* Mr – now Captain – Ledbury who had promised her marriage she flatly refused to do so.

"Of course, there was not a soul there who had not made up his or her mind that Captain Ledbury *had* met Mary Newton in the lane, and had heard from her that all his love-letters to her were now in her father's hands, and that the old man meant to use these in order to extort money from him.

"Fearing the exposure and disgrace of so sensational a breach of promise action, and not having the money with which to meet Mat Newton's preposterous demands, he probably lost control over himself, and in a moment of impulse and mad rage had silenced the old man for ever.

"I assure you that at the adjourned inquest everybody expected to see Captain Ledbury in the custody of two constables. The police in the interim had been extremely reticent, and no fresh details of the extraordinary case had found its way into the papers, but fresh details of a sensational character were fully expected, and I can assure you the public were not disappointed.

"It is no use my telling you all the proceedings of that second most memorable day; I will try and confine myself to the most important points of this interesting mystery.

"I must tell you that the story told by the landlord of the Fernhead Arms was fully corroborated by several witnesses, all of whom testified to the fact that the old man came back from his visit to Fernhead Towers in a terrible fury, swearing to bring disgrace upon the scoundrel who had ruined his daughter.

"What occurred during that visit was explained by Edward Sanders, the butler at The Towers. According to the testimony of this witness, there was a large house-party staying with Sir John Fernhead to celebrate the engagement of his daughter; the party naturally included Captain Mervin Ledbury, his brother, Lord Walterton, with the latter's newly married young wife, also many neighbours and friends.

"At about six o'clock on Monday evening, it appears, a disreputable-looking old man, who Edward Sanders did not know, but who gave the name of Newton, rang at the front door bell of The Towers and demanded to see Mr Ledbury. Sanders naturally refused to admit him, but the old man was so persistent, and used such strange language, that the butler, after much hesitation, decided to apprise Captain Ledbury of his extraordinary visitor.

"Captain Ledbury, on hearing that Old Man Newton wished to speak to him, much to Sanders' astonishment, came downstairs and elected to interview his extraordinary visitor in the dining-room, which was then deserted. Sanders showed the old man in, and waited in the hall. Very soon, however, he heard loud and angry voices, and the next moment Captain Ledbury threw open the dining-room door, and said:

"'This man is mad or drunk; show him out, Sanders.'

"And without another word the Captain walked upstairs, leaving Sanders the pleasant task of 'showing the old man out'. That this was done very speedily and pretty roughly we may infer from Old Man Newton's subsequent fury, and the threats he uttered even while he was being 'shown out'.

"Now you see, do you not?" continued the man in the corner, "that this evidence seemed to add another link to the chain which was incriminating young Mr Ledbury in this terrible charge of murdering Old Man Newton.

"The young man himself was now with his regiment stationed at York. It appears that the house-party at Fernhead Towers was breaking up on the very day of Old Man Newton's strange visit thither. Lord and Lady Walterton left for town on the Tuesday morning, and Captain Ledbury went up to York on that very same fatal night.

"You must know that the small local station of Fernhead is quite close to The Towers. Captain Ledbury took the late local train there for Ayrsham Junction after dinner that night, arriving at the latter place at 9.15, with the intention of picking up the Midland express to the North at 10.15 p.m. later on.

"The police had ascertained that Captain Ledbury had got out of the local train at Ayrsham Junction at 9.15, and aimlessly strolled out of the station. Against that, it was definitely proved by several witnesses that the young man did catch the Midland express at 10.15 p.m., and travelled up north by it.

"Now, there was the hitch, do you see?" added the funny creature excitedly. "Samuel Holder overheard a conversation in the fatal lane between Mary Newton and the stranger, whom everybody by now believed to be Captain Ledbury. Good! That was between 9 p.m. and 10 p.m., and, as it happened, the young man does seem to have unaccountably strolled about in the neighbourhood whilst waiting for his train; but remember that when Sam Holder left the stranger waiting in the lane, and went back towards Ayrsham in order to try and find Old Man Newton, he distinctly heard Ayrsham church clock striking ten.

"Now, the lane where the murder occurred is two and a half miles from Ayrsham Junction station, therefore it could not have been Captain Ledbury who was there lying in wait for the old man, as he could not possibly have had his interview with old Mat, quarrelled with him and murdered him, and then caught his train two and a half miles further on, all in the space of fifteen minutes.

"Thus, even before the final verdict of 'wilful murder against some person or persons unknown', the case against Captain Mervin Ledbury had completely fallen to the ground. He must also have succeeded in convincing Sir John Fernhead of his innocence, as I see by the papers that Miss Fernhead has since become Mrs Ledbury.

"But the result has been that the Ayrsham tragedy has remained an impenetrable mystery.

"'Who killed Old Man Newton? and why?' is a question which many people, including our clever criminal investigation department, have asked themselves many a time.

"It was not a case of vulgar assault and robbery, as the old man was not worth robbing, and the few coppers he possessed were found intact in his waistcoat pocket.

"Many people assert that Samuel Holder quarrelled with the old man and murdered him, but there are three reasons why that theory is bound to fall to the ground. Firstly, the total absence of any motive. Samuel Holder could have no possible object in killing the old man, but still, we'll waive that; people do quarrel – especially if they are confederates, as these two undoubtedly were – and quarrels do sometimes end fatally. Secondly, the weapon which caused the old man's death – a heavily leaded cane of foreign make, with solid silver ferrule.

"Now, I ask you, where in the world could a village carpenter pick up an instrument of that sort? Moreover no one ever saw such a thing in Sam Holder's hands or in his house. When he walked to the Fernhead Arms in order to try and find the old man, he had nothing of the sort in his hand, and in spite of the most strenuous efforts on the part of the police, the history of that cane was never traced.

"Then, there is a third reason why obviously Sam Holder was not guilty of the murder, though that reason is a moral one; I am referring to Mary Newton's attitude at the inquest. She lied, of that there could not be a shadow of doubt; she was determined to shield her former lover, and incriminated Sam Holder only because she wished to save another man.

"Obviously, old Newton went out on that dark, wet night in order to meet someone in the lane; that someone could not have been Sam Holder, whom he met anywhere and everywhere, and every day in his own house.

"There! you see that Sam Holder was obviously inno-cent, that Captain Ledbury could not have committed the murder, that surely Mary Newton did not kill her own father, and that in such a case, common sense should have come to the rescue, and not have left this case, what it now is, a tragic and impenetrable mystery."

"But," I said at last, for indeed I was deeply mystified, "what does common sense argue? – the case seems to me absolutely hopeless."

He surveyed his beloved bit of string for a moment, and his mild blue eyes blinked at me over his bone-rimmed spectacles.

"Common sense," he said at last, with his most apologetic manner, "tells me that Ayrsham village is a remote little place, where a daily paper is unknown, and where no one reads the fashionable intelligence or knows anything about birthday honours."

"What *do* you mean?" I gasped in amazement.

"Simply this, that no one at Ayrsham village, certainly not Mary Newton herself, had realized that one of the Mr Ledburys, whom all had known at The Limes four years ago, had since become Lord Walterton."

"Lord Walterton!" I ejaculated, wholly incredulously.

"Why, yes!" he replied quietly. "Do you mean to say you never thought of that? that it never occurred to you that Mary Newton may have admitted to her father that Mr Ledbury had been the man who had so wickedly wronged her, but that she, in her remote little village, had also no idea that the Mr Ledbury she meant was recently made, and is now styled, Lord Walterton?

"Old Man Newton, who knew of the gossip which had coupled his daughter's name, years ago, with the younger Mr Ledbury, naturally took it for granted that she was referring to him. Moreover, we may take it from the girl's subsequent attitude that she did all she could to shield the man whom she had once loved; women, you know, have that sort of little way with them.

"Old Newton, fully convinced that young Ledbury was the man he wanted, went up to The Towers and had the stormy interview, which no doubt greatly puzzled the young Hussar. He undoubtedly spoke of it to his brother, Lord Walterton, who, newly married and of high social position, would necessarily dread a scandal as much as anybody.

"Lord Walterton went up to town with his young wife the following morning. Ayrsham is only forty minutes from London. He came down in the evening, met Mary in the lane, asked to see her father, and killed him in a moment of passion, when he found that the old man's demands were preposterously unreasonable. Moreover, Englishmen in all grades of society have an innate horror of being bullied or blackmailed; the murder probably was not premeditated, but the outcome of rage at being browbeaten by the old man.

"You see, the police did not use their common sense over so simple a matter. They naturally made no enquiries as to Lord Walterton's movements, who seemingly had absolutely nothing to do with the case. If they had, I feel convinced that they would have found that his lordship would have had some difficulty in satisfying everybody as to his whereabouts on that particular Tuesday night.

"Think of it, it is so simple – the only possible solution of that strange and unaccountable mystery."

# The Affair at the Novelty Theatre

## 1

"Talking of mysteries," said the man in the corner, rather irrelevantly, for he had not opened his mouth since he sat down and ordered his lunch, "talking of mysteries, it is always a puzzle to me how few thefts are committed in the dressing-rooms of fashionable actresses during a performance."

"There have been one or two," I suggested, "but nothing of any value was stolen."

"Yet you remember that affair at the Novelty Theatre a year or two ago, don't you?" he added. "It created a great deal of sensation at the time. You see, Miss Phyllis Morgan was, and still is, a very fashionable and popular actress, and her pearls are quite amongst the wonders of the world. She herself valued them at £10,000, and several experts who remember the pearls quite concur with that valuation.

"During the period of her short tenancy of the Novelty Theatre last season, she entrusted those beautiful pearls to Mr Kidd, the well-known Bond Street jeweller, to be restrung. There were seven rows of perfectly matched pearls, held together by a small diamond clasp of 'art-nouveau' design.

"Kidd and Co. are, as you know, a very eminent and old-established firm of jewellers. Mr Thomas Kidd, its present sole representative, was sometime president of the London Chamber of Commerce and a man whose integrity has always been held to be above suspicion. His clerks, salesmen, and bookkeeper had all been in his employ for years, and most of the work was executed on the premises.

"In the case of Miss Phyllis Morgan's valuable pearls, they were restrung and reset in the back shop by Mr Kidd's most valued and most trusted workman, a man named James Rumford, who is justly considered to be one of the cleverest craftsmen here in England.

"When the pearls were ready, Mr Kidd himself took them down to the theatre, and delivered them into Miss Morgan's own hands.

"It appears that the worthy jeweller was extremely fond of the theatre; but, like so many persons in affluent circumstances, he was also very fond of getting a free seat when he could.

"All along he had made up his mind to take the pearls down to the Novelty Theatre one night, and to see Miss Morgan for a moment before the performance; she would then, he hoped, place a stall at his disposal.

"His previsions were correct. Miss Morgan received the pearls, and Mr Kidd was on that celebrated night accommodated with a seat in the stalls.

"I don't know if you remember all the circumstances connected with that case, but, to make my point clear, I must remind you of one or two of the most salient details.

"In the drama in which Miss Phyllis Morgan was acting at the time, there is a brilliant masked ball scene which is the crux of the whole play; it occurs in the second act, and Miss Phyllis Morgan, as the hapless heroine dressed in the shabbiest of clothes, appears in the midst of a gay and giddy throng; she apostrophizes all and sundry there, including the villain, and has a magnificent scene which always brings down the house, and nightly adds to her histrionic laurels.

"For this scene a large number of supers are engaged, and in order to further swell the crowd, practically all the available stage hands have to 'walk on' dressed in various coloured dominoes, and all wearing masks.

"You have, of course, heard the name of Mr Howard Dennis in connection with this extraordinary mystery. He is what is usually called 'a young man about town', and was one of Miss Phyllis Morgan's most favoured admirers. As a matter of fact, he was generally understood to be the popular actress's *fiancée*, and as such, had of course the *entrée* of the Novelty Theatre.

"Like many another idle young man about town, Mr Howard Dennis was stage-mad, and one of his greatest delights was to don nightly a mask and a blue domino, and to 'walk on' in the second act, not so much in order to gratify his love for the stage, as to watch Miss Phyllis Morgan in her great scene and to be present, close by her, when she received her usual salvo of enthusiastic applause from a delighted public.

"On this eventful night – it was on 20th July last – the second act was in full swing; the supers, the stage hands, and all the principals were on the scene, the back of the stage was practically deserted. The beautiful pearls, fresh from the hands of Mr Kidd, were in Miss Morgan's dressing-room, as she meant to wear them in the last act.

"Of course, since that memorable affair, many people have talked of the foolhardiness of leaving such valuable jewellery in the sole charge of a young girl – Miss Morgan's dresser – who acted with unpardonable folly and careless-ness, but you must remember that this part of the theatre is only accessible through the stage door, where sits enthroned that incorruptible dragon, the stage doorkeeper.

"No one can get at it from the front, and the dressing-rooms for the supers and lesser members of the company are on the opposite side of the stage to that reserved for Miss Morgan and one or two of the principals.

"It was just a quarter to ten, and the curtain was about to be rung down, when George Finch, the stage doorkeeper, rushed excitedly into the wings; he was terribly upset, and was wildly clutching his coat, beneath which he evidently held something concealed.

"In response to the rapidly whispered queries of the one or two stage hands that stood about, Finch only shook his head excitedly. He seemed scarcely able to control his impatience, during the close of the act, and the subsequent prolonged applause.

"When at last Miss Morgan, flushed with her triumph, came off the stage, Finch made a sudden rush for her.

"'Oh, madam!' he gasped excitedly, 'it might have been such an awful misfortune! The rascal! I nearly got him, though! but he escaped – fortunately it is safe – I have got it –!'

"It was some time before Miss Morgan understood what in the world the otherwise sober stage doorkeeper was driving at. Everyone who heard him certainly thought that he had been drinking. But the next moment from under his coat he pulled out, with another ejaculation of excitement, the magnificent pearl necklace which Miss Morgan had thought safely put away in her dressing-room.

"'What in the world does all this mean?' asked Mr Howard Dennis, who, as usual, was escorting his *fiancée*. 'Finch, what are you doing with madam's necklace?'

"Miss Phyllis Morgan herself was too bewildered to question Finch; she gazed at him, then at her necklace, in speechless astonishment.

"'Well, you see, madam, it was this way,' Finch managed to explain at last, as with awestruck reverence he finally deposited the precious necklace in the actress' hands. 'As you know, madam, it is a very hot night. I had seen everyone into the theatre and counted in the supers; there was nothing much for me to do, and I got rather tired and very thirsty. I seed a man loafing close to the door, and I ask him to fetch me a pint of beer from round the corner, and I give him some coppers; I had noticed him loafing round before, and it was so hot I didn't think I was doin' no harm.'

"'No, no,' said Miss Morgan impatiently. 'Well!'

"'Well,' continued Finch, 'the man, he brought me the beer, and I had some of it – and – and – afterwards, I don't quite know how it happened – it was the heat, perhaps – but – I was sitting in my box, and I suppose I must have dropped asleep. I just remember hearing the ring-up for the second act, and the call-boy calling you, madam, then there's a sort of a blank in my mind. All of a sudden I seemed to wake with the feeling that there was something wrong somehow. In a moment I jumped up, and I tell you I was wide awake then, and I saw a man sneaking down the passage, past my box, towards the door. I challenged him, and he tried to dart past me, but I was too quick for him, and got him by the tails of his coat, for I saw at once that he was carrying something, and I had recognized the loafer who brought me the beer. I shouted for help, but there's never anybody about in this back street, and the loafer, he struggled like old Harry, and sure enough he managed to get free from me and away before I could stop him, but in his fright the rascal dropped his booty, for which Heaven be praised! and it was your pearls, madam. Oh, my! but I did have a tussle,' concluded the worthy doorkeeper, mopping his forehead, 'and I do hope, madam, the scoundrel didn't take nothing else.'

"That was the story," continued the man in the corner, "which George Finch had to tell, and which he subsequently repeated without the slightest deviation. Miss Phyllis Morgan, with the light-heartedness peculiar to ladies of her profession, took the matter very quietly; all she said at the time was that she had nothing else of value in her dressing-room, but that Miss Knight – the dresser – deserved a scolding for leaving the room unprotected.

"'All's well that ends well,' she said gaily, as she finally went into her dressing-room, carrying the pearls in her hand.

"It appears that the moment she opened the door, she found Miss Knight sitting in the room, in a deluge of tears. The girl had overheard George Finch telling his story, and was terribly upset at her own carelessness.

"In answer to Miss Morgan's questions, she admitted that she had gone into the wings, and lingered there to watch the great actress' beautiful performance. She thought no one could possibly get to the dressing-room, as nearly all hands were on the stage at the time, and of course George Finch was guarding the door.

"However, as there really had been no harm done, beyond a wholesome fright to everybody concerned, Miss Morgan readily forgave the girl and proceeded with her change of attire for the next act. Incidentally she noticed a bunch of roses, which were placed on her dressing-table, and asked Knight who had put them there.

"'Mr Dennis brought them,' replied the girl.

"Miss Morgan looked pleased, blushed, and dismissing the whole matter from her mind, she proceeded with her toilette for the next act, in which, the hapless heroine having come into her own again, she was able to wear her beautiful pearls around her neck.

"George Finch, however, took some time to recover himself; his indignation was only equalled by his volubility. When his excitement had somewhat subsided, he took the precaution of saving the few drops of beer which had remained at the bottom of the mug, brought to him by the loafer. This was subsequently shown to a chemist in the neighbourhood, who, without a moment's hesitation, pronounced the beer to contain an appreciable quantity of chloral."

## 2

"The whole matter, as you may imagine, did not affect Miss Morgan's spirits that night," continued the man in the corner, after a slight pause.

220

"'All's well that ends well,' she had said gaily, since almost by a miracle, her pearls were once more safely round her neck.

"But the next day brought the rude awakening. Something had indeed happened which made the affair at the Novelty Theatre, what it has ever since remained, a curious and unexplainable mystery.

"The following morning Miss Phyllis Morgan decided that it was foolhardy to leave valuable property about in her dressing-room, when, for stage purposes, imitation jewellery did just as well. She therefore determined to place her pearls in the bank until the termination of her London season.

"The moment, however, that, in broad daylight, she once more handled the necklace, she instinctively felt that there was something wrong with it. She examined it eagerly and closely, and, hardly daring to face her sudden terrible suspicions, she rushed round to the nearest jeweller, and begged him to examine the pearls.

"The examination did not take many moments: the jeweller at once pronounced the pearls to be false. There could be no doubt about it; the necklace was a perfect imitation of the original, even the clasp was an exact copy. Half-hysterical with rage and anxiety, Miss Morgan at once drove to Bond Street, and asked to see Mr Kidd.

"Well, you may easily imagine the stormy interview that took place. Miss Phyllis Morgan, in no measured language, boldly accused Mr Thomas Kidd, late president of the London Chamber of Commerce, of having substituted false pearls for her own priceless ones.

"The worthy jeweller, at first completely taken by surprise, examined the necklace, and was horrified to see that Miss Morgan's statements were, alas! too true. Mr Kidd was indeed in a terribly awkward position.

"The evening before, after business hours, he had taken the necklace home with him. Before starting for the theatre, he had examined it to see that it was quite in order. He had then, with his own hands, and in the presence of his wife, placed it in its case, and driven straight to the Novelty, where he finally gave it over to Miss Morgan herself.

"To all this he swore most positively; moreover, all his *employés* and workmen could swear that they had last seen the necklace just after closing time at the shop, when Mr Kidd walked off towards Piccadilly, with the precious article in the inner pocket of his coat.

"One point certainly was curious, and undoubtedly helped to deepen the mystery which to this day clings to the affair at the Novelty Theatre.

"When Mr Kidd handed the packet containing the necklace to Miss Morgan, she was too busy to open it at once. She only spoke to Mr Kidd through her dressing-room door, and never opened the packet till nearly an hour later, after she was dressed ready for the second act; the packet at that time had been untouched, and was wrapped up just as she had had it from Mr Kidd's own hands. She undid the packet, and handled the pearls; certainly, by the artificial light she could see nothing wrong with the necklace.

"Poor Mr Kidd was nearly distracted with the horror of his position. Thirty years of an honest reputation suddenly tarnished with this awful suspicion – for he realized at once that Miss Morgan refused to believe his statements; in fact, she openly said that she would – unless immediate compensation was made to her – place the matter at once in the hands of the police.

"From the stormy interview in Bond Street, the irate actress drove at once to Scotland Yard; but the old-established firm of Kidd and Co. was not destined to remain under any cloud that threatened its integrity.

"Mr Kidd at once called upon his solicitor, with the result that an offer was made to Miss Morgan, whereby the jeweller would deposit the full value of the original neck-lace, i.e. £10,000, in the hands of Messrs Bentley and Co., bankers, that sum to be held by them for a whole year, at the end of which time, if the perpetrator of the fraud had not been discovered, the money was to be handed over to Miss Morgan in its entirety.

"Nothing could have been more fair, more equitable, or more just, but at the same time nothing could have been more mysterious.

"As Mr Kidd swore that he had placed the real pearls in Miss Morgan's hands, and was ready to back his oath by the sum of £10,000, no more suspicion could possibly attach to him. When the announcement of his generous offer appeared in the papers, the entire public approved and exonerated him, and then turned to wonder who the perpetrator of the daring fraud had been.

"How came a valueless necklace in exact imitation of the original one to be in Miss Morgan's dressing-room? Where were the real pearls? Clearly the loafer who had drugged the stage doorkeeper, and sneaked into the theatre to steal a necklace, was not aware that he was risking several years' hard labour for the sake of a worthless trifle. He had been one of the many dupes of this extraordinary adventure.

"Macpherson, one of the most able men on the detective staff, had, indeed, his work cut out. The police were extremely reticent, but, in spite of this, one or two facts gradually found their way into the papers, and aroused public interest and curiosity to its highest pitch.

"What had transpired was this:

"Clara Knight, the dresser, had been very rigorously cross-questioned, and, from her many statements, the following seemed quite positive.

"After the curtain had rung up for the second act, and Miss Morgan had left her dressing-room, Knight had waited about for some time, and had even, it appears, handled and admired the necklace. Then, unfortunately, she was seized with the burning desire of seeing the famous scene from the wings. She thought that the place was quite safe, and that George Finch was as usual at his post.

"'I was going along the short passage that leads to the wings,' she exclaimed to the detectives, 'when I became aware of someone moving some distance behind me. I turned and saw a blue domino about to enter Miss Morgan's dressing-room.

"'I thought nothing of that,' continued the girl, 'as we all know that Mr Dennis is engaged to Miss Morgan. He is very fond of "walking on" in the ballroom scene, and he always wears a blue domino when he does; so I was not at all alarmed. He had his mask on as usual, and he was carrying a bunch of roses. When he saw me at the other end of the passage, he waved his hand to me and pointed to the flowers. I nodded to him, and then he went into the room.'

"These statements, as you may imagine, created a great deal of sensation; so much so, in fact, that Mr Kidd, with his £10,000 and his reputation in mind, moved heaven and earth to bring about the prosecution of Mr Dennis for theft and fraud.

"The papers were full of it, for Mr Howard Dennis was well known in fashionable London society. His answer to these curious statements was looked forward to eagerly; when it came it satisfied no one and puzzled everybody.

"'Miss Knight was mistaken,' he said most emphatically, 'I did not bring any roses for Miss Morgan that night. It was not I that she saw in a blue domino by the door, as I was on the stage before the curtain was rung up for the second act, and never left it until the close.'

"This part of Howard Dennis' statement was a little difficult to substantiate. No one on the stage could swear positively whether he was 'on' early in the act or not, although, mind you, Macpherson had ascertained that in the whole crowd of supers on the stage, he was the only one who wore a blue domino.

"Mr Kidd was very active in the matter, but Miss Morgan flatly refused to believe in her *fiancée*'s guilt. The worthy jeweller maintained that Mr Howard Dennis was the only person who knew the celebrated pearls and their quaint clasp well enough to have a facsimile made of them, and that when Miss Knight saw him enter the dressing-room, he actually substituted the false necklace for the real one; while the loafer who drugged George Finch's beer was – as everyone supposed – only a dupe.

"Things had reached a very acute and painful stage, when one more detail found its way into the papers, which, whilst entirely clearing Mr Howard Dennis' character, has helped to make the whole affair a hopeless mystery.

"Whilst questioning George Finch, Macpherson had ascertained that the stage door-keeper had seen Mr Dennis enter the theatre some time before the beginning of the celebrated second act. He stopped to speak to George Finch for a moment or two, and the latter could swear positively that Mr Dennis was not carrying any roses then.

"On the other hand a flower-girl, who was selling roses in the neighbourhood of the Novelty Theatre late that memorable night, remembers selling some roses to a shabbily dressed man, who looked like a labourer out of work. When Mr Dennis was pointed out to her she swore positively that it was not he.

"'The man looked like a labourer,' she explained. 'I took particular note of him, as I remember thinking that he didn't look much as if he could afford to buy roses.'

"Now you see," concluded the man in the corner excitedly, "where the hitch lies. There is absolutely no doubt, judging from the evidence of George Finch and of the flower-girl, that the loafer had provided himself with the roses, and had somehow or other managed to get hold of a blue domino, for the purpose of committing the theft. His giving drugged beer to Finch, moreover, proved his guilt beyond a doubt.

"But here the mystery becomes hopeless," he added with a chuckle, "for the loafer dropped the booty which he had stolen – that booty was the false necklace, and it has remained an impenetrable mystery to this day as to who made the substitution and when.

"A whole year has elapsed since then, but the real necklace has never been traced or found; so Mr Kidd has paid, with absolute quixotic chivalry, the sum of £10,000 to Miss Morgan, and thus he has completely cleared the firm of Kidd and Co. of any suspicion as to its integrity."

### 3

"But then, what in the world is the explanation of it all?" I asked bewildered, as the funny creature paused in his narrative and seemed absorbed in the contemplation of a beautiful knot he had just completed in his bit of string.

"The explanation is so simple," he replied, "for it is obvious, is it not? that only four people could possibly have committed the fraud."

"Who are they?" I asked.

"Well," he said, whilst his bony fingers began to fidget with that eternal piece of string, "there is, of course, old Mr Kidd; but as the worthy jeweller has paid £10,000 to prove that he did not steal the real necklace and substitute a false one in its stead, we must assume that he was guiltless. Then, secondly, there is Mr Howard Dennis."

"Well, yes," I said, "what about him?"

"There were several points in his favour," he rejoined, marking each point with a fresh and most complicated knot; "it was not he who bought the roses, therefore it was not he who, clad in a blue domino, entered Miss Morgan's dressing-room directly after Knight left it.

"And mark the force of this point," he added excitedly.

"Just before the curtain rang up for the second act, Miss Morgan had been in her room, and had then undone the packet, which, in her own words, was just as she had received it from Mr Kidd's hands.

"After that Miss Knight remained in charge, and a mere ten seconds after she left the room she saw the blue domino carrying the roses at the door.

"The flower-girl's story and that of George Finch have proved that the blue domino could not have been Mr Dennis, but it was the loafer who eventually stole the false necklace.

"If you bear all this in mind you will realize that there was no time in those ten seconds for Mr Dennis to have made the substitution *before* the theft was committed. It stands to reason that he could not have done it afterwards.

"Then, again, many people suspected Miss Knight, the dresser; but this supposition we may easily dismiss. An uneducated, stupid girl, not three-and-twenty, could not possibly have planned so clever a substitution. An imitation necklace of that particular calibre and made to order would cost far more money than a poor theatrical dresser could ever afford; let alone the risks of ordering such an ornament to be made.

"No," said the funny creature, with comic emphasis, "there is but one theory possible, which is my own."

"And that is?" I asked eagerly.

"The workman, Rumford, of course," he responded triumphantly. "Why! it jumps to the eyes, as our French friends would tell us. Who other than he, could have the opportunity of making an exact copy of the necklace which had been entrusted to his firm?

"Being in the trade he could easily obtain the false stones without exciting any undue suspicion; being a skilled craftsman, he could easily make the clasp, and string the pearls in exact imitation of the original; he could do this secretly in his own home and without the slightest risk.

"Then the plan, though extremely simple, was very cleverly thought out. Disguised as the loafer –"

"The loafer!" I exclaimed.

"Why, yes! the loafer," he replied quietly; "disguised as the loafer, he hung round the stage door of the Novelty after business hours, until he had collected the bits of gossip and information he wanted; thus he learnt that Mr Howard Dennis was Miss Morgan's accredited *fiancée*; that he, like everybody else who was available, 'walked on' in the second act; and that during that time the back of the stage was practically deserted.

"No doubt he knew all along that Mr Kidd meant to take the pearls down to the theatre himself that night, and it was quite easy to ascertain that Miss Morgan – as the hapless heroine – wore no jewellery in the second act, and that Mr Howard Dennis invariably wore a blue domino.

"Some people might incline to the belief that Miss Knight was a paid accomplice, that she left the dressing-room unprotected on purpose, and that her story of the blue domino and the roses was prearranged between herself and Rumford, but that is not my opinion.

"I think that the scoundrel was far too clever to need any accomplice, and too shrewd to put himself thereby at the mercy of a girl like Knight.

"Rumford, I find, is a married man: this to me explains the blue domino, which the police were never able to trace to any business place, where it might have been bought or hired. Like the necklace itself, it was 'home-made'.

"Having got his properties and his plans ready, Rumford then set to work. You must remember that a stage door-keeper is never above accepting a glass of beer from a friendly acquaintance; and, no doubt, if George Finch had not asked the loafer to bring him a glass, the latter would have offered him one. To drug the beer was simple enough; then Rumford went to buy the roses, and, I should say, met his wife somewhere round the corner, who handed him the blue domino and the mask; all this was done in order to completely puzzle the police subsequently, and also in order to throw suspicion, if possible, upon young Dennis.

"As soon as the drug took effect upon George Finch, Rumford slipped into the theatre. To slip a mask and domino on and off is, as you know, a matter of a few seconds. Probably his intention had been – if he found Knight in the room – to knock her down if she attempted to raise an alarm; but here fortune favoured him. Knight saw him from a distance, and mistook him easily for Mr Dennis.

"After the theft of the real necklace, Rumford sneaked out of the theatre. And here you see how clever was the scoundrel's plan: if he had merely substituted one necklace for another there would have been no doubt whatever that the loafer – whoever he was – was the culprit – the drugged beer would have been quite sufficient proof for that. The hue and cry would have been after the loafer, and, who knows? there might have been someone or something which might have identified that loafer with himself.

"He must have bought the shabby clothes somewhere; he certainly bought the roses from a flower-girl; anyhow, there were a hundred and one little risks and contingencies which might have brought the theft home to him.

"But mark what happens: he steals the real necklace, and keeps the false one in his hand, intending to drop it sooner or later, and thus sent the police entirely on the wrong scent. As the loafer, she was supposed to have stolen the false necklace, then dropped it whilst struggling with George Finch. The result is that no one has troubled about the loafer; no one thought that he had anything to do with the substitution, which was the main point at issue, and no very great effort has ever been made to find that mysterious loafer.

"It never occurred to anyone that the fraud and the theft were committed by one and the same person, and that that person could be none other than James Rumford."

# The Tragedy of Barnsdale Manor

1

"We have heard so much about the evils of Bridge," said the man in the corner that afternoon, "but I doubt whether that fashionable game has ever been responsible for a more terrible tragedy than the one at Barnsdale Manor."

"You think, then," I asked, for I saw he was waiting to be drawn out, "you think that the high play at Bridge did have something to do with that awful murder?"

"Most people think that much, I fancy," he replied, "although no one has arrived any nearer to the solution of the mystery which surrounds the tragic death of Mme Quesnard at Barnsdale Manor on the 23rd September last.

"On that fateful occasion, you must remember that the house party at the Manor included a number of sporting and fashionable friends of Lord and Lady Barnsdale, among whom Sir Gilbert Culworth was the only one whose name was actually mentioned during the hearing of this extraordinary case.

"It seems to have been a very gay house party indeed. In the daytime Lord Barnsdale took some of his guests to shoot and fish, whilst a few devotees remained at home in order to indulge their passion for the modern craze of

Bridge. It was generally understood that Lord Barnsdale did not altogether approve of quite so much gambling. He was not by any means well off; and although he was very much in love with his beautiful wife, he could ill afford to pay her losses at cards.

"This was the reason, no doubt, that Bridge at Barnsdale Manor was only indulged in whilst the host himself was out shooting or fishing; in the evenings there was music or billiards, but never any cards.

"One of the most interesting personalities in the Barnsdale *ménage* was undoubtedly madame Nathalie Quesnard, a sister of Lord Barnsdale's mother, who, if you remember, was a Mademoiselle de la Trémouille. This Mme Quesnard was extremely wealthy, the widow of a French West Indian planter, who had made millions in Martinique.

"She was very fond of her nephew, to whom, as she had no children or other relatives of her own, she intended to leave the bulk of her vast fortune. Pending her death, which was not likely to occur for some time, as she was not more than fifty, she took up her abode at Barnsdale Manor, together with her companion and amanuensis, a poor girl named Alice Holt.

"Mme Quesnard was seemingly an amiable old lady, the only unpleasant trait in her character being her intense dislike of her nephew's beautiful and fashionable young wife. The old Frenchwoman, who, with all her wealth, had the unbounded and innate thriftiness peculiar to her nation, looked with perfect horror on Lady Barnsdale's extravagances, and above all on her fondness for gambling; and subsequently several of the servants at the Manor testified to the amount of mischief the old lady strove to make between her nephew and his young wife.

"Mme Quesnard's dislike for Lady Barnsdale seems, moreover, to have been shared by her dependent and companion, the girl Alice Holt. Between them, these two ladies seem to have cordially hated the brilliant and much-admired mistress of Barnsdale Manor.

"Such were the chief inmates of the Manor last September, at the time the tragedy occurred. On that memorable night Alice Holt, who occupied a bedroom immediately above that of Mme Quesnard, was awakened in the middle of the night by a persistent noise, which undoubtedly came from her mistress' room. The walls and floorings at the old Manor are very thick, and the sound was a very confused one, although the girl was quite sure that she could hear Mme Quesnard's shrill voice raised as if in anger.

"She tried to listen for a time, and presently she heard a sound as if some piece of furniture had been knocked over, then nothing more. Somehow the sudden silence seemed to have frightened the girl more than the noise had done. Trembling with nervousness she waited for some few minutes, then, unable to bear the suspense any longer, she got out of bed, slipped on her shoes and dressing-gown, and determined to run downstairs to see if anything were amiss.

"To her horror she found on trying her door that it had been locked on the outside. Quite convinced now that something must indeed be very wrong, she started screaming and banging against the door, determined to arouse the household, which she, of course, quickly succeeded in doing.

"The first to emerge from his room was Lord Barnsdale. He at once realized that the shrieks proceeded from Alice Holt's room. He ran upstairs helter-skelter, and as the key had been left in the door, he soon released the unfortunate girl, who by now was quite hysterical with anxiety for her mistress.

"Altogether, I take it, some six or seven minutes must have elapsed from the time when Alice Holt was first alarmed by the sudden silence following the noise in Mme Quesnard's room until she was released by Lord Barnsdale.

"As quickly and as coherently as she could, she blurted forth all her fears about her mistress. I can imagine how picturesque the old Manor House must have looked then, with everybody, ladies and gentlemen, and servants, crowding into the hall, arrayed in various *négligé* attire, asking hurried questions, getting in each other's way, and all only dimly to be seen by the light of candles, carried by some of the more sensible ones in this motley crowd.

"However, in the meanwhile, Lord Barnsdale had managed to understand Alice Holt. He ran downstairs again and knocked at his aunt's door; he received no reply – he tried the handle, but the door was locked from the inside.

"Genuinely frightened now, he forced open the door, and then recoiled in horror.

"The window was wide open, and a brilliant moonlight streamed into the room, weirdly illumining Mme Quesnard's inanimate body, which lay full length upon the ground. Hastily begging the ladies not to follow him, Lord Barnsdale quickly went forward and bent over his aunt's body.

"There was no doubt that she was dead. An ugly wound at the back of her head, some red marks round her throat, all testified to the fact that the poor old lady had been assaulted and murdered. Lord Barnsdale at once sent for the nearest doctor, whilst he and Miss Holt lifted the unfortunate lady back to bed.

"The messenger who had gone for the doctor was at the same time instructed to deliver a note, hastily scribbled by Lord Barnsdale, at the local police station.

"That a hideous crime had been committed, with burglary for its object, no one could be in doubt for a moment. Lord Barnsdale and two or three of his guests had already thrown a glance into the next room, a little boudoir, which Mme Quesnard used as a sitting-room. There the heavy oak bureau bore silent testimony to the motive of this dastardly outrage. Mme Quesnard, with the unfortunate and foolhardy habit peculiar to all French people, kept a very large quantity of loose and ready money by her. That habit, mind you, is the chief reason why burglary is so rife and so profitable all over France.

"In this case the old lady's national characteristic was evidently the chief cause of her tragic fate; the drawer of the bureau had been forced open, and no one could doubt for a moment that a large sum of money had been abstracted from it.

"The burglar had then obviously made good his escape through the window, which he could do quite easily, as Mme Quesnard's apartments were on the ground floor. She suffered from shortness of breath, it appears, and had a horror of stairs; she was, moreover, not the least bit nervous, and her windows were usually barred and shuttered.

"One very curious fact, however, at once struck all those present, even before the arrival of the detectives, and that was, that the old lady was partially dressed when she was found lying on the ground. She had slipped on an elaborate dressing-gown, had smoothed her hair, and put on her slippers. In fact, it was evident that she had in some measure prepared herself for the reception of the burglar.

"Throughout these hasty and amateurish observations conducted by Lord Barnsdale and two of his male guests, Alice Holt had remained seated beside her late employer's bedside sobbing bitterly. In spite of Lord Barnsdale's entreaties she refused to move; and wildly waved aside any attempt at consolation offered to her by one or two of the older female servants who were present.

"It was only when everybody at last made up their minds to return to their rooms, that someone mentioned Lady Barnsdale's name. She had been taken ill and faint the evening before, and had not been well all night. Jane Barlow, her maid, expressed the hope that her ladyship was none the worse for this awful commotion, and must be wondering what it all meant.

"At this, suddenly, Alice Holt jumped up, like a madwoman.

"'What it all means?' she shrieked, whilst everyone looked at her in speechless horror. 'It means that that woman has murdered my mistress, and robbed her. I know it – I know it – I know it!'

"And once more sinking beside the bed, she covered her dead mistress' hand with kisses, and sobbed and wailed as if her heart would break."

"You may well imagine the awful commotion the girl's wild outburst had created in the old Manor House. Lady Barnsdale had been taken ill the previous evening, and, of course, no one had breathed a word of it to her, but equally, of course, it was freely talked about at Barnsdale Manor, in the neighbourhood, and even so far as in the London clubs.

"Lord and Lady Barnsdale were very well known in London society, and Lord Barnsdale's adoration for his beautiful wife was quite notorious.

"Alice Holt, after her frantic outburst, had not breathed another word. Silent and sullen she went up to her room, packed her things, and left the house, where, of course, it became impossible that she should stay another day. She refused Lord Barnsdale's generous offer of money and help, and only stayed long enough to see the detectives and reply to the questions they thought fit to put to her.

"The whole neighbourhood was in a fever of excitement; many gossips would have it that the evidence against Lady Barnsdale was conclusive, and that a warrant for her arrest had already been applied for.

"What had transpired was this:

"It appears that the day preceding the tragedy, Bridge was, as usual, being played for, I believe, guinea-points. Lord Barnsdale was out shooting all day, and though the guests at the Manor were very loyal to their hostess, and refused to make any positive statements, there seems to be no doubt that Lady Barnsdale lost a very large sum of money to Sir Gilbert Culworth.

"Be that as it may, nothing further could be gleaned by enterprising reporters fresh from town; the police were more than usually reticent, and everyone eagerly awaited the opening of the inquest, when sensational developments were expected in this mysterious case.

"It was held on September the 25th, in the servants' hall of Barnsdale Manor, and you may be sure that the large room was crowded to its utmost capacity. Lord Barnsdale was, of course, present, so was Sir Gilbert Culworth, but it was understood that Lady Barnsdale was still suffering from nervous prostration, and was unable to be present.

"When I arrived there, and gradually made my way to the front rank, the doctor who had been originally summoned to the murdered lady's bedside was giving his evidence.

"He gave it as his opinion that the fractured skull from which Mme Quesnard died was caused through her hitting the back of her head against the corner of the marble-topped washstand, in the immediate proximity of which she lay outstretched, when Lord Barnsdale first forced open the door. The stains on the marble had confirmed him in that opinion. Mme Quesnard, he thought, must have fallen, owing to an onslaught made upon her by the burglar; the marks round the old lady's throat testified to this, although these were not the cause of death.

"After this there was a good deal of police evidence with regard to the subsequent movements of the unknown miscreant. He had undoubtedly broken open the drawer of the bureau in the adjoining boudoir, the door of communication between this and Mme Quesnard's bedroom being always kept open, and it was presumed that he had made a considerable haul both in gold and notes. He had then locked the bedroom door on the inside and made good his escape through the window.

"Immediately beneath this window, the flower-bed, muddy with the recent rain, bore the imprint of having been hastily trampled upon; but all actual footmarks had been carefully obliterated. Beyond this, all round the house the garden paths are asphalted, and the burglar had evidently taken the precaution to keep to these asphalted paths, or else to cross the garden by the lawns.

"You must understand," continued the man in the corner, after a slight pause, "that throughout all this preliminary evidence, everything went to prove that the crime had been committed by an inmate of the house or at any rate by someone well acquainted with its usages and its *ménage*. Alice Holt, whose room was immediately above that of Mme. Quesnard, and who was, therefore, most likely to hear the noise of the conflict and to run to her mistress's assistance, had been first of all locked up in her room. It had, therefore, become quite evident that the miscreant had commenced operations from inside the house, and had entered Mme Quesnard's room by the door, and not by the window, as had been at first supposed.

"But," added the funny creature excitedly, "as the old lady had, according to evidence, locked her door that night, it became more and more clear, as the case progressed, that she must of her own accord have admitted the person who subsequently caused her tragic death. This was, of course, confirmed by the fact that she was partially dressed when she was subsequently found dead.

"Strangely enough, with the exception of Alice Holt, no one else had heard any noise during the night. But, as I remarked before, the walls of these old houses are very thick, and no one else slept on the ground floor.

"Another fact which in the early part of the inquest went to prove that the outrage was committed by someone familiar with the house, was that Ben, the watchdog, had not raised any alarm. His kennel was quite close to Mme Quesnard's windows, and he had not even barked.

"I doubt if the law would take official cognizance of the dumb testimony of a dog; nevertheless, Ben's evidence was in this case quite worthy of consideration.

"You may imagine how gradually, as these facts were unfolded, excitement grew to fever pitch, and when at last Alice Holt was called, everyone literally held their breath, eagerly waiting to hear what was coming.

"She is a tall, handsome-looking girl, with fine eyes and a rich voice. Dressed in deep black she certainly looked an imposing figure as she stood there, repeating the story of how she was awakened in the night by the sound of her mistress' angry voice, of the noise and sudden silence, and also of her terror, when she found that she had been locked up in her room.

"But obviously the girl had more to tell, and was only waiting for the coroner's direct question.

"'Will you tell the jury the reason why you made such an extraordinary and unwarrantable accusation against Lady Barnsdale?' he asked her at last, amid breathless silence in the crowded room.

"Everyone instinctively looked across the room to where

Lord Barnsdale sat between his friend Sir Gilbert Culworth and his lawyer, Sir Arthur Inglewood, who had evidently come down from London in order to watch the case on his client's behalf. Alice Holt, too, looked across at Lord Barnsdale for a moment. He seemed attentive and interested, but otherwise quite calm and impassive.

"I, who watched the girl, saw a look of pity cross her face as she gazed at him, and I think, when we bear in mind that the distinguished English gentleman and the poor paid companion had known each other years ago, when they were girl and boy together in old Mme Quesnard's French home, we may make a pretty shrewd guess why Alice Holt hated the beautiful Lady Barnsdale.

"'It was about six o'clock in the afternoon,' she began at last, in the same quiet tone of voice. 'I was sitting sewing in madame's boudoir, when Lady Barnsdale came into the bedroom. She did not see me, I know, for she began at once talking volubly to madame about a serious loss she had just sustained at Bridge; several hundred pounds, she said.'

"'Well?' queried the coroner, for the girl had paused, almost as if she regretted what she had already said. She certainly threw an appealing look at Lord Barnsdale, who, however, seemed to take no notice of her.

"'Well,' she continued with sudden resolution, 'madame was very angry at this; she declared that Lady Barnsdale deserved a severe lesson; her extravagances were a positive scandal. "Not a penny will I give you to pay your gambling debts," said madame; "and, moreover, I shall make it my business to inform my nephew of your goings-on whilst he is absent."

"'Lady Barnsdale was in a wild state of excitement. She begged and implored madame to say nothing to Lord Barnsdale about it, and did her very best to try to induce her to help her out of her difficulties, just this once more. But madame was obdurate. Thereupon Lady Barnsdale turned on her like a fury, called her every opprobrious name under the sun, and finally flounced out of the room, banging the door behind her.

"'Madame was very much upset after this,' continued Alice Holt, 'and I was not a bit astonished when directly after dinner she rang for me, and asked to be put to bed. It was then nine o'clock.

"'That is the last I saw of poor madame alive.

"'She was very excited then, and told me that she was quite frightened of Lady Barnsdale – a gambler, she said, was as likely as not to become a thief, if opportunity arose. I offered to sleep on the sofa in the next room, for the old lady seemed quite nervous, a thing I have never known her to be. But she was too proud to own to nervousness, and she dismissed me finally, saying that she would lock her door, for once: a thing she scarcely ever did.'

"It was a curious story, to say the least of it, which Alice Holt thus told to an excited public. Cross-examined by the coroner, she never departed from a single point of it, her calm and presence of mind being only equalled through-out this trying ordeal by that of Lord Barnsdale, who sat seemingly unmoved whilst these terrible insinuations were made against his wife.

"But there was more to come. Sir Gilbert Culworth had been called; in the interests of justice, and in accordance with his duty as a citizen, he was forced to stand up and, all unwillingly, to add another tiny link to the chain of evidence that implicated his friend's wife in this most terrible crime.

"Right loyally he tried to shield her in every possible way, but cross-questioned by the coroner, harassed nearly out of his senses, he was forced to admit two facts – namely, that Lady Barnsdale had lost nearly £800 at Bridge the day before the murder, and that she had paid her debt to himself in full, on the following morning, in gold and notes.

"He had been forced, much against his will, to show the notes to the police; unfortunately for the justice of the case, however, the numbers of these could not be directly traceable as having been in Mme Quesnard's possession at the time of her death. No diaries or books of accounts of any kind were found. Like most French people, she arranged all her money affairs herself, receiving her vast dividends in foreign money, and converting this into English notes and gold, as occasion demanded, at the nearest money-changer's that happened to be handy.

"She had, like a great many foreigners, a holy horror of banks. She would have mistrusted the Bank of England itself; as for solicitors, she held them in perfect abhorrence. She only went once to one in her life, and that was in order to make a will leaving everything she possessed unconditionally to her beloved nephew, Lord Barnsdale.

"But in spite of this difficulty about the notes, you see for yourself, do you not? how terribly strong was the circumstantial evidence against Lady Barnsdale. Her losses at cards, her appeal to Mme Quesnard, the latter's refusal to help her, and finally the payment in full of the debt to Sir Gilbert Culworth on the following morning.

"There was only one thing that spoke for her, and that was the very horror of the crime itself. It was practically impossible to conceive that a woman of Lady Barnsdale's refinement and education should have sprung upon an elderly woman, like some navvy's wife by the docks, and then that she should have had the presence of mind to jump out of the window, to obliterate her footmarks in the flower-bed, and, in fact, to have given the crime the look of a clever burglary.

"Still, we all know that money difficulties will debase the noblest of us, that greed will madden the sanest and most refined. When the inquest was adjourned, I can assure you that no one had any doubt whatever that within twenty-four hours Lady Barnsdale would be arrested on the capital charge."

### 3

"But the detectives in charge of the case had reckoned without Sir Arthur Inglewood, the great lawyer, who was watching the proceedings on behalf of his aristocratic clients," said the man in the corner, when he had assured himself of my undivided attention.

"The adjourned inquest brought with it, I assure you, its full quota of sensation. Again Lord Barnsdale was present, calm, haughty, and impassive, whilst Lady Barnsdale was still too ill to attend. But she had made a statement upon oath, in which, whilst flatly denying that her interview with the deceased at 6 p.m., had been of an acrimonious character as alleged by Alice Holt, she swore most positively that all through the night she had been ill, and had not left her room after 11.30 p.m.

"The first witness called after this affidavit had been read was Jane Barlow, Lady Barnsdale's maid.

"The girl deposed that on that memorable evening preceding the murder, she went up to her mistress' room at about 11.30 in order to get everything ready for the night. As a rule, of course, there was nobody about in the bedroom at that hour, but on this occasion when Jane Barlow entered the room, which she did without knocking, she saw her mistress sitting by her desk.

"'Her ladyship looked up when I came in,' continued Jane Barlow, 'and seemed very cross with me for not knocking at the door. I apologized, then began to get the room tidy; as I did so I could see that my lady was busy counting a lot of money. There were lots of sovereigns and banknotes. My lady put some together in an envelope and addressed it, then she got up from her desk and went to lock up the remainder of the money in her jewel safe.'

"'And this was at what time?' asked the coroner.

"'At about half past eleven, I think, sir,' repeated the girl.

"'Well,' said the coroner, 'did you notice anything else?'

"'Yes,' replied Jane, 'whilst my lady was at her safe, I saw the envelope in which she had put the money lying on the desk. I couldn't help looking at it, for I knew it was ever so full of banknotes, and I saw that my lady had addressed it to Sir Gilbert Culworth.'

"At this point Sir Arthur Inglewood jumped to his feet and handed something over to the coroner; it was evidently an envelope which had been torn open. The coroner looked at it very intently, then suddenly asked Jane Barlow if she had happened to notice anything about the envelope which was lying on her ladyship's desk that evening.

"'Oh yes, sir!' she replied unhesitatingly, 'I noticed my lady had made a splotch, right on top of the "C" in Sir Gilbert Culworth's name.'

"'This, then, is the envelope,' was the coroner's quiet comment, as he handed the paper across to the girl.

"'Yes, there's the splotch,' she replied. 'I'd know it anywhere.'

"So you see," continued the man in the corner, with a chuckle, "that the chain of circumstantial evidence against Lady Barnsdale was getting somewhat entangled. It was indeed fortunate for her that Sir Gilbert Culworth had not destroyed the envelope in which she had handed him over the money on the following day.

"Alice Holt, as you know, heard the conflict and raised the alarm much later in the night, when everybody was already in bed, whilst long before that Lady Barnsdale was apparently in possession of the money with which she could pay back her debt.

"Thus the motive for the crime, so far as she was concerned, was entirely done away with. Directly after the episode witnessed by Jane Barlow, Lady Barnsdale had a sort of nervous collapse, and went to bed feeling very ill. Lord Barnsdale was terribly concerned about her; he and the maid remained alternately by her bedside for an hour or two; finally Lord Barnsdale went to sleep in his dressing-room, whilst Jane also finally retired to rest.

"Ill as Lady Barnsdale undoubtedly was then, it was absolutely preposterous to conceive that she could after that have planned and carried out so monstrous a crime, without any motive whatever. To have locked Alice Holt's door, then gone downstairs, forced her way into the old lady's room, struggled with her, to have jumped out of the window, and run back into the house by the garden, might have been the work of a determined woman, driven mad by the desire for money, but became absolutely out of the question in the case of a woman suffering from nervous collapse, and having apparently no motive for the crime.

"Of course Sir Arthur Inglewood made the most of the fact that no mud was found on any shoes or dress belonging to Lady Barnsdale. The flower-bed was very soft with the heavy rain of the day before, and Lady Barnsdale could not possibly have jumped even from a ground-floor window and trampled on the flower-bed, without staining her skirts.

"Then there was another point which the clever lawyer brought to the coroner's notice. As Alice Holt had stated in her sworn evidence that Mme Quesnard had owned to being frightened of Lady Barnsdale that night, was it likely that she would *of her own accord* have opened the door to her in the middle of the night, without at least calling for assistance?

"Thus the matter has remained a strange and unaccountable puzzle. It has always been called the 'Barnsdale Mystery' for that very reason. Everyone, somehow, has always felt that Lady Barnsdale did have something to do with that terrible tragedy. Her husband has taken her abroad, and they have let Barnsdale Manor; it almost seems as if the ghost of the old Frenchwoman had driven them forth from their own country.

"As for Alice Holt, she maintains to this day that Lady Barnsdale was the culprit, and I understand that she has not yet given up all hope of collecting a sufficiency of evidence to have the beautiful and fashionable woman of society arraigned for this hideous murder."

## 4

"Will she succeed, do you think?" I asked at last.

"Succeed? Of course she won't," he retorted excitedly. "Lady Barnsdale never committed that murder; no woman, except, perhaps, an East-end factory hand, could have done it at all."

"But then –" I urged.

"Why, then," he replied, with a chuckle, "the only logical conclusion is that the robbery and the murder were not committed by the same person, nor at the same hour of the night; moreover, I contend that there was no premeditated murder, but that the old lady died from the result of a pure accident."

"But how?" I gasped.

"This is my version of the story," he said excitedly, as his long bony fingers started fidgeting, fidgeting with that eternal bit of string. "Lady Barnsdale, pressed for money, made an appeal to Mme Quesnard, which the latter refused, as we know. Then there was an acrimonious dispute between the two ladies, after which came the dinner hour, then madame, feeling ill and upset, went up to bed at nine o'clock.

"Now my contention is that undoubtedly the robbery had been committed before that, between the dispute and madame's bedtime."

"By whom?"

"By Lady Barnsdale, of course, who, as the mistress of the house, could come and go from room to room without exciting any comment; who, moreover, at 6 p.m. was hard pressed for money, and who but a few hours later was handling a mass of gold and banknotes.

"But the strain of committing even an ordinary theft is very great upon a refined woman's organization. Lady Barnsdale has a nervous breakdown. Well! what is the most likely thing to happen? Why! that she should confess everything to her husband, who worships her, and no doubt express her repentance at what she had done.

"Then imagine Lord Barnsdale's horror! The old lady had not discovered the theft before going to bed. That was only natural, since she was feeling unwell, and was not likely to sit up at night counting her money; the lock of the bureau drawer having been tampered with would perhaps not attract her attention at night.

"But in the morning, the very first thing, she would discover everything, at once suspect the worst, and who knows? make a scandal, talk of it before Alice Holt, Lady Barnsdale's archenemy, and all before restitution could be made.

"No, no, that restitution must be made at once; not a minute must be lost, since any moment might bring forth discovery, and perhaps an awful catastrophe.

"I take it that Mme Quesnard and her nephew were on very intimate terms. He hoped to arouse no one by going to his aunt's room, but in order to make quite sure that Alice Holt, hearing a noise in her mistress' room, should not surreptitiously come down, and perhaps play eavesdropper at the momentous interview, he turned the key of the girl's door as he went past, and locked her in.

"Then he knocked at his aunt's door (gently, of course, for old people are light sleepers), and called her by name. Mme Quesnard, recognizing her nephew's voice, slipped on her dressing-gown, smoothed her hair, and let him in.

"Exactly what took place at the interview it is, of course, impossible for any human being to say. Here even I can but conjecture," he added, with inimitable conceit, "but we can easily imagine that, having heard Lord Barnsdale's confession of his wife's folly, the old lady, who as a Frenchwoman was of quick temper and unbridled tongue, would indulge in not very elegant rhetoric on the subject of the woman she had always disliked.

"Lord Barnsdale would, of course, defend his wife, and the old lady, with feminine obstinacy, would continue the attack. Then some insulting epithet, a word only, perhaps, roused the devoted husband's towering indignation – the meekest man on earth becomes a mad bull when he really loves, and the woman he loves is insulted.

"I maintain that the old lady's death was really due to a pure accident; that Lord Barnsdale gripped her by the throat, in a moment of mad anger, at some hideous insult hurled at his wife; of that I am as convinced as if I had witnessed the whole scene. Then the old lady fell, hit her head against the marble, and Lord Barnsdale realized that he was alone at night in his aunt's room, and that he had killed her.

"What would anyone do under the circumstances?" he added excitedly. "Why, of course, collect his senses and try to save himself from what might prove to be consequences of the most awful kind. This Lord Barnsdale thought he could best do by giving the accident, which looked so like murder, the appearance of a burglary.

"The lock of the desk in the next room had already been forced open; he now locked the door on the inside, threw open the shutter and the window, jumped out as any burglar would have done; and, being careful to obliterate his own footmarks, he crept back into the house, and thence into his own room, without alarming the watchdog, who naturally knew his own master. He was, of course, just in time before Alice Holt succeeded in rousing the household with her screams.

"And thus you see," he added, "there are no such things as mysteries. The police call them so, so do the public, but every crime has its perpetrator, and every puzzle its solution. My experience is that the simplest solution is invariably the right one."

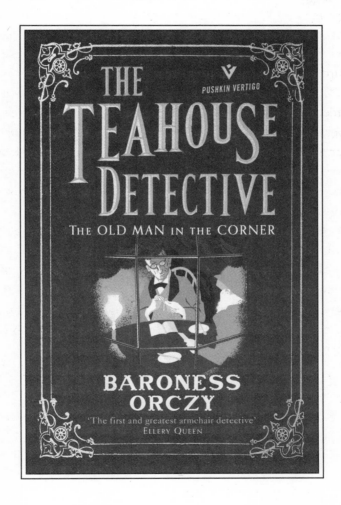

## AVAILABLE AND COMING SOON
## FROM PUSHKIN VERTIGO

**Jonathan Ames**
*You Were Never Really Here*

**Augusto De Angelis**
*The Murdered Banker*
*The Mystery of the Three Orchids*
*The Hotel of the Three Roses*

**Olivier Barde-Cabuçon**
*Casanova and the Faceless Woman*

**María Angélica Bosco**
*Death Going Down*

**Piero Chiara**
*The Disappearance of Signora Giulia*

**Frédéric Dard**
*Bird in a Cage*
*The Wicked Go to Hell*
*Crush*
*The Executioner Weeps*
*The King of Fools*
*The Gravediggers' Bread*

**Friedrich Dürrenmatt**
*The Pledge*
*The Execution of Justice*
*Suspicion*
*The Judge and His Hangman*

**Martin Holmén**
*Clinch*
*Down for the Count*
*Slugger*

**Alexander Lernet-Holenia**
*I Was Jack Mortimer*

**Margaret Millar**
*Vanish in an Instant*

**Boileau-Narcejac**
*Vertigo*
*She Who Was No More*

**Leo Perutz**
*Master of the Day of Judgment*
*Little Apple*
*St Peter's Snow*

**Soji Shimada**
*The Tokyo Zodiac Murders*
*Murder in the Crooked Mansion*

**Masako Togawa**
*The Master Key*
*The Lady Killer*

**Emma Viskic**
*Resurrection Bay*
*And Fire Came Down*
*Darkness for Light*

**Seishi Yokomizo**
*The Inugami Clan*
*Murder in the Honjin*